DEADLY DECEPTION

O'HALLERAN SECURITY INTERNATIONAL, VOLUME 3

TJ LOGAN

DEADLY DECEPTION by TJ Logan

Published by TJL Creative Works LLC, 2019

Copyright © 2019 TJ Logan

tjloganauthor.com

First edition: October 16, 2019

Paperback ISBN: 9781076467812

Cover Art: Wicked Smart Designs

Editor: Chris Kridler

Deadly Deception is a work of fiction. Similarities to real people, places, or events are entirely coincidental. All rights reserved. Other than quotes used in reviews, no part of this book may be reproduced or used in whole or in part without written permission from the author.

DEDICATION

Deadly Deception is dedicated to my amazing sister-in-law, Lisa, who recently retired as a Supervisory Special Agent, after twenty-seven years of dedicated service to the Federal Bureau of Investigation. I can't possibly include all of the impressive accomplishments listed on her resume, but I will do my best to hit some high points.

Her extensive investigative experience includes fugitives, espionage, foreign counterintelligence, domestic terrorism, and civil rights. The Hillsborough County, Florida Bar Association recognized her as the Federal Law Enforcement Officer of the Year, for her investigation and the successful prosecution of two active duty U.S. Army personnel for Espionage. She is also a graduate of the Department of Defense Polygraph Institute and served as the Polygraph Examiner for the Knoxville and Anchorage FBI Field Offices, as well as the Chief Security Officer for the Anchorage FBI Field Office.

Lisa won the Jefferson Award from the University of Virginia for research she and Dr. David Matsumoto conducted in verbal and nonverbal indicators of deception and veracity. With a ninety-percent success rate, their techniques have proven to be extremely successful.

Lisa's last assignment was at the FBI Academy as an instructor for the National Academy. While there, she was designated as an adjunct professor for the University of Virginia, where she taught *Interviewing Strategies through Statement Analysis*, *Analysis of Verbal and Nonverbal Behavior and Investigative Interviewing and Interrogation*. This class was created specifically for the National Academy by combining the microfacial expressions and emotional leakage with the techniques of statement analysis. She also lectured nationally and internationally on these topics to various law enforcement departments and agencies.

Not one to sit idly by, Lisa now provides this training as an Independent Consultant for Humintell. She also assists law enforcement departments and agencies with investigative and interview strategies.

The premise for *Deadly Deception* came to me during a conversation with Lisa about her work. The more I learned about her fascinating research and some of her cases, I just knew I had to create a character that would do her justice. Voila! Andréa Swain began to form in my mind. Andi is a brilliant, complicated, tough as nails heroine who has dedicated her life to serving her country.

Lisa, your willingness to share your vast knowledge with me, even when it meant "dumbing down" your research so I could understand it, or answering the same question multiple times, is what brought Andi Swain to life. *Deadly Deception* would not be the story it is without your insights and knowledge. You are amazing, and I am so glad my brother was smart enough to marry you! I love you!

ACKNOWLEDGMENTS

To my friends, Rick and Jeanette, and Dawn. Joel and I have shared happy times, sad times, and crazy times with each of you. We even trusted you to help us buy a house sight unseen when we live in the opposite corner of the country! You guys continue to bring laughter, joy, and unending support to my life. For that, and so many other things, I will love you forever.

To Joel, you are my person, and I love you.

CHAPTER ONE

Lieutenant Commander and Navy SEAL Jonathan O'Halleran leaned over the territory map in his tent. He tilted his head at the faint yet distinctive sound of a helicopter approaching from the other side of the ridge.

Communications were BFU right now ... beyond fucked up. Instead of them receiving an advanced transmission with details, the incoming chopper's movements had been relayed from one forward operating base, or FOB, to the next as it progressed across the miles-long ridgeline. No one could tell him the purpose for this unexpected visit, but he'd find out soon enough. Only thing he *did* know—it was a "friendly," meaning it wasn't coming in to blow them to smithereens. So that was a bonus.

His second-in-command, Senior Chief Tyrone Jefferson, aka Sherm, straightened and moved to the opening in the tent. Powerfully built like a Sherman tank, he'd been tagged with the nickname during BUD/S, Basic Underwater Demolition/Seal training. The six-month SEAL training course was brutal, and only the toughest survived.

He was a big, bald badass with skin the color of deep

umber and unrivaled levels of patience, and Jonathan trusted him with his life. Having been around awhile and seen things others couldn't begin to imagine, Sherm liked to think he was in charge. There was a string of truth to it. He seemed to know what Jonathan wanted or needed before he ever said a word. Not that he'd ever tell the big guy that. No sense stroking his already polished ego.

"Sounds like our company's arriving, Homer," his senior chief said over his shoulder.

In the field, his guys all called Jonathan Homer. His roommate at the Naval Academy stuck him with it when he noticed his tattered, dog-eared copy of Homer's *Odyssey* sitting on his desk. Could've been worse. One guy who was pretty much bald by the age of eighteen got stuck with being called Gramps.

Jonathan tucked his pencil behind his ear and stood shoulder-to-shoulder with Sherm as they watched the chopper swoop down into the valley. The skill of the guys who managed to maneuver those beasts always impressed the hell out of him.

Three Seabees, Navy guys who managed all the inbound logistics for the FOB, and some men from the Afghan National Police kicked up dust as they rushed to take up defensive positions outward from the landing zone, or LZ, as it was called in the field. On this FOB, the LZ was a generous term for a rough-hewn circle of rocks on the craggy valley floor between the Hindu Kush and Safed Kuh mountains in Afghanistan—the far-from-glamorous location of FOB Nugent and SEAL TEAM Seven's current home.

Most times, when a helo came in, it never even powered down. They just swooped in, hovered over the pad with their load, dropped it, then hauled ass. Not this time.

Cloying dust, dirt and gravel kicked up by the powerful MH-60R helicopter temporarily obscured the large emblem on its side as it settled gracefully. Before the long blades came to a stop, the side door rolled open, and two men in desert camouflage hopped out. Jonathan squinted. Even from two hundred yards away, the Red Cross armbands with their stark white backgrounds stood out against the bland landscape.

Shit. The International Red Cross had many responsibilities in areas of armed conflict, only one of which was tracking down and notifying deployed personnel if a family member became seriously ill or died. Surprise visits from them were never a good thing, and everyone knew it.

Marilyn flickered through his mind and, just as quickly, he shoved his concern aside. She'd said her last checkup went "spectacularly great" ... her exact words. That left Denny, his petty officer. His dad had been battling cancer for several months.

The guys on his team abandoned their intensely physical game of touch football to form a shirtless wall of testosterone and heightened awareness in front of the newcomers.

Jonathan turned back to the table. He had an op to plan and very little time to pull it together.

"Looks like the boys are giving them a good vetting." Sherm dropped the tent flap and went back to reviewing the map with Jonathan.

The guys on his team weren't being dickheads, they were being vigilant. People operating in this part of the world learned the hard way to distrust strangers. Even those wearing the Red Cross insignia.

A knock rattled the brace post. Powder-fine, yellowish-beige sand drifted down through several small holes. The shit was everywhere. Seriously. Everywhere.

"Enter." Jonathan kept his voice low yet forceful. He'd learned at the Academy that volume and intensity were not the same thing.

The flap lifted, and their two visitors stepped inside. The men's eyes widened as they looked up at Jonathan and Sherm.

Jonathan was six four and Sherm was about six five and a half. Both had to hunch over to keep their heads from brushing the top of the tent. Experienced warriors, they quickly took in every detail, every nuance of the newcomers and scanned them for any possible threat.

The dark-haired guy spoke first.

"I am Tomas Rickard and this"—he indicated the man at his right—"is Renaugh Boivin. We are with the International Committee of the Red Cross. We are here to see Lieutenant O'Halleran."

His smooth French accent seemed out of place in such an unrefined, uncivilized environment. Almost as much as their pristine, perfectly starched battledress.

Rickard stiffened his spine as if mustering his courage and made a move to step around Sherm.

The big man flattened his hand against the visitor's chest. His dark, war-battered skin was a striking contrast against the clean uniform shirt.

"That's far enough, fellas." The senior chief crossed his arms over his chest, dominating the space around him. "Let's see some ID."

Rickard shook his head and muttered something in French to his partner. Boivin, proving he was the smarter man, had already pulled his identification from his pocket and was handing it to Sherm.

Jonathan stepped up next to Sherm and glared down at Rickard.

"Bitch all you want, Rickard, but it's standard operating procedure to produce your identification when arriving at any outpost. Even if you are wearing that armband." *That's right, I understood every word you said. You arrogant little ass.* "But of course, you already knew that, didn't you?"

Rickard hesitated, then mumbled an insincere apology before quickly regaining his haughtiness.

"Are you Lieutenant Jonathan O'Halleran?" Even though he was about a whole foot shorter, the guy still somehow managed to look down his nose at Jonathan.

"I am." He crossed his arms and lifted a brow. "Why the hell did they send you two out here?"

Red Cross messages were delivered to the FOB commander electronically. Since theirs was currently making a goodwill visit to the local village, Jonathan was left in charge.

"Yes, well, you see ... " Rickard swallowed hard. A bead of sweat snaked down the side of his face. "We have been having, um ... technical issues with our electronics."

Ah. No wonder. If it wasn't for shitty, outdated equipment, this snotty prick and his seemingly mute buddy wouldn't be anywhere near a dangerous outlying base like this one.

Rickard's hand trembled as he pulled a handkerchief from his pocket. He swiped it across his face, over the back of his neck, then stuffed it out of sight.

"Who'd you boys piss off?" Sherm asked.

"Excuse me?" Rickard's brows drew together.

"Never mind." Jonathan waved it off. "Tell the senior chief who your message is for, and he'll go grab him."

Jonathan turned his back to them and yanked the pencil from behind his ear. The makeshift table groaned when he spread his hands atop it, then resumed making notes on the map spread out before him.

Rickard's eyes darted from Sherm back to him. "The message is for you, Lieutenant O'Halleran."

Jonathan straightened, tossed his pencil down, then slowly turned back to the smaller man. He tilted his chin at Sherm, who stepped over and closed the tent flap, leaving a group of curious SEALS standing on the other side.

Rickard stepped forward and held out a large manila envelope. Jonathan took it from him, then moved to the far side of the tent, the closest he would get to having any privacy. He flipped open his knife and sliced it across the top of the envelope, then pulled out an official-looking document. After plowing through a bunch of formal military and introductory language, he got to the meat of the letter.

August Ten: Thirteen Seventeen hours, Marilyn O'Halleran arrived at Skagit Bay Memorial Hospital via ambulance.
August Ten: Thirteen Thirty-Two hours, Marilyn O'Halleran underwent an emergency cesarean section, performed by Dr. Stephen Barrister, OB/GYN.
August Ten: Fourteen Thirteen hours, a female infant was airlifted to the Neonatal Intensive Care Unit at Seattle Children's Hospital.
August Ten: Fourteen Sixteen hours, as a result of severe hemorrhaging, Marilyn O'Halleran did not survive the rigors of birth.
Official TOD: 1416 HRS PST

Sounds of life on the FOB ceased. Colors faded to varying shades of gray. The ever-present smells of military life—sweat, spent brass, musty canvas, dust and dirt—ceased to exist.

A gaping chasm tore open inside his gut and threatened to double him over. All his hopes, dreams, and plans for a life with the woman he'd known since childhood were sucked into its cold, dark abyss. Marilyn, *his* Marilyn, was gone. Forever.

His mind dragged him back to the last time he saw her. It was a month ... no, two months ago during a staticky video call. She was so happy and excited about him coming home soon. Her blue eyes twinkled the way they always did, and she was positively glowing. It almost hurt to look at her.

Marilyn's bright light had been extinguished, and he hadn't been there for her. She'd always been there for him, always been a big part of his life. How the hell was he supposed to move forward without her in it?

Jonathan forced a deep, silent breath and shoved his emotions to the far, darkest corners of his soul. Locked them down tight until he felt *nothing*.

He slogged through the rest of the letter. Logistical details, travel schedules, even condolences. Training and experience kicked in, and he fell into take-care-of-business mode. He handed Sherm the letter on his way to his rack, grabbed his duffle, dropped it on the old cot and stuffed his few belongings inside.

His friend's eyes skimmed across the pages. The hand holding the letter fell to his side.

"What can we do, Homer? Anything, just name it." He meant it, too. No matter what Jonathan asked of him, he would make it happen. Problem was, even Sherm couldn't bring Marilyn back.

Words were impossible. A riot of emotions—jammed up like a fist in his throat—choked him as they tried to hammer their way through. He couldn't let that happen. His senior chief knew the protocol and would step up to command the team until Jonathan's replacement arrived.

Voice subdued, Sherm glanced at the letter, then back at him. "Says here you have a baby girl."

Jonathan faltered midway through pulling on his tactical vest. He waited for the words to flip some sort of internal switch that would kick-start his emotions. It never happened. They pinged off him like a bullet ricocheting off a cliff face, leaving behind nothing but a superficial scar.

He turned to Sherm, held his hand out, palm up.

His friend hesitated, looked like he wanted to say something else. Finally, he handed over the letter and quietly turned to step out of the tent. The flap lifted, and questioning murmurs from the group congregated outside snuck through before it dropped back into place.

Jonathan looked at the paperwork one more time, then carefully slid it back into the envelope and tucked it into the side pocket of his bag. By rote, he finished strapping on his vest, yanked the zipper on his duffle and threw it over his shoulder. He grabbed the rest of his gear, took a last look around his quarters—knowing nothing would ever be the same again—and jammed on his helmet, careful not to look at the picture of Marilyn tucked inside the lining. He threw open the tent flap and, out of habit, slipped on his wraparound sunglasses. It wasn't as if the bright August sun had even registered.

Having conveyed the news, Sherm waited with the rest of the team just outside the tent. Their faces held varying degrees of anguish, pity and even frustration. These were men used to being in control. In this, like him, they had none. A few of them murmured words of condolence and apologies for his loss. Others stood in stunned silence. At one time or another, most of them had met Marilyn. Everyone loved her. Why the hell wouldn't they? She embodied everything good and pure about the world.

"Back it up, guys." Voice somber, Sherm walked ahead of him, a sort of human plow clearing everyone in their path.

Eyes fixed on the horizon, Jonathan put one foot in front of the other. The crunching of rocks beneath their boots was drowned out by his heartbeat pounding between his ears. Surprising, since he was certain his heart had just been ripped from his chest. There was no high-pitched whine from the helicopter engine. No *whop whop whop* from the long, spinning rotor blades. Gone was the oppressive heat, the parched landscape, the concern about imminent threats.

He navigated the small incline to the helipad.

Rickard and Boivin were already seated inside the helo. Having dropped their bomb, they'd hightailed it back to the relative safety of the helicopter. He had no right to hate these men, to blame them. After all, they were only the harbingers of doom, not the creators.

Knowing he couldn't leave without saying ... *something*, Jonathan rolled his shoulders, then turned to his team.

"Senior Chief's in charge. He'll fill you in on what you need to know."

As one, they straightened and snapped a salute.

He clenched his jaw, returned their salute, then, with a last nod to his men, he turned, hunched over and walked to the helo, oblivious to the sand pelting his face as dust and debris whipped around him. After he climbed in next to Rickard, the door rattled shut, the blades sped up, and the chopper lifted.

The ground fell away below him, and his team disappeared from sight. Jonathan's head thumped back against the equipment panel. As they flew low over the snow-dusted, jagged peaks, he closed his eyes and tried to conjure up Marilyn's smiling face. Instead, only three little words pounded around inside him like a wrecking ball, destroying everything in its path.

"Did not survive."

CHAPTER TWO

Andi Swain silently fumed as her boss explained why he'd yanked her back to the States, away from her duties in Afghanistan.

"You've been over there for the better part of three years, Andi. That's why I brought you back." As the head of the NSA, it was safe to assume, Jeffrey Burke rarely had to explain himself.

He didn't understand. She had no business being back in DC. Her expertise was needed on the front lines. Not to mention, she fit in better there, knew how to function. Here? *Home?* She was a five-foot-nine-and-a-half-inch fish out of water.

"Jeffrey, I still have work to do over there. We're getting ready to round up the leaders of the Al-Mu'min Brotherhood. They're going to need me there for statement analysis." After all their years of work, they were so damned close.

The Al-Mu'min Brotherhood, the "Guardian of the Faith," was one of the most bloody, vicious arms of ISIS currently operating in Afghanistan and parts of Pakistan. They'd sworn their allegiance to the caliph, Jalaal Abdul-

Azeem, a political religious leader, a self-professed successor to the Islamic prophet Muhammad. His authority over his people was absolute and unimpeachable. They had one goal and one goal only—to enlarge the Islamic state by any means necessary. Not even an ocean would stop them from expanding their caliphate.

"Are you done?" He tossed his pen on his desk and leaned back in his chair with a loud *SQUE-E-E-EAK*.

"Jesus." Eyes squeezed tight, Andi drew her shoulders up around her ears as the grating sound scraped up her spine. "I've been gone three years, and you still haven't done anything about that?" She tipped her chin toward his chair. "I'm sure you could requisition a replacement. Hell, I'd be happy to buy you a brand-new one."

"Nice try, Swain, but I'm not letting you change the subject." Jeffrey leaned forward and crossed his arms on his desk.

Oh, well. Worth a try.

"Thanks to your hard work, the Brotherhood's leadership is in shambles and their strength is dwindling." He flipped her thick file shut. "You are the best at what you do, but everyone needs a break now and then."

"Fine, I'll take a couple weeks to buy some new tactical gear, maybe pick up a new weapon, then I'll head back over." Surely, he didn't expect her to stay here longer than *that*.

"You're *not* hearing me, Andi." Her boss had that look on his face—the one that told her he wasn't going to budge. "You're done."

"Damn it, Jeffrey, I—" She sat forward.

He held up his hand.

"I have an assignment for you here in the States." He handed her a folder with the distinctive "Top Secret" red border and markings.

"You're the only one seeing that." He pointed at the file in her hand, then gave her a one of *those* looks. The kind that said listen up, because he was about to share something important. "Since you're the only person I trust with this assignment."

Okay, so that was pretty frickin' nice to hear. Having Jeffrey Burke's trust was the thing of fantasies. Like having a friend who happened to be a leprechaun with a magic lamp who rode a flying carpet from one pot of gold to the next. His faith in her touched her deeply, in a part of her she kept walled off good and tight, a place she allowed very few things to penetrate.

Ten minutes later, her boss finished outlining her next assignment. He sat back in his old chair, fingers steepled beneath his chin, and looked at her in that eerie *way* of his. Like he could see the gears in her brain working.

"Let me make sure I've got this straight." Andi leaned closer. "You think O'Halleran Security International, one of the top security agencies in the world, an agency responsible for the creation of some of the most advanced surveillance and detection equipment out there—who also happens to have a stellar reputation for problem-solving—needs my help finding who gave up the details of a secret FBI operation?"

"Don't misunderstand me, Andi." He leaned forward, elbows on his desk, fingers laced together. "I trust Beckett O'Halleran and the people who work for him not only with my life, but the life of every single person involved in every single op I've ever assigned to his company. If I didn't, I wouldn't work with the man."

"If that's true, then why send me in? What do they need me for?" She'd never met the head of OSI, but he was one of the most highly respected people in the intelligence community. Surely he had the resources to nail the person responsible for getting his brother shot.

"I think your skill set could be an asset to their organization."

"Isn't there someone from the FBI NA you can send?" She waved her hand in the general direction of Quantico, where the FBI National Academy was located. "I need to finish what I started."

"It's that, or you stay here and train new recruits on your interrogation methodology."

Her head dropped back on a loud groan.

"Training?" He couldn't be serious. Andi wasn't one to brag, but she was considered one of the most effective interviewers in the world. Being kept here to run training would be a waste of her years of experience and expertise. Not to mention, she'd go out of her damn mind.

"How does Beckett O'Halleran feel about me sticking my nose in their family business?" Everyone knew what a tight bunch the O'Hallerans were.

"He wants someone outside the family on this one. Someone who can look at things through a different lens. I suggested you, and he was in one hundred percent agreement."

"Fine." She sighed. "Guess I'm headed to California."

OSI's main training facility and offices were located on a large, isolated chunk of land near the coast.

"Actually, you'll be working with one of his brothers out of their new field office in Washington State."

Oh no. Andi did not like where this was going. While in Afghanistan, she'd had a less-than-pleasant encounter with an O'Halleran. One who blamed her for the nightmare that took place early one freezing cold morning near the border between the Nangarhar Province and Pakistan. What were the chances it was him? Surely there must be other O'Hallerans in the world. And anyway, he'd come across as the kind of guy who wouldn't know how to live a life outside the Navy.

Jeffrey dipped his chin to the folder in her lap. She flipped it open, and none other than Navy SEAL Lieutenant Commander Jonathan O'Halleran's photo stared up at her.

Her body tensed. *Son of a bitch.*

"Problem?" Jeffrey asked, one eyebrow arched high.

Hell, yeah!

"No problem at all." She forced her jaw to relax. After all, how hard could it be to work with a man who had zero respect for her or her life's work? A guy who'd gotten in her face and blamed her for the death of his friend. Yep. Easy. Piece of cake.

Their confrontation had left her with a whispering uncertainty about herself and her abilities. Which really pissed her off. All the more reason she needed to be back over there, where she could prove she could still do her job. That she was still effective. That her work, and by extension, she mattered.

Of course, her boss knew nothing about it. A man in his position had bigger problems to deal with than the drama of Andi's wounded psyche.

"Good. He hasn't been brought into the loop yet, but he'll be briefed before you arrive." Jeffrey flipped open a file on his desk. "There's one more thing I need you to do for me."

She waited.

"Go home and dig out your best evening gown. I need you at the annual Capitol Hill holiday fundraiser tomorrow night."

"Oh, come on, Jeffrey." He couldn't be serious. The man knew how much she hated getting dressed up. She especially hated watching all those sycophants kissing each other's asses one minute, then stabbing each other in the back the next.

"I need you to evaluate a couple individuals for me." He

wrote the names on a small piece of paper. "Memorize that, then destroy it." He pointed at the note in her hand. "As usual, everything we've discussed here stays in this room. Understood?"

"Understood." Andi couldn't refuse an opportunity to ply her craft. It was her kryptonite, and Jeffrey knew it. Hell, for that, she'd even throw on a stupid gown.

"Anything else I can do to for you, oh great and powerful leader?" Being snarky with a guy who could make a person disappear with the snap of his fingers was probably not her brightest move. But ever since he'd recruited her straight from college, they'd had a unique relationship. It always felt more father-daughter than boss-employee.

As much as she hated to admit it, Andi kinda liked it, especially since she'd never had anything close to it with her real hard-ass of a father. And she would be taking *that* pathetic little piece of intel to her grave.

"That's it." One side of his mouth lifted as he slipped on his reading glasses. With a wave of his hand, he shooed her away and started rifling through the mountain of paperwork on the side of his desk.

Andi sighed. She pushed up from the chair and turned to leave his office.

"Close the door behind you, would you please, Andi?" He shot her a look over the top of his glasses. *"Close* it. Don't *slam* it."

She gave him a cheeky grin, then made a production of quietly pulling it closed.

Nancy Raymond, Burke's longtime assistant, was back at her desk. When Andi arrived, she was at lunch.

"Hey there, Ms. Raymond." Andi paused at the side of her desk.

The older woman's fingers halted over the keyboard. She swiveled her chair and smiled up at Andi. "Andi! How are you? It's good to see you. You've been missed around here."

Andi wasn't sure she believed that last part.

"I'm doing great." No sense lamenting to this poor woman about how miserable she was being back here. After all, they were friendly, not friends.

"That's wonderful. Well, welcome back." Nancy turned back to her desk and resumed what she was doing. And just like that, their little reunion was over.

"Thanks." Andi walked the few feet to her small office and unlocked the door. The motion-sensor overhead fluorescents flickered on. She looked around the colorless, nondescript space. With the exception of a fine layer of dust over everything, it was exactly the same. The last time she was in this room was two days before she'd deployed overseas. She hated it. It always felt like a trap she might never escape from.

There'd been a week here and there when she'd been back to the States. Most recently when her father died. She'd avoided the office and stayed in the States just long enough to clear out his house. The only things she'd kept were her mother's wedding ring, currently on a chain around her neck, and the hand-carved cherry-wood box containing her father's medals, which she'd shoved onto the top shelf at the back of her closet. Everything else was donated to the first charity willing to pick it up.

Andi wanted nothing to do with it.

Circling behind her desk, she dropped her worn backpack on the floor, rolled out the chair, then plopped onto it with a hard sigh. She thought of the paperwork sitting on her boss's desk and shuddered. Was that her future?

She turned and stared up at the shelf. Stacked in a row, like good little soldiers, were the binders she'd grudgingly maintained during her ten years of service to the Agency.

She pulled one down and flipped it open. The first page was an outline she could use to establish a course of study.

Ugh. Course of study. Kill me now.

After traveling almost twenty-four hours straight, including an oppressive stop in Bahrain, she was in no mood to deal with this right now.

Hell with it. I have until tomorrow. Who was she kidding? She'd already made her decision.

Andi scooped up her pack and tossed it over a shoulder. She stepped out of her office and locked the door. Like a human version of Whac-a-Mole, heads popped up in cubicles as she headed to the elevator. Not a single familiar face in the bunch. She refused to be depressed by that or let it make her feel like an outsider. *Nothing new there.* Sheesh. She'd only been back in the States a few hours and was already feeling maudlin.

An hour later, she sat unmoving in bumper-to-bumper traffic. Her mind flashed back to another traffic jam she, her two-man protection detail, and their interpreter had been stuck in. They were on a one-lane gravel and dirt road—a wide goat trail, really—en route to the village of Sh'ar Langar. Instead of cars blocking their way, it had been a herd of goats. The owner had been in no hurry to move along, especially when he noticed a woman in the back seat.

She hadn't been at the secured location five minutes when Lieutenant Commander Jonathan O'Halleran, the leader of SEAL Team Seven and her soon-to-be sort-of boss, had stormed in, dark, menacing and pissed as hell. He'd literally dragged in a high-ranking officer from the Brotherhood responsible for the ambush that killed one man and wounded three others a few days earlier. The dead man happened to be a friend of O'Halleran's.

While Andi was there to glean as much information as possible from the prisoner, the SEAL wanted to beat the answers out of the man in typical muscle-head fashion.

She understood his desire to exact retribution, but it was

counterproductive. The more you hit these guys, the quieter they got. The Brotherhood's hatred for the *infidels,* the *invaders,* was bone-deep and went back generations. Their leaders were motivated by their deep religious beliefs, based on their warped interpretation of the Koran. They used the promise of property, great wealth and, most importantly, family honor to entice new foot soldiers to their cause.

When she'd ordered him to stand down, O'Halleran had loomed over her, a raging storm cloud of testosterone and disgust. He'd flat-out blamed her and her "fucked-up methods" for what had happened.

She'd stood her ground, had given no indication his accusations burrowed under her skin like a sand flea. Instead, she'd stuck out her chin, thrown back her shoulders and told him to go to hell. Whether he liked it or not, her job was to get answers, and her method had proven to be much more effective than knocking the crap out of people.

A horn honked, jarring her from her memories.

"What an ass."

Like she'd done many times since, she shoved all of it—the hurt and guilt, the self-recrimination, the questions about what she could've done differently—to a special compartment at the back of her mind.

Andi finally pulled into her condo parking lot and zipped around the corner to find a car parked in her assigned space. Perfect. A quick look around, and she backed her rental into an open *Visitor* spot. Wasn't like she needed her own spot. She didn't even own a car. Why bother? Making payments on something she would never drive made zero sense.

She grabbed her backpack and duffle, then shoved open the door. The late afternoon sun streamed through the bare branches of the nearby trees, casting long, skeleton-like shadows over the sides of the building. Biting wind sliced through her thin jacket, reminding her how much she hated

DC in the winter. Andi was self-aware enough to know the starkness and bitter cold were exaggerated by her passionate dislike for being anywhere near all the bullshit associated with the nation's capital.

The corrugated metal stairs clanked under her boots as she hustled up to her second-floor unit. Her condo was freezing and had that stale, closed-up feeling. Bands of soft, golden light filtered through the partially closed blinds, highlighting the dust covering everything. Dust was a constant in her life these days—Afghanistan, her office, here ...

Andi cranked up the heat on her way into the small living room, then set her backpack and duffle on the floor. She dropped onto the couch. Her head fell back with a deep sigh, and her eyes drifted shut.

When she opened them again, the room was awash in subdued moonlight. She glanced at her watch, surprised to discover she'd slept right through the usual dinner hour.

"Usual." She snorted. What the hell was that?

With a groan, she stood, stretched her hands over her head, leaned side to side, then bent forward to touch her toes. Military travel really did a number on a person's back.

Her stomach growled, a not-so-subtle reminder she hadn't eaten since ... Andi tilted her head. When *was* the last time she'd eaten? *Oh yeah*. She snapped her fingers. She'd choked down a protein bar with a bottle of water right after she'd strapped into the drop-down seat in the belly of that C130 cargo plane out of Bahrain.

She dug through her closet for a heavier coat, scooped her keys off the table, grabbed her wallet, then headed out to do something she hadn't done in almost three years.

"Ugh, grocery shopping."

CHAPTER THREE

Matthew Roberson scanned the room of DC politicians and financial high rollers until he found his boss, Senator Preston Etheridge. Even from a distance, the man looked downright presidential.

At the relatively young age of forty-five, the esteemed senator from Georgia had already risen to the chairmanship of the U.S. Senate Select Committee on Intelligence.

Matt considered it quite a feather in his own cap. Without him, Etheridge would still be a junior senator from just another backward Southern state dreaming of invites to functions like this and vying for a position on any small committee that would take him. Instead, the man was here, in a ballroom schmoozing with the very young CEO of a Fortune 100 tech company and his incredibly homely wife.

Uh-oh. Looked like his boss was losing interest. Time for Matt to swoop in and save the day. He maneuvered his way around veterans in wheelchairs, women wearing long gowns—their trains draped all over the damn floor—and more than one drunk congressman and lobbyist. As he approached his boss, he pulled his cell phone from his pocket.

"Sir." He turned to the couple and held up his phone. "I apologize. The senator has a very important phone call."

"Oh, certainly." This from the ugly wife.

"I do apologize for this untimely interruption." The senator turned up the dial on his smooth Southern accent and actually kissed the back of her hand. "The government never sleeps." He winked at her, then flashed one of his signature "vote for me" smiles.

She giggled and blushed as her husband shook the senator's hand.

Matt forced himself not to roll his eyes. Instead, he smiled, took the senator by the elbow and steered him away.

"You looked like you could use a rescue, sir." Only two years younger than his boss, Matt was called an ass-kisser by some. Like he gave a shit. He was merely showing the appropriate level of respect for a man who intended to accomplish great things. As his personal aide, Matt planned to be right there next to him when he moved into the Oval Office, a critical member of his team and a huge factor in his success. He would do anything, stop anyone, who got in the way of that goal.

"Thanks, Matt." The senator turned his back to the room, wedged his finger into the collar of his tux shirt and gave it a tug. "That guy is as dry as the creek bed behind my granddaddy's house in the middle of summer."

Matt laughed because ... well ... it was expected.

"I can only imagine." He looked at his watch. "Sir, I think it would be fine for you to leave now."

Though he'd fought to get included in this crowd, the senator always felt a bit out of place. Not everyone felt compelled to laugh at his good ol' boy euphemisms the way Matt did.

A familiar spark lit his boss's eyes just as the corner of his mouth lifted.

"Ya know what, Matt?" He tugged his cuffs down and straightened his bow tie. "I think I just might stay a bit longer."

Uh-oh. Matt had seen that look before.

He followed his boss's gaze to a tall, strikingly beautiful woman on the other side of the room. She had short, dark hair and wore a turquoise dress. Her gown was understated, in contrast with the other women in the room, who seemed to be trying too hard. Not one sequin or feather in sight, nor was it cut so low as to be in poor taste.

"Do you think that's wise, sir? You have a committee meeting tomorrow morning at eight thirty." Though he was married to a "sweet Georgia peach," his boss had a reputation as a bit of a skirt-chaser.

"A man's got needs, Matthew." His boss winked at him, clapped him on the shoulder and sauntered away.

Shit. Matt could already see how this would play out. The senator would call him from some hotel outside the beltway at the ass-crack of dawn to come get him and his latest conquest. He would, of course, pick them up at the loading dock. And if he was really lucky, the press or some moron with a cell phone looking to make an easy buck or grab his fifteen minutes of fame wouldn't get a shot of his *married* boss and some broad doing the walk of shame past a bunch of delivery trucks and overflowing garbage cans.

Screw that. Tomorrow's committee meeting was too important, and as the chairman, it's not like people wouldn't notice if the senator crawled in late. Matt was already spending too damn much of his time deflecting quiet criticism and making excuses for him.

He grabbed a glass of champagne from a passing waiter and headed toward his boss.

As he drew near, he heard the woman ask, "And where *is* your lovely wife, Senator Etheridge?"

"Why, she's back in Georgia. She hasn't taken much of a likin' to life in DC."

He laid on the Southern charm so thick, Matt could practically smell pecan pie in the air.

"Well, I'm sorry to hear that." Her dark brow lifted. "I think she could learn a lot by being here."

Matt was sure she'd meant it as a dig, but the lady was hard to read. He watched and listened to them interact a few more minutes before stepping closer.

She turned and noticed him.

"Matthew Roberson," he said as he extended a hand. "Senator Douglas's personal aide."

Her firm, confident handshake surprised him. If he had to guess, the smooth muscles in her arms were not built in a gym. In heels, she was slightly taller than Matt, and her direct eye contact was oddly unsettling, as if she were sizing him up.

The senator was barking up the wrong tree with this one. She wasn't another needy, vapid political groupie who would fall at his feet. No, this woman radiated intelligence and had an alluring edginess about her.

"Mr. Roberson." She released his hand. "Must be a tough job keeping up with this one." One corner of her mouth lifted, and she tilted her head at his boss.

"It's a privilege to work for the senator."

"I'm sure it is." She didn't sound convinced.

"I'm sorry, I didn't catch your name." Matt liked to know everything about the people who entered the senator's universe—even peripherally.

"That's because I didn't throw it." She waited a beat, then turned back to his boss. "So, Senator, what is it you're working on these days?"

For the next few minutes, the senator bragged about the cutting-edge defense technology he was promoting and bills he'd introduced. Not that it took much to get him going.

Politicians were inherently narcissists who loved the sound of their own voices.

"If it weren't for Jef—"

Matt coughed, cutting off what would surely be another of his boss's diatribes about Jeffrey Burke standing in his way. The NSA chief's people had a knack for being everywhere and nowhere, and there wasn't a wall in this town that didn't have ears.

"So," Matt turned to her, "what is it you do, Ms. ... ?"

"I work for the government."

No help there—practically everyone in DC worked for the government in some capacity.

She cleverly deflected the senator's persistent invites to join him for cocktails or dinner by playing to his ego with questions about his work, all the while watching him with those measuring eyes of hers.

There's something about her ...

Matt didn't believe for a minute she was the least bit interested in the senator's political agenda. No, there was something else going on, but he had no idea what.

She glanced over at the clock on the wall.

"Well, I've got an early appointment in the morning." She slipped the skinny strap of her purse over her tanned, fit shoulder. "It's been ... enlightening, Senator."

"Are you sure you don't have time to grab a quick drink?" His boss curled his fingers under her elbow.

She glanced down at his hand, then back up at him. The look she shot his boss held a warning.

The senator's hand fell away, along with his politician's smile.

Interesting.

"Mr. Roberson." Her eyes slowly swept to Matt. "Good luck with"—she looked sideways at his boss then back to him —"everything."

"Oh, yes ... well, it was nice *almost* meeting you." Matt chuckled and smiled.

She did not.

"Senator." A quick nod to his boss and she turned and walked away without a backward glance. Proof there was at least one woman in DC immune to his boss's charm.

As much as he would've liked a few extra minutes to learn more about the mysterious woman, he was thankful she left. Without his boss.

"What the blazin' hell, Matt?" Etheridge turned on him. "I was this close"—he held his thumb and index finger about an inch apart—"to closin' the deal with her when you showed up."

Huh. Not the impression he'd gotten, but he knew better than to say that out loud.

"Sorry about that, sir." Matt set his still-full glass down on a nearby table. "What was her name, anyway?"

"Ya know somethin' ... " His boss's brows drew together. "I don't think she ever told me her name."

Unusual, in a town where who you knew meant more than what you knew.

"Well, maybe you'll bump into her at another fundraiser." Matt didn't believe that for a minute.

The bars around the room were shutting down, and folks were starting to leave. Few people wanted to be at one of these things without access to alcohol.

"How about I give you a ride home, Senator." A giant pain in the ass, but the only way to ensure the man went home alone. Unlike his boss, Matt didn't have a huge townhouse in the city paid for by his rich daddy-in-law. Nor did he have a driver waiting to pick him up and take him into the office every day.

"Now that's awful darn nice of you, Matt." He clapped

him on the back, and they joined the crowd filtering out of the ballroom.

He pulled up the senator's calendar on his phone and went over his schedule as they made their way down the long, carpeted corridor.

"As I mentioned, at eight thirty you've got your committee meeting. Noon, you have lunch with Senators Riley and Tomlinson. Committee readjourns at two thirty and goes until whenever you finish up the required items on the agenda."

The senator sighed. "Have my driver pick me up at seven forty-five tomorrow morning. That oughta give me time to pull together what I need for the meeting."

"Already done, sir. Everything you'll need is in a sealed envelope in the middle of your desk."

The senator stopped and glared at him. "Now how the hell would you know what I need?"

This was where things got tricky. Hidden behind his boss's charming, country bumpkin façade was a devious intelligence and dark, violent streak. A dangerous combination. Matt had to walk a fine line between making sure he was indispensable and encroaching on forbidden territory.

"We spoke about it once before, and I took copious notes." He didn't break eye contact, didn't shift his weight, nothing.

A big, slow smile broke across his boss's face. "Well, alrighty then. That's what I like to hear."

Another clap to the back and they started walking again. They approached the lobby, and the senator came to an abrupt stop. His lips pinched, and his jaw jumped.

Matt spotted the object of his boss's disdain. Jeffrey Burke stood with his executive assistant, smiling and shaking hands with Beckett O'Halleran, president and founder of O'Halleran Security International.

The senator had a deep dislike for Burke. The well-respected NSA chief was a constant thorn in his side, calling his proposed budget cuts uninformed, dangerous even, to U.S. assets here and overseas. He'd been able to get most of his boss's cuts kicked to the curb. He'd even had the stones to confront the senator about his hound-dog behavior, said it jeopardized national security. The man was scary powerful, even by DC standards.

In an effort to avoid an embarrassing scene, Matt said, "Senator, if you'll wait here, I'll have my car brought around."

He pushed through the revolving door and handed the ticket to the valet.

"Good evening, Matthew." An edge of danger always seemed to hover just below the surface of Burke's deep, smooth voice.

Matt's spine stiffened. He swallowed hard and forced a smile before turning around.

"Good evening, Mr. Burke." He dipped his chin at the middle-aged woman standing a few feet away. "Mrs. Raymond."

"I see you managed to save your boss from himself once again." He kept his voice low—for their ears only—but it did nothing to diminish the power saturating his words.

"I'm not sure I understand what you mean, sir." Matt had gotten really good at playing dumb, being temporarily blind and suffering from selective hearing.

"Let's just say the woman your boss was just trying to"—he hesitated, then tugged on his gloves—"get to know better is a friend of mine. For that, and many other reasons I won't go into, she is *not* someone he wants to mess with."

Who the hell was she to the NSA chief? Could they be romantically involved? It wasn't a stretch. Burke was a single, wealthy forty-eight-year-old with the physique of a guy in his mid-thirties. Not to mention, he wielded a great deal of power. And who didn't want to be near that?

Rumor had it, he was brutally loyal to those people close to him. Matt oftentimes wondered what that would feel like. Then he'd remind himself he was working for a man who was great in his own right. A man with an express ticket to the White House. Their time would come.

"I'm sure the senator was only—"

Burke stepped into his personal space. "Are we ... understood?"

Matt cursed himself when he stumbled back a step. This was not a man you showed weakness to.

"Yes, sir. Very clear." Any lame defense he might have offered was choked off by the man's authoritative power.

"Have a good evening then, Matthew." Burke turned and escorted his assistant toward a waiting car.

The valet climbed out of Matt's car and handed him the keys. Matt slipped him a five-spot and turned to the door.

What the hell?

His boss, a powerful United States senator, appeared to be hiding behind a giant potted plant.

He held up one finger to the valet. "Give me a minute." Then he headed back inside.

Face sweating and drained of color, his boss skulked in the corner.

"Sir, is there—"

"Who's the guy drivin' that car?"

"What guy?" He looked over his shoulder at the wide front doors. "What car?"

"That one, right there." He pointed toward the car Burke was just shutting the door to. "Ya damn chuckle-headed fool."

His country-boy accent became exaggerated whenever he was stressed.

"I have no idea." Eyes narrowed, Matt turned back to him. "Is there something I should know, sir?"

Etheridge scanned the lobby, then yanked him by the arm into the nearby coat closet. Fur coats and jackets were ripped from hangers as he swiped through the racks. Having apparently assured himself no one was hiding, he paced and tugged at his bottom lip.

Matt had seen this behavior before. Right before the shit hit the fan and he was stuck cleaning up a mess.

He gripped Matt by the arms and yanked him close, nose-to-nose.

"We have to find out who he is." A chilling combination of fury and panic coated his words.

"Why is that, Senator?"

"The guy drivin' that car was at that place—The Farm—when I was there and ... " He released his hold and stepped back. "I'm pretty sure he saw me coming out of the VIP quarters after I was ... well ... ya know ... with one of their little gals up there."

Son. Of. A. Bitch. This was not good. Not good at all.

CHAPTER FOUR

Jonathan looked at his watch. Nine thirty. Ashling would be asleep by now. Guilt washed over him because he couldn't deny he'd stayed late on purpose. Which made him the world's shittiest father.

He picked up his cell and called his folks.

"Hello." Michaleen O'Halleran's deep voice rumbled through the phone.

"Hey, dad."

"Jonathan, how are you, son?" Knowing his dad, that's not what he really wanted to ask. The more likely question was, "*Where* are you?"

"I'm fine. Just wanted to let you know I'm headed home."

"I'll let your mother know."

"Thanks."

"Sure thing."

Jonathan had never been much of a talker, but he'd loved the conversations he'd shared with his father. Now, they always seemed stilted, awkward. It never used to be that way ... before.

"How is she?" Jonathan asked.

"She's perfect, is how she is. Get yourself home and you can see for yourself." His dad wasn't one to heap on guilt, but he did have a way of getting his point across.

"Be there shortly." Jonathan hung up, powered down his laptop and shoved it in his backpack. Shame prickled over his skin as he stashed the bottle and shot glass in his bottom drawer. He clicked off his desk lamp and locked his office.

Other than a few accent lights here and there, the inside of the building was dark. Empty. Similar to how he felt most days.

O'Halleran Security International's northwest offices were located in a former timber mill. Even after all the renovations, the scent of cut pine and cedar clung to the old place like a ghost. The massive, unassuming brick building was surrounded by several acres of wooded land on the outskirts of the small town of Whidbey Cove. Now that additional operatives had been hired and teams formed, the thick woods would provide excellent training options.

OSI was the brainchild of his oldest brother, Beck. He'd started the business after leaving the Bureau. Their teams specialized in private security, close protection, national and international hostage retrieval, tracking and cybersecurity.

As a Navy SEAL ... scratch that ... as a *former* Navy SEAL, Jonathan was more than qualified. Although, these days, he spent more time in the office than in the field. Since he'd only been back in the States a grand total of about eight months during the past several years, this new life would take some getting used to. For a lot of reasons.

Jonathan couldn't help wondering if things would've turned out differently had he been here when ... He scrubbed his hand down his face and tried to ignore the way his insides twisted every time he thought about the *what-ifs*.

After setting the master alarm, he climbed in his truck. He fired it up, backed out of his spot and headed to his parents' house a few minutes away. Convenient, since he and Ashling had been living with them since her release from the Neonatal Intensive Care Unit three months ago.

The time she'd spent there was the most torturous two and a half months of his entire life. And she wasn't out of the woods yet. The doctors wanted to wait until her six-month follow-up exam before declaring her one hundred percent healthy. One month to go and every single second ticked by in Jonathan's head like the click of a trigger in a psychological game of Russian roulette.

As he made his way through the small onetime fishing village of Whidbey Cove, he was flooded with memories of when they were kids and used to spend all their time cruising around on their bikes, fishing down at the bay or exploring the woods surrounding the town. Everyone knew the six O'Halleran kids.

It was the perfect place to raise children.

Ashling's angelic face floated through his mind, and he smiled. He loved his little girl so much, it scared the holy living hell out of him. He would never survive losing her, too. And still, no matter how hard he tried to distance himself from her, he just couldn't pull it off.

The half-empty bottles of scotch he kept in his office and bedroom were humiliating testaments to the constant push-pull of emotions: guilt, anger, betrayal, grief, fear. He carried —and buried—all of them inside.

Jonathan rolled down the window and took a deep breath. Cool night air slapped him in the face and yanked him from his dark thoughts.

He cruised down the quiet main street. Miller's Department Store looked about the same. As kids, they used to fold shirt boxes in the basement for five cents apiece. Posh's Five and Dime, where a quarter could get you a bagful of candy, was still there, too. Stombaugh's Drug Store was on the corner where it had always been. Walking inside was like stepping back in time. You could still get an old-fashioned cherry coke or a homemade root beer float at the original soda fountain in the back by the pharmacy.

At the only light in town, he hung a left and took the road that wound along the bay. His parents' property was about two miles outside of town, one hundred fifty acres of wooded paradise overlooking the Puget Sound and the San Juan Islands in the distance.

Jonathan's truck bumped its way over the ruts and potholes of the long dirt and gravel private road that led up to the house. Their dad said they forced people to slow down. As he crested the hill, his headlights swept across the front of the large structure and passed over his folks. They sat in their usual spots—side by side in a couple of cedar Adirondack chairs his dad built years ago. Puffs of smoke from the one pipe a day his dad was allowed to have curled overhead.

As far back as he could remember, his parents always made a point to end their evenings doing something together. Marilyn had always said they would do the same thing one day. She'd had a lot of ideas, and Jonathan had been content to go along with all of them. Anything to make Marilyn happy.

Her family had lived on the large parcel of land next to theirs. She was an only child and her parents adored her. She was their princess, and she looked like one. Blond hair, big blue eyes, rosy cheeks and an easy smile. She'd never had a care in the world. Or so Jonathan had thought.

They'd met the first day of second grade when he'd ended up sitting next to her on the bus. She'd chattered his ear off the whole way and, by the time they arrived at school, he knew everything about her. Whether he wanted to or not.

Jonathan shook off the cobweb of memories, parked and

turned off his car. He gave himself a minute, listened to the clicks and pings of his cooling engine. The *screech* of an owl as it swept down from a tall tree for its nightly hunt. The rustle of the evergreens surrounding the property. If you listened carefully, you could hear the far-off sound of a lonely ship's deep horn as it navigated its way through the dark, tumultuous waters of the sound.

Jonathan took another deep breath as if to steel himself against the bombardment of emotions to come. He opened the door, swung his long legs out and walked around to the front porch. *Clunk clunk clunk,* he took the wide steps two at a time.

"Hi, honey. Let me warm you up something to eat." His mom started to get up, and he noticed the baby monitor on the table next to her.

Jonathan help up his hand. "Don't worry about it, mom. I already ate something."

Not since lunch, but no way was he telling her that. She'd tie him down and force food down his throat. Molly O'Halleran could do it, too. His mom might only be five foot two, but she had the strength of a mother's love on her side. These days, he practically had to force *himself* to eat.

She flashed him one of her worried looks—the one he'd seen too many times over the past few months—then settled back in her chair.

His dad laced his fingers with hers and kissed her knuckles before setting their joined hands on the arm of the chair.

"He's a grown man, honey. He can feed himself." Then he gave her a soft smile—the one reserved just for her.

She relented but wasn't happy about it. Jonathan was pretty sure he heard her *harrumph*.

"Well, good night." He turned to walk inside and was stopped by his father's voice.

"You're going in to check on her, right?" One of those questions that wasn't really a question.

"Of course." He pulled the door open and stopped. His back to them, hesitant, he asked, "Is she really okay?"

"Yes, honey, she's really okay." His mother's voice was rich with understanding and a grandmother's love. "Perfect, in fact."

Jonathan knew if he turned around he would see concern or, God forbid, pity on their faces, so he didn't. He just nodded and walked through the door. He toed off his boots, hung his coat on a hook, then headed upstairs.

Ashling's nursery was at the end of the hall, next to his parents' room. Made it easier for his mom, who'd been doing most of the work—one, because she knew what the hell she was doing, and two, because Jonathan was gone a lot, getting the office up and operational.

Liar. You're gone a lot because you're avoiding your daughter and all the emotions that go with her. Unfortunately, he wasn't sure how to change that or if he even could.

He set his bag on the floor outside his room, then approached her door on silent feet.

The top of her little head was barely visible through the narrow opening. His fingers dragged across the door as it swung open, and he stepped into the room. The smell of baby powder and baby shampoo softened the air.

The soft carpet muffled his steps as he moved to her crib. He stood and stared down at the most beautiful creature on the planet. Rounded cheeks framed a tiny button nose. Beneath it, little pink, bow-shaped lips puckered and unpuckered, as if anticipating a bottle. She'd taken to sleeping on her back, arms spread overhead, her little hands curled tight. Jonathan reached in and stroked over the tiny dimples forming along her little knuckles. He loved seeing them—they were a sign she was gaining weight. *Thank God.* For so long, she'd been too thin, too small, too sick. But his baby girl was a fighter. She'd had to be.

She opened her fist and curled her fingers around his thumb and, with a sleepy little sigh, held on tight. He smiled and stayed there for several minutes, allowing himself to enjoy the connection. Much easier to do during quiet, private moments like this.

With her dark hair, Ashling favored the O'Halleran side of the family. Ashamed as he was to admit it, that made it slightly easier. He wasn't sure how he'd handle it if she was a carbon copy of her mother.

Why did you do it, Marilyn? It was the same question he'd asked himself more times than he could count, ever since the doctors told him what happened.

CHAPTER FIVE

Andi stifled a yawn, then caught her reflection in the mirrored elevator door. *Yikes.* She tucked her short hair over her ears and tried to ignore the dark circles under her eyes. Thanks to multiple time changes, her internal clock was all kinds of screwed up. Sleep had proven to be an elusive creature since she'd arrived in the States, and it showed.

She rolled her shoulders and stretched her neck side to side. Tension from all the crazy travel, that's all it was. After all, she had no reason to be nervous; if anything, she had the advantage here. The man she was about to meet with had no idea who she was. Well ... not yet anyway.

The doors whispered open on the top floor.

She took a deep breath, hitched her backpack higher up her shoulder and stepped out.

A pretty woman looked up from her desk. A big smile lit her face. A sparkly pencil had been stabbed through a messy bun teetering atop her head.

"Hi, there. Can I help you?" Her voice was all sunshine and rainbows.

"Yes. Andi Swain to see Jonathan O'Halleran."

"Andi Swa—" Her eyes widened. "You're Andi?"

"Yes. Well, my real name is Andréa, but I go by Andi."

"You're a woman." Though it seemed impossible, her smile got even bigger.

"Since the day I was born," Andi said.

A mischievous clarity brightened the young woman's features.

"Oh ... oh, no ... this is too perfect." She snorted and started laughing. Her shoulders shook to the point Andi was afraid the pencil would fly out and send white-blond hair tumbling all over the place.

"Excuse me?" Andi wasn't sure she'd said anything funny. Then again, she'd been living in a war zone for a long time—maybe she'd missed something.

"I'm sorry." She tried to get control of herself. "It's just that he's expecting a man. Not that it would matter to him." She tipped her head toward the set of large wooden doors over her right shoulder. "You're going to love him," she gushed.

Highly doubtful, Andi thought.

"He's a great boss and has no problem working with women. When I first started here, he made sure I knew he didn't expect me to fetch his coffee or pick up his dry cleaning or ... " She tilted her head, tapped her pen against her lip. "Hmm, come to think of it, I don't think he's really the dry-cleaning type."

With a quick shake of her head, she rambled onward, "Anyway, what I'm trying to say is, he's not one of those chauvinist guys who thinks women are lesser humans or some such silliness. It's just ... well, I just know he's going to be very surprised to see you."

You have no idea.

"I'm sorry." She stood and circled the desk with her hand

out. "I'm Christina and, in case you haven't figured it out yet, I can be a bit chatty."

The woman was a perky bundle of energy. Andi was exhausted just listening to her.

"Would you like some water or tea, coffee maybe?"

"No, thank you. I'm fine." One more cup of coffee and Andi's heart might explode.

"Please, make yourself at home. I'll let him know you're here." Christina tapped on the big wooden door and disappeared inside.

Drawn to the fire crackling in a massive fireplace, Andi crossed the dark reclaimed wood floors. Pinecones recently tossed in the fire surrounded her with the earthy scent of the woods she'd driven through on her way here. The expansive stacked stone wall surrounding the fireplace was made up of varying shades of white, beige and brown. Split wood loaded neatly into cubbies on either side looked like artwork. Whether on purpose or by accident, she couldn't be sure. The whole look was very structured, yet not.

She turned and took in the rest of the large space. A huge, dark leather sofa, two chairs in a soft oatmeal-colored fabric and a beautiful, huge, wooden coffee table complemented the clean lines and warm wood top of Christina's desk. Beyond the elevator, three large, polished wood doors the same color as the floors lined the main corridor. At the end, there was what appeared to be a large conference room, and there were hallways to the left and right.

The entire top floor had a warm, welcoming, masculine feel to it. Not in a hunting-lodge-dead-animal-heads-on-the-wall kind of way, though. Not that she would have a problem with that. It was just ... comfortable. Not what you'd expect from one of the world's most successful security organizations. And a far cry from the tents and huts she'd been living and working in for the past few years.

Andi liked it. A lot.

"Andi?" Christina's voice drew her away from the fire.

Good thing she showed up when she did. A few more minutes, and Andi might've curled up on the sofa and fallen asleep. Not the best way to make a first, well, second impression.

"You can go in now." Christina bit the inside of her cheek and whispered, "I didn't tell him you were—"

"A woman?" Andi interjected.

Christina nodded, a co-conspirator's smile firmly in place.

I think I'm going to like this woman.

"That's fine," Andi said. He would find out soon enough.

She took a bracing breath and firmed her shoulders. *Here goes nothin'.* She twisted the knob and pushed open one of the big wooden doors.

A large man turned from where he'd been poking at a fire in another massive fireplace. Silhouetted by the flames, he looked like some kind of ancient warrior. His glare skewered her from across the room. No doubt he wondered what the hell *she* was doing there. Call it petty, but she gained a certain gleeful satisfaction at the look of disbelief on his face. Every instinct she had told her this man was seldom surprised by anything.

He slowly replaced the poker in the stand. Then, like a large predator who'd scented its prey, he stalked closer.

Andi thought back to their first and only meeting in that bombed-out stone hut. She'd assumed all the tactical gear and weaponry he'd been wearing created the illusion of size. Boy, had she been wrong.

Jonathan O'Halleran was a big man, well over six feet. The scraggly, dark beard and shaggy hair he'd sported while in-theater had been trimmed to GQ perfection. His broad chest and shoulders currently tested the load strength of what had to be a custom-made button-up shirt. No way was that thing off-the-rack. If his sleeves weren't rolled up, she'd probably find an embroidered monogram on the cuff. She also wouldn't have noticed the trident logo peeking out from beneath the dark hair or the huge gold aviator watch shining on his wrist. He wasn't fooling her with that starched oxford, groomed face and fancy watch. Deep down, this man was as far from civilized as a person could get.

She thrust her hand forward.

"Andi Swain." She strengthened her voice to cover her jangling nerves.

"What the hell are you doing here?" He crossed his arms over his chest.

Nope. Not happy to see her. He obviously still blamed her for his friend's death.

"I'm sure you already know exactly why I'm here." He was delusional if he expected Andi to cower under his macho gruffness.

A few more seconds of scowling, then he took hold of her outstretched hand. Calluses earned from hours at the gun range and hand-to-hand practice matched her own. He might have a big fancy office, but he didn't spend all of his time there.

His grip was firm but not too tight. No doubt in deference to her being a woman.

Whatever.

An unexpected warmth traveled up her arm, and unnerving tingles crept around in her belly.

Uh ... Andi ... hello. He's a widower ... with a kid. Yeah, she'd read all about that in his file. Not to mention he harbored a deep dislike for her.

In the wake of that little reminder, the unwelcome sensations created by his touch fizzled.

Andi gave three quick, strong pumps and let go. She slipped her resume from her bag and handed it to him. The fact OSI agreed to bring her in sight unseen said a lot about Burke's relationship with Beckett O'Halleran.

Jonathan looked down at the single piece of paper.

"*Andréa* Swain, huh?" His eyebrow cocked up. "What happened to Agent Jones?"

"Agent Jones ceased to exist upon leaving Afghanistan. And please, call me Andi." No one called her Andréa.

Dark blue eyes scanned her up and down. "Why?"

"Why what?"

"Why Andi and not Andréa?" He circled behind his big desk. "Let me guess, too girlie for a big, tough interrogations tactics specialist like you?"

Ouch. Direct hit. The ultra-feminine name had always seemed like an ill-fitting, itchy suit. She was just Andi, the person who was more comfortable sending lead downrange at a target or hanging out with guys in the field than she was shopping or doing lunch.

"It's not relevant to my job here. Nor is it any of your business." She lifted her chin, challenging him to press further.

Narrowed eyes searched hers. Most people probably quaked under such intense focus.

Do your best, buddy. He had nothing on her father.

"When it comes to working at OSI, everything about you is relevant." He indicated the chair in front of his desk. "Sit, *Andréa.*"

Even after settling into his big leather chair, he dominated the space.

"Please," she mumbled under her breath as she sat, then put her backpack on the floor next to her.

"What was that?" He looked up from her resume.

"As I said before, I prefer Andi. It's what I've been called since my father brought me home from the hospital." The closest she would get to being the son her father always wanted but never had. *Cliché much?*

Good ol' dad.

Colonel Hampton "Sabretooth" Swain, often referred to by his peers as "the toughest SOB ever to bless the ranks of the United States Army," had only ever loved two things—her mother and the Army—in that order.

Her entire damn life, until the day he died, she'd spent trying to be someone the hard-ass colonel could love ... or even like. Turned out to be a complete waste of time. She could never be a son and could never bring her mother back.

Not once in all that time had he ever stopped to consider Andi's loss.

Of course, she'd never tell Jonathan O'Halleran any of that. Not that he'd care.

She met his eyes. *Be cordial. Keep smiling.* If she was going to be successful, she couldn't risk alienating this man. A tall order, considering their history.

He tilted his head.

"I'm sensing there's a story there." His deep voice rolled across the room and wrapped around her like warm caramel. And, boy, did she like caramel.

"Nope, no story. Just a nickname." Uncomfortable with the idea he might be able to see things she'd rather keep hidden, Andi scrubbed all emotion from her features. A handy trick in her line of work, where a person's veracity could be determined by the simplest verbal cue or muscle twitch.

He picked up a slim gold pen and gave it a twist. The delicate instrument looked out of place in his large, scarred hand as he jotted something in a file. Something about her bad attitude, most likely.

Andi spent so much time with guys in the field, she never paid much attention to their hair. Hell, outside of work, she never paid much attention to *them*. Too complicated. But something about the way Jonathan's dark hair fell over his forehead as he scribbled a note made her want to brush it out of his eyes and run her fingers through it. And just how ridiculously girlie was that?

I'm just tired. That's all it was. Okay, and maybe a little horny. When was the last time she'd had sex, anyway?

Focus, Andi. Now was so not the time for thoughts like that.

A few very long minutes later, he set the pen down, closed the file and looked up at her. It was then she noticed a few strands of gray at his temples that weren't there before. No doubt a testament to what he'd been through the past several months.

"So, tell me, Andréa, why did you agree to consult for OSI?"

She'd die a thousand painful deaths before she ever admitted how the sound of her given name crossing his lips touched a feminine part of her she'd tried to deny most of her life. Especially since he did it just to needle her.

"Jeffrey and your brother thought OSI could benefit from adding someone with my expertise and skill set to your team to help identify the person responsible for what happened to your brother." Take that, you mouth-breathing Neanderthal.

"I guess I'm surprised. That they still think that, I mean." His square jaw jumped, and he pierced her with his cold, midnight-blue stare. "Considering the one instance I know of, your professed expertise was no help and actually led to a supreme clusterfuck. If I remember correctly, one person died, and three were seriously wounded."

And there it was.

"Listen, *Mister* O'Halleran, if you don't think you can work with me, take it up with Burke and your brother." Andi was sick of this volley of veiled insults. Especially since she had enough of her own doubts about what she should've or could've done differently.

"Oh, believe me, I will." He leaned forward. His disgust reached across the desk and coated her like black tar. "Until then, it looks like I'm stuck with you."

She lifted her chin. "Looks like we're stuck with each other."

CHAPTER SIX

Jonathan wasn't happy about her being there, but he had to give her credit. Andréa Swain had guts. Which should come as no surprise, considering she'd spent the last three-plus years working in a part of the world that could chew up and spit out even the toughest souls.

Jeffrey Burke had some major juice behind him. So when he recommended her to Beck, his brother had brought her on board without hesitation. Too bad he hadn't seen fit to send her resume to him before she arrived. Jonathan wouldn't have been taken by surprise when she strolled into his office.

After reading over the list of credentials on her resume, he had to grudgingly admit to being impressed. Not to mention, when a guy like Burke referred to someone as "the best of the best," you sat up and took notice.

That said, even the best fucked up sometimes.

The memory of their first encounter almost two years ago gnawed at the frayed edges of his conscience. Amped up on adrenaline, frustrated and pissed, not just at her but at the whole fucked-up war, he'd acted like a dickhead. His brutish behavior with her was an anomaly. That's not who he was. Jonathan studied things from every angle, considered every possibility before he reacted. He lived for control. His mom would kick his ass if she knew how he'd treated her that day and how he was treating her now.

There was just something about this particular woman ...

He stared across the desk at her.

"According to my brother, you'll be here for six months." Unless he came up with a legitimate reason to get rid of her sooner.

"Think you can handle that?" She cocked up a brow. "After all, keeping all that righteous indignation bottled up might become painful."

Face blank, hands crossed in her lap, she watched him.

"You can stop analyzing me, Andréa." Jonathan knew enough about her area of expertise to know that was exactly what she was doing.

The woman was fierce, yet he'd picked up on the way her shoulders stiffened a fraction every time he used her real name. He'd also noticed the shadow that crept through her eyes when she mentioned her father. Yeah. Definitely a story there.

"Ah, so you've read at least one of my studies." Her smirk did little to hide the combination of surprise and delight.

"This is my brother's company. So yes, I did my due diligence." Trust outside his family was hard-earned. She would have to work doubly hard. "And now that I know your *real* name, I'll do even more."

"Do your best. I've got nothing to hide."

Maybe professionally, but he got the sense there were skeletons in her personal closet she'd rather not have dragged out into the light of day. If they interfered with her ability to do her job, she was gone.

"I'm about to go over my expectations." He held out a legal pad and pen. "You might want to take notes."

"Thanks, I've got one." Andi leaned over and dug a well-worn leather notebook and pen from her pack. She flipped it open, clicked the pen and waited for him to begin.

Jonathan spent the next several minutes detailing her responsibilities, as well as their extensive goals and expectations for her during her time at OSI. The combination of her top-secret clearance and Burke's endorsement would allow her access to their system ... with one exception. Any and all information about members of the family was strictly off limits.

Protecting the family was always their number one priority.

"Any questions?" He dropped his pen on his desk as he sat back, elbows on the arms of his chair, fingertips tapping together.

"Not at this time." She clicked the pen to close it and flipped her notebook shut.

"You can get started tomorrow morning." He stood and rounded his desk.

"I'd like to get started today, if possible." She wedged her notebook inside, then grabbed her pack, stood and hefted it over her shoulder.

He looked at his watch. "It's almost five o'clock, and most everyone will be heading home soon. I'd prefer you wait until tomorrow."

"Don't trust me, huh?" One corner of her mouth lifted.

Not even a little.

"When you get here tomorrow, Christina will get you badged, set up in an office and make sure you have the accesses you need."

Andréa drew back her shoulders and looked him straight in the eye.

"I *will* find out who's responsible for what happened to your brother and his partner. And as much as you might hate me for what happened to your friend, you can't possibly know how I feel about it."

With that, she turned and left his office.

The door whispered shut behind her, and Jonathan leaned his hip against the side of his desk. He glanced down at her resume, then back at the door.

"You are a complicated woman, Andréa Elizabeth Swain." And beautiful and mysterious and sexy as hell.

"Shit." He scrubbed his hand down his face.

There was a light tap on his door before Christina and her big energy bubble blew into the room. Even with her rough past, she still managed to be upbeat and positive. If he had to guess, it was in spite of her past, sort of her way of giving a big middle finger to all the shit she'd survived.

She was a force of nature, and Jonathan patted himself on the back every day for seeing past her harried exterior to the administrative wonder hidden below. OSI's northwest branch would not function without her, and anyone who underestimated her was an idiot.

"I'm getting ready to go. Did you need anything?" She moved over to the fireplace and tossed a log on top. Bright red embers broke apart and shifted. Sparks crackled and sprinkled upward.

"No, thanks, I'm good." He turned back to his desk. "Make sure someone walks you to your car."

"Duh." She rolled her eyes as she brushed her hands together, then walked to the door. "Open or closed?"

"Closed, please."

"Closed it is. Night, Boss Man." She waggled her fingers in a little wave and shut the door quietly behind her.

Jonathan pulled open his bottom drawer and grabbed the bottle and shot glass. He walked over and dropped into the large leather chair in front of the fireplace. Feet propped on the stone hearth, he crossed his ankles, filled the glass and tossed back the golden-brown liquid.

The first one always burned—like a warning shot intended to stop him from going any further.

What the hell was he doing thinking about another woman?

A second shot—a little less burn.

It had been six months since Marilyn died. Due to back-to-back deployments, it had been over a year since the last time he'd seen her. He'd talked to her once via internet video, but the connection had been shitty, and they'd had to cut it short. Hell, the only way he even found out she was pregnant was from an e-mail she'd sent him about two months after his last leave. What the hell kind of husband did that make him?

A third shot—no burn at all.

Like most spouses of spec ops guys, she'd built a life that didn't include him. Jonathan would never say the words aloud, but it had begun to feel like the only thing they'd had in common was their past ... and the baby she carried.

His fingers gripped the neck of the bottle where it rested on the arm of the chair. Fire flashed off its contents. The other hand rested on his abs, the shot glass held loosely in his grasp. He stared, unblinking, into the flames as he was dragged into the past.

After he'd unfolded himself from the Red Cross chopper, he'd flown to Kabul. There, he'd jumped on a C130 to Bagram Airfield, then another to Landstuhl, Germany. Finally, five sleepless, hazy days later, he'd landed at Sea-Tac Airport.

His mom and dad had picked him up and driven him straight to the hospital. After he'd stuffed himself into a too-small set of scrubs, the NICU nurse had showed him how to wash and scrub his arms and hands. Protocols satisfied, she'd led him down the quiet hallway and turned into one of the small rooms. The lights were dimmed, and a lone incubator stuck out from the wall. A steady hum and the rhythmic hiss from the ventilator provided a backdrop to the quiet beeps from a heart monitor. He'd stood, frozen in the doorway, and stared at that damn machine. With each blink of the small heart icon on the screen, he'd begun to feel his own heart beating again.

When his feet finally decided to cooperate, he'd approached the clear plastic crib with a strange mixture of dread and elation. Inside was this amazing, teeny-tiny creation who was a part of him and a part of Marilyn. Pads with teddy bears printed on them covered her eyes; tubes and wires came from her nose, mouth, the top of her head, the back of her hand. For several minutes, he'd watched her little chest rise and fall with each pulse of the ventilator. Crushed by the weight of responsibility and overcome by an onslaught of emotions, he'd flattened his hands atop his daughter's incubator and broken down. At some point his parents came in, because it was his father's strong arms banded around him that kept him from collapsing to the floor in a sobbing heap.

A while later, as he'd sat vigil by his sleeping daughter, his mother held his hand and gently reminded him that his baby girl needed a name.

"We never even got the chance to talk about it," Jonathan managed to croak out. He'd been downrange and unable to communicate with the *real* world.

"It's okay, honey." She'd squeezed his hand. "The right name will come to you."

And it had—Ashling Marilyn O'Halleran. The unique name was Irish for a dream or a vision. It seemed appropriate.

Two and a half very long, very stressful months later, she'd finally been released from the NICU. With the help of a nurse, he'd tucked her into her special preemie car seat, triple-checked the restraints were fastened properly, then proceeded to drive to the house like he had a shipment of eggs rolling around loose in his backseat. He'd been less nervous driving a Humvee through IED-infested countryside than he had been navigating the damn gravel road up to his folks' house.

Huge smiles lit their faces as they jogged down the wide wood steps and flagstone walk to meet him in the driveway. He'd loaded his dad's arms with BSE—baby support equipment—then unstrapped Ashling from her car seat and carefully handed her to his mom. He'd been keeping his daughter at arm's length ever since.

CHAPTER SEVEN

Andi cursed and wished a pox upon Jeffrey Burke as she stared out across the sea of files, paperwork and unwatched DVDs covering her huge desk. Her worst nightmare had come to life.

"I'm sorry there are so many." With an apologetic smile, Christina handed her two more. "Jonathan wanted you to have them so you could get started doing ... well ... " She waved her hand over the stacks. "Whatever it is that you do."

"What is it you do, anyway?" Behind Christina, a small woman with dark auburn hair and mischievous green eyes leaned against the doorjamb. "Hi." She stepped into the office, hand outstretched. "I'm Jonathan's sister, Emily. You're Andi, right?"

Before Andi had time to answer, the diminutive dynamo delivered a handshake bigger than you'd expect from someone her size.

"Sorry, I didn't mean to eavesdrop. I was actually coming to introduce myself and overheard Christina." Emily helped herself to one of the chairs in front of Andi's desk. "I know you're an interrogator of some sort but not sure what that really means."

Andi was used to being on her own. Being around these two peppy people would take some getting used to.

"We prefer to call it statement analysis and analysis of nonverbal behaviors." The word "interrogator" tended to turn people off. "You sure you want to hear this? Some people find it ... tedious."

Their responses of "definitely" and "absolutely" overlapped.

She set aside a stack of files and crossed her arms on her desk.

"Statement analysis is when I examine written statements, transcripts of interviews, even the choice and structure of an interviewee's words. It's all based on the premise that word use and grammar structures differ when people lie as opposed to when they tell the truth. By carefully analyzing these things, I can identify veracity, ascertain motive and detect deception."

Christina slowly sat in the chair next to Emily.

"The use of minimizing adverbs—*simply, only, just, merely*—editing adverbs like *then, so, later, next, after that, until,* and intensifying words or phrases such as *really, I swear,* and *honest to God* serve one purpose. They're meant to convince you of something, not convey any real information."

They both gave her wide-eyed blank looks. She got that a lot when she talked about her work. Best not to go into equivocations and spatial details.

"Simply put, what a person says or writes and how they say or write it matters."

"Fascinating." Emily beamed. "The other one ... "

"Nonverbal behaviors."

"Yeah, what's that about?" She scooted to the front edge

of the chair, leaned her elbow on the front of the desk, her chin in her hand.

Andi loved talking about her work, so it was fun when someone else seemed genuinely interested.

"I watch videotaped statements looking for two things, emblematic gestures and ones associated with the face." She tried to clarify. "An example of emblematic behavior is like ... let's say you flip someone the bird." She held up her middle finger. Knowing her luck, Jonathan would choose that moment to walk by and think she was flipping off his little sister. "Everyone knows what that means, right?"

The two women smiled and nodded.

"Or if you do this"—she made a circle with her index finger and thumb—"it means everything is A-OK. You know what the person means without them having to say the word."

"Oh, so you're also looking at gestures and things like that?"

"That's part of it, yes. Then we have ones associated with the face, the micro-expressions. They're signs of hidden or repressed emotions."

"I saw on a TV show once where they said if someone looks up and to the left, they're probably lying." Christina said.

"Actually, in our studies, we've determined that is a fallacy." Television shows seldom got it right. "A better example would be saying the word 'yes' but ever so slightly shaking your head 'no.' The word is in conflict with the gesture. That said, emblematic gestures are culturally specific. For example, in Bulgaria and some of the more remote parts of Pakistan where I've worked, 'yes' and 'no' are reversed."

She shared the story of the Navy spy ship, the USS Pueblo, captured by the North Koreans in 1968. The ship was stripped of every piece of high-tech equipment, and the eighty-three-member crew was taken hostage.

"During their eleven months in captivity, they were beaten, tortured and forced to sit for propaganda photos. In one, several of the men are shown extending their middle fingers. Because the emblematic gesture is English in its derivation, the North Koreans didn't recognize it for what it was—a hint to the American government that they'd been coerced. In all likelihood, they never would've figured it out if *Time* magazine hadn't run the picture with a caption giving away what they were doing."

Andi didn't think they needed to know that all it did was piss off the North Koreans. As a result, the torture the men endured became worse.

"Interesting side note, the North Koreans reverse-engineered a lot of the technology they stole. And they are still in possession of the USS Pueblo." The assholes had it on display for all to see. A sort of feather in their cap for having defeated, in some small way, the mighty forces of the U.S. Navy.

"Holy crap," Emily said. "That is fascinating."

Christina nodded in agreement.

"Bottom line is, when motivated people lie and face consequences when caught, clues to deception emerge and appear in a lot of different ways: facial expressions, gestures and body language, voice and verbal style, as well as the actual words spoken. We refer to it as *leakage,* and it occurs simultaneously. Investigators can be trained to identify these indicators and use them, coupled with good, old-fashioned investigative work—taking witness statements, forensics, and other evidence—to close their cases."

On those rare occasions Andi was able to watch the news, she couldn't help analyzing the talking heads. Presidential debates were another great opportunity to fine-tune her skill.

"What a fascinating way to make a living." Emily leaned forward and whispered, "Think you can teach me your ways so I can use them against my pain-in-the-butt brothers?"

Andi chuckled. "I'm not really sure how it can help you, unless you think one of them is lying to you."

"No, never that." She frowned and fell back in her chair with a huff. "They're just bossy and overbearing and can't seem to grasp the concept that I *can* actually take care of myself. It's so friggin' annoying."

What must it be like having siblings to complain about?

"Oh, shoot!" Christina tapped her earpiece and bolted up from the chair as if she'd received a shock. "O'Halleran Security International. How can I help you?" Her words faded and her ponytail flew out behind her as she darted back to her desk.

"She certainly has a lot of energy." Andi sat back in her chair. "Makes me feel old."

"Oh, please." Emily scoffed. "I saw you running at lunch today. In the rain, no less." She shivered, like it was the worst possible thing a person could endure and that Andi might be a little bit crazy for doing it.

"I take it you're not a fan of running?"

"Uh, no. Not even a little." Emily chuckled. "If you ever see me running, you probably should run, too. It means something with large teeth and claws is chasing me."

Andi laughed, and it felt great. "I think I like you, Emily."

"I think I like you, too, Andi." Her smile made her look like a little imp up to no good. She must keep all those big brothers of hers on their toes.

"Emily, Ricky's looking for you." Speaking of big brothers ... Like a sexy fog, Jonathan's deep voice found its way over and around all the stacks and piles on her desk. "Something about CAC cards for a couple of the guys?" His words may have been directed at his sister, but his eyes were on Andi.

Great.

"Oh, good." Emily sprang up out of the chair, oblivious to the tension clogging the air. "It was great meeting you, Andi. Let's go get drinks sometime, okay?"

"Absolutely." Andi smiled at her. "And it was great meeting you, too."

Jonathan stopped his sister with a hand on her shoulder.

"Em, did you get the brakes on your car taken care of?" His voice was low and gentle in a way she'd never heard before.

"With Dad, you and Mason constantly harping on me about it, how could I forget?" Emily sighed dramatically, rolled her eyes and looked back at Andi. "See what I mean?"

"It's because we love you, squirt." Jonathan tugged on his sister's hair.

"Yeah, yeah, whatever. I love you, too." She rolled her eyes again, stood on tiptoes and gave him a quick peck on the cheek. Then she headed toward the basement, where Ricky and the other computer guys worked.

Not having windows would make Andi nuts, but those guys seemed to thrive in the cold, dark space.

Jonathan shook his head. A smile broke out across his handsome face as he watched his little sister march away.

It was the most beautiful, tender moment she'd ever witnessed in her life. She couldn't help but be a touch jealous of her new friend. Must be nice to have someone care so much about you.

By the time he turned back to her, his demeanor had changed. The smile was a thing of the past, and the caring big brother was replaced by the man who couldn't wait for Andi to fail.

"You need to understand something, Andréa. My sister is—"

"Strong, independent, intelligent?" His tone put an immediate end to Andi's private little pity party. Facing off against the man now looming in her doorway required she be at her best.

"Yes, she is all of those things. She is also very stubborn and unaware of the dangers that await her in the world she is so determined to take on." He moved into her office and continued. "I would appreciate it if you didn't encourage her."

"Encourage her? I'm not sure I know what you mean." Did he think she was going to corrupt his baby sister or something?

"She's ... not like you." Two more steps brought him closer still.

"You don't know anything about me."

"I've learned a lot about you since you got here."

This should be good.

"I have no doubt you did." He wouldn't be the man she thought he was if he hadn't. Besides, he wasn't big on trust, especially with her.

"Father was Colonel Hampton Swain. Mother, Bethany Swain. An only child, you're thirty years old, were born in Southern Pines, North Carolina, while your father was stationed at Fort Bragg." His eyes stayed on her as he recited the facts of her life.

"You graduated *magna cum laude* from Jacksonville State University, where you earned a double major in psychology and criminal justice, then went on to achieve your master's in criminology at the University of Alabama. While there, Jeffrey Burke recruited you to work for the National Security Agency. You excelled, moving quickly up the ranks. You're highly respected for your investigative skills, specifically statement analysis and analysis of nonverbal behaviors."

She leaned back in her chair and crossed her arms and legs, striving for a look of indifference.

"For the past three years, you have been assigned to

multiple forward operating bases throughout Afghanistan and parts of Pakistan. You've been responsible for gathering intel that, I'm told, saved hundreds of lives." He paused. "Right up until it didn't."

Her right eye twitched. She cursed herself.

"What does any of that have to do with your sister?" Andi slowly stood and rounded her desk, pretty sure she wasn't going to like what he had to say.

"She's innocent, fragile, and we take care of our own." He moved closer, dragging the scent of pine and man along with him.

Energy crackled and the tension in the air thickened as the space closed between them.

"Oh." She jammed her hands onto her hips. "And since I'm an outsider, I'm a threat to her. Is that it?"

He stepped into her personal space, towering over her. "Something like that."

Heat pumped from his big body, and she could see the lighter blue striations spearing out from the center of his irises.

Andi's hands dropped, and she closed the remaining space. "Whether you want to accept it or not, your sister is a grown woman. She can make her own decisions."

Her heartbeat faltered, and her nipples pebbled against her T-shirt. All it would take is one deep breath, and her breasts would brush against his chest. She was tempted to do it, just to get a reaction from him, but she wasn't sure she'd survive it herself. Pretty ridiculous, considering the circumstances and nature of their ... relationship.

He looked down. Dark blue eyes traveled over her face like a touch. Distrust and something else, something hotter battled for control within.

"She hasn't seen what you've seen, been where you've been." His harsh whisper skittered across her nerve endings.

His eyes narrowed. His head tilted to one side. "You're hard, tough, immune to the nightmares of war, aren't you? You've learned to shut off your emotions for the job. Maybe you never learned how to turn them back on."

He said it as if stating fact. As if he had any clue how she felt. Andi schooled her features, gave away none of her doubts or fears, hid her longing to be accepted and loved for who she was.

"Emily is naïve to that kind of ugliness, and it's my job to protect her. I won't have her exposed to it by anyone, especially you."

Especially you? Her chin drew back as if she'd been slapped.

Unable to reconcile his harsh words with the way he made her feel when he stood so close, she stepped back and leaned her butt against the front of her desk, putting some much-needed space between them.

"Are you worried I'm going to regale your baby sister with my blood-splashed stories of war? Or tell her how a good man was slaughtered in some godforsaken shithole of a village because of me? Or, no, maybe I'll work my devilish magic and turn your sister into an emotionless automaton, just like me."

She hesitated, her voice low, almost afraid to ask. "Is that honestly what you think of me?"

When he didn't respond right away, Andi realized how much she'd been hoping, deep down, he would be different. That maybe, just maybe he would see through her armor to the hurt and loneliness she kept hidden inside.

What an idiot. Why did she give a shit what he thought of her?

She swallowed past the disappointment lodged in her throat as she moved behind her desk and sat. "If we're through here ... I've got work to do."

"Look." He plowed his fingers through his hair. "Andréa, I'm—"

"It's Andi, and I got the message—stay away from your sister." Shocked when rare tears threatened, she bit the inside of her cheek. She would not give this man the satisfaction of knowing how much he'd hurt her.

She grabbed a file from the stack, snapped it open and, without looking up, said, "Please close the door on your way out."

After a moment, there were muffled footsteps, and her door quietly clicked shut.

She dropped back against her chair and turned to the window behind her desk. The sky was gray, and a heavy drizzle continued to soak everything. A low mist crept around evergreen and fir trees towering nearby.

An involuntary tear streamed down her face, and she thought back to the last time she'd cried. She was ten years old and had come home to find an ambulance in her next-door neighbor's driveway. The nice old lady who lived there, the one who made cookies for her and waved at her every day as she walked to and from the bus stop, had died.

Her father's words to her that day plowed through her mind.

"Toughen up, Andi. No one likes a crybaby. You don't want people thinking you're weak, do you?"

No, she didn't.

Andi dashed the useless tear from her cheek with the back of her hand and did what she did best, "toughened up" and got back to work.

CHAPTER EIGHT

Jonathan tossed back the shot, promising himself it would be his one and only tonight. The smooth whiskey warmed its way down his throat to his belly and outward.

He sat at his desk and thought back over his confrontation with Andi. He'd been walking down the hall when he heard her and Emily laughing together. His first thought had been, what the hell could they possibly have to laugh about? No two women could be more different. Then, as he'd been doing since the day Emily was born, his overprotective big-brother instincts kicked in.

In her typical ballsy fashion, Andi hadn't backed down an inch. But there'd been something in her eyes, in the minuscule sag of her shoulders. She was all brass and ballsy on the outside, but he was sure something was eating away at her just below the surface.

Shit knows he could relate. There were times it took every ounce of discipline and control he possessed to keep his conflicted feelings from blowing him into a million pieces.

His cell phone rang, and he dug it from his pocket.

"Hey, Mom."

"Hi, honey." Her voice held a smile. "I just wanted to make sure you didn't forget that Dad and I are going to Darby's release party tonight."

"Yeah, I remembered." How the hell could he forget? Dread had been gnawing at his gut all day.

Tonight would be the first time he was completely responsible for Ashling, without his parents as a buffer. It terrified him. More accurately, the thought of getting too close and losing his baby girl terrified him.

Pretty fucking pathetic.

"I'll wrap things up here and head home," he said.

"Excellent! I'm really excited to pick up this wine allotment. It's supposed to be one of his best yet." His folks weren't big drinkers, but they'd joined Darby English's wine club after their first tasting. A couple of his brothers were members as well. The vintner had since become a good friend of the family.

"Sounds great, mom." These days, he had a hard time mustering up excitement about anything.

"Jonathan, sweetie, you're going to be fine. *She's* going to be fine." Their mom had a sixth sense about when one of her children was struggling or hurting. "You have to trust me on this."

"I know, and I do. It's just ... " How could he tell her he'd rather sit here, in the dark, and finish off the bottle of whiskey currently tempting him from inside the drawer? Or that he couldn't look at his daughter without being slammed by anger at her mother, then feeling like shit for even having thoughts like that about his dead wife?

He couldn't. Instead, he simply said, "I'll be home in thirty minutes."

His mom sighed and let him off the hook. "We'll see you soon, honey."

Jonathan hung up and put the shot glass back in the drawer, next to the bottle. He shoved himself up from the chair and tucked his phone back in his pocket. Heavy boots sank into the thick carpet as he crossed to the fireplace, checked the embers to ensure they were all burned out, then slid the glass doors shut. After grabbing his stuff, he took a last look around, then secured his office.

Rather than drive around the bay, he took the long way home. Stalling? Yes. Did it make him feel like a coward? Absolutely.

Damp, crisp air snuck through the partially open windows of his truck as it wound its way up and around the curves of the narrow two-lane road. Large, old-growth trees, like nature's sentinels, arched overhead, mingling with newer evergreens, oaks and pines to block out most of the stars.

Jonathan loved these woods, had spent a good portion of his childhood exploring them. Lately, he'd been drawn, once again, to the solitude they conveyed. To the temporary peacefulness they offered.

His tranquility was interrupted when a large deer burst through the trees on the embankment to his right and planted itself in the middle of the road.

Jonathan's arms stiffened, and his foot slammed on the brakes. All four tires locked up and screamed across the blacktop. The big truck shuddered to a stop, jerked forward, then back. The stench of burnt rubber billowed past his windows.

No more than two feet from his front bumper, the doe turned and stared at him. Fog blew from her flared nostrils as his headlights flashed off her big brown eyes. For a few minutes, she stood her ground, unblinking, watching him. As if assessing his next move. He realized why when she slowly turned back toward the woods. The leaves of a dense blackberry bush quivered and snapped. A long-legged, knobby-kneed fawn about three feet tall, its spots almost faded, worked its way out of the thorny brush before it trotted across the road. Not until her baby was safely ensconced in the woods on the other side did the doe turn back to Jonathan. Their eyes locked for another moment. She blinked, twitched one ear, then hurried after the fawn.

Air burst from Jonathan's lungs, and his grip loosened from the wheel. For the longest time, he stared into the murky woods where they'd disappeared, the rumble of the idling engine the only sound cutting through the chill air.

A quick shake of his head, and he put the car in gear. The look in the doe's eyes stayed with him the entire way home. She'd boldly stared him down, as if daring him to move. Willing to take on any adversary to keep her offspring safe.

If Jonathan were the kind of guy who believed in signs, he might think it was the universe's way of kicking him in the ass with regard to his own child. A sort of *get your shit together* message.

Ridiculous.

He turned off the road and headed up the hill to the house. Emily's jeep sat off to the side of the driveway. Probably going to the release party with their parents. He parked, grabbed his stuff and headed inside.

The front door clicked shut, and his mother called out. "Is that you, honey?"

"Depends which 'honey' you're talking about." See? He could pretend everything was fine. He kicked off his boots and shoved them to the side. Their mom wasn't picky about much, but she was downright militant about her no-boots-in-the-house rule.

"Hey." Emily walked around the corner from the dining room, a bowl of ice cream in her hand.

"Hey, squirt. What's wrong?"

"What makes you think anything's wrong?" She avoided

eye contact by scooping a spoonful into her mouth. Atypical of her usual take-no-prisoners approach to ... well ... everything.

He tilted his head in the direction of the bowl. "You only eat ice cream when something's bugging you."

"Huh-uh." She stabbed at the ice cream like it had wronged her in some way.

Jonathan crossed his arms and waited. Emily would bust at the seams if she tried keeping anything inside.

"Fine!" The spoon dropped into the bowl with a *clank,* and she threw up her free hand.

"Mason's a jerk, and I think you should fire him." She turned, stomped into the family room and dropped down on the couch.

Here we go again. About once a month she complained to him about Mason. He doesn't respect her. He treats her like a child. He's bossy. One time, she even complained his hair was too long. They were always butting heads about something. As long as it didn't interfere with their work, Jonathan tried to stay out of it.

"Okay." He sighed and followed her. "What did the devil Mason do now?"

"That ... that egotistical, bossy—" Emily leaned forward, clunked the bowl on the coffee table, then flopped back against the sofa. "He had the nerve to tell me I should get rid of my Jeep and get something more reliable."

She crossed her arms over her chest with an honest-to-God harrumph. His kid sister elevated pouting to an art form.

"You *should* get something more reliable." He set his back-pack on the floor and sat on the edge of the large, sturdy coffee table in front of her. Their dad built it to withstand a houseful of aggressive, physical boys. "That POS is always in the shop."

Her chin drew back with an indignant intake of air, and she gave him a fierce scowl.

"How *dare* you call my car a piece of ... " She glanced around him toward the kitchen where their mother was, then leaned close to whisper, "*Shit.* And you're taking *his* side?"

"I'm not taking anyone's side, Em. It just so happens that, in this instance, I agree with Mason."

"Traitor." She grumbled under her breath, her scowl still firmly in place.

He chuckled.

"What are you doing here, anyway?" He nudged her knee with his. "You going to the tasting with Mom and Dad?"

"I thought I'd come over and help you out with Ashling." Her expression softened, and she laid her much smaller hand over his. "I know how freaked out you get at the idea of taking care of her by yourself."

His sister was a real sweetheart. When she wasn't being a royal pain in the butt.

"I'm sure you have something better to do." His family worried about Jonathan's inability to cope with being alone with his daughter. Knowing that made him feel like the worst kind of failure. Especially since they were right.

"I didn't, but ... " She smirked and smacked the back of his hand. "Now that you've insulted my beloved jeep ... "

"I'm being serious here, Em." Jonathan was embarrassed to admit he knew very little about his sister's social life these days. Ever since arriving home, he'd been so absorbed in his own shit, he hadn't given much thought to anyone else.

"Dude, have you ever known me to do something I didn't want to do?" One eyebrow quirked up high in question. "Besides, I love hanging out with my baby niece. After all, we O'Halleran girls have to stick together."

Emily reached forward, grabbed the bowl and held out the spoon. "Want some?"

Jonathan smiled and shook his head. His shoulders relaxed and, as he watched his sister scrape up the last drop of melting ice cream, all he could think was how he'd dodged a bullet. Pathetic, how badly he'd wanted ... needed his kid sister to stick around. One of these days, though, he was going to have to man up and face his responsibilities.

CHAPTER NINE

Matt swiped his access card, and the gate arm lifted. He half-heartedly waved and returned the parking garage attendant's smile. His mind was focused on the wheels he was about to set in motion. He'd pondered all the options and ramifications deep into the early morning hours. Bottom line—it had to be done. The witness had to be found, and he had to be stopped.

He made his way to the third floor and pulled into his reserved spot. One of the perks of being the senator's right-hand guy. No coincidence he'd chosen the one closest to the elevator and within view of the surveillance cameras. Nothing was too good for his baby, a brand-new Mercedes C-class sedan he'd busted his ass to earn.

The engine hummed quietly, and the heater blew warm air to keep him from freezing his ass off. He slipped his personal cell phone, along with the plain white business card, from his breast pocket. For one minute, two, three, he stared down at it. After taking a deep, bracing breath and slowly releasing it, he entered the phone number. With each ring, his heart rate increased.

A gravel-voiced man answered. "Yeah."

"This is ... Mr. Smith." Anonymity was key until he knew more about this guy. "I was given your number by a business associate of mine. He told me you were the best at what you do."

"That's right." The private investigator certainly didn't lack confidence.

"He also assured me you knew the importance of exercising discretion." If there was even a hint the guy couldn't keep his mouth shut, this conversation was over. Too much was at stake. *Everything* was at stake.

"Wouldn't be the best if I didn't." His voice had an almost lazy quality to it. As if he could care less whether Matt hired him or not.

"Good. Excellent." He scoped out the parking garage. Other than a guy jogging to catch the elevator, there was no one around. "I need someone found."

"Name?" The PI asked.

"Well, that's the problem. I don't know his name." Matt had had no luck trying to find out on his own.

"Where does he work?"

"I don't know that either," Matt said.

A heavy sigh filtered through the phone. "What *do* you know?"

"I can give you a description of him and his car, as well as the first two numbers on his license plate." Now that he said it out loud, Matt began to wonder if this was a futile effort.

It sounded like a pen clicked in the background. "Give me what you've got, and I'll see what I can find out."

Matt relaxed back into the supple leather seat, unaware every muscle in his body had constricted. He gave him the information, then asked, "What about payment?" He would be paying for this with his own money, so it mattered. It mattered a whole hell of a lot. Because, unlike his boss, he didn't have unlimited funds.

"My standard rate is three hundred fifty an hour, plus expenses." He rattled the amount off without hesitation. Like it wasn't an outlandish sum. "You pay me when I find him."

When, not if. Matt was reassured by the man's confidence.

"Time is of the essence. So when should I contact you again?" The senator was freaking out that the guy who saw him was still *out there somewhere,* able to destroy him.

"You don't. I'll contact you." And with that, the line went dead.

Matt's hand dropped to his lap, and he sat there, staring at the *reserved spot* sign on the wall in front of his car. *No turning back now.* He envisioned himself freely strolling the halls of the White House. Coming and going from the Oval Office at will. A smile spread unbidden across his face. Yeah, all this hassle would definitely be worth it.

CHAPTER TEN

Andi sat in the darkened conference room and scribbled notes on her pad as she watched another videotaped statement. For the eleventh time in three minutes, the interviewee scrubbed his hand over his eyes and cleared his throat. *Stalling*. The moron was a horrible liar.

"Knock, knock."

She grabbed the remote and paused the interview and turned to find Mason Croft silhouetted in the doorway. She didn't know much about him, but he seemed like a good guy. Quick-witted, deadly as hell, and completely clueless to the fact Emily had a thing for him. Though her friend had never said the words and would likely deny the truth of it, Andi recognized the signs.

"That guy"—he pointed at the image frozen on the large screen—"was a real piece of work." He shook his head. "Dumber than a box of rocks."

She smiled and glanced at her pad. "Name's Clayton Marks." Then up at him. "You've seen him before?"

"Yeah, we busted him about a year ago as part of a high-end auto theft ring. Local cops didn't have the resources to handle it, so OSI stepped in."

"Wait. You're telling me this guy's already behind bars?" She pointed her pencil over her shoulder.

He nodded. "Asshole pulled a gun on a woman loading groceries into her brand-new Mercedes. Made her give up the keys, then took off. If I remember correctly, he got fifteen years without possibility of parole."

Andi didn't like the thoughts that began to swirl around in her head. She grabbed another DVD, popped it in and fast-forwarded.

"What about this woman? Know anything about her?" She waited, hoping her suspicions were wrong.

He stepped farther into the room.

"She was busted for forging passports, driver's licenses, immigration papers, you name it. Damn good at it, too. Except when she was strung-out on coke. Then she was just batshit crazy."

"Do you have a second to look at a few more?" She rifled through the stack of DVDs.

"Sure." He plopped down in the chair across from her and watched snippets from five more interviews.

"Why are you watching videos of folks we've already put away?"

That son of a bitch.

"That's a damn good question." Andi shoved up from her chair, sent it rolling across the room until it bumped into the wall. She'd been under the impression these were all active cases. "Excuse me." She switched off the projector, grabbed her notepad and scooped up the DVDs.

"Um ... sure, no problem." Mason followed behind as she stomped down the hallway.

She charged into Jonathan's office and slammed the door,

leaving a no doubt confused Mason standing on the other side.

Jonathan looked up from his desk.

"Ever hear of knocking, Andréa?" He dropped his pen and sat back in his chair.

"Just what the hell do you think you're doing?" She stopped at the front edge of his desk.

He slowly rose from his chair.

"Afraid I'm going to need more information before I can answer that."

Errrrgh.

Her urge to smack the smug look off his face competed with her desire to crawl across the desk and wrap herself around him like a spider monkey. What the hell was wrong with her?

"You know exactly what I'm talking about. You've been testing me, haven't you?"

He hesitated, and damned if it didn't sting knowing she was right. Pushing aside the disappointment, she latched on to her anger.

"How many of the twenty-three interviews you asked me to watch were actually from solved cases?" Andi asked.

"All but three." He answered without hesitation, a challenge in his voice.

She shook her head. How the hell was she going to prove she knew what she was doing if he didn't give her the chance?

"The person responsible for getting your brother shot is still waltzing around out there, and you're wasting my time with crap like this?" She dumped the DVDs on his desk. "Maybe if you weren't in such a hurry to get rid of me, you might actually see that I can help. But noooo, the almighty Jonathan O'Halleran would rather sit in judgment over the rest of us mere mortals."

Andi knew she should probably shut up, but she was sick of this game.

"You know what? I'll make you a deal. I've made notes on every single one of these interviews." She tossed her notepad on top of the DVDs and pointed at it. "Why don't you compare my findings against the actual case files. If I got even one wrong ... one"—she held up one finger—"I'll pack my stuff and be out of here before you can say 'I'm an arrogant asshole.'"

Jonathan didn't respond right away, just carefully straightened and stacked the DVDs.

She held her breath, unsure if she wanted him to accept the challenge so she could finally prove herself to him or reject it outright and send the message he finally trusted her.

He did neither.

He picked up her notepad and handed it to her. "Even if I believe you about these, that doesn't mean I'm willing to forget what happened over there."

It always comes back to that.

Andi firmed her shoulders against the weight of his disdain. There was no way to defend herself or set the record straight without divulging top-secret information. And she wasn't willing to break the law for anyone. Besides, a part of her *needed* him to believe her ... without having to offer proof. Stupid, but there it was.

"That said, I'll have Emily get you the video interviews from the guys working the op with Caleb." He indicated the chair in front of his desk.

She chose to stand.

He shook his head and sat, mumbling something about stubborn women.

"We feel pretty confident none of them are involved, but I want you to do a statement analysis for each one and report back to me with your findings."

"How many are we talking about?"

"There were eight team members on the ground, including Caleb's canine partner, Power." He tugged on his earlobe. "I wasn't in the States when it went down." His jaw rippled beneath his beard, and his shoulders seemed to tense. If they weren't so damn big, she probably wouldn't have noticed. "If you want any details, I suggest you speak to Caleb directly."

Andi knew from reviewing the timeline that Jonathan had been overseas when Caleb was almost killed. His family had decided not to tell him until he was safely back in the States. One moment of distraction could've cost him his life. Having served in the same hellacious region, she agreed it was absolutely the right decision.

"I'll talk to him and start working on those statements." She turned to leave.

"Andréa." She'd given up on correcting him but not because she loved the way her name sounded crossing his lips.

Liar, liar, pants on fire.

He picked up his pen, then looked up at her. "Let me know if you need anything else."

Andi gave a quick nod and returned to her office. She propped her hip against her windowsill, crossed her arms and gazed out at the view, awed by the streaks of the setting sun spearing sideways through the trees. Maybe now, she could finally make some progress on this case.

The phone on her desk rang. She slid off the sill and snatched up the receiver. "Andi Swain."

"Hey, Andi, it's Caleb." The guy always sounded so happy and upbeat. Hard to believe he was related to the surly guy down the hall.

Emily had gushed about how he'd married his "soul mate," which made him the "luckiest guy in the world." Apparently, those had been his exact words to his little sister ... and anyone else who would listen. Hard to believe he used to be a no-commitment kinda guy.

"My brother said you wanted to chat with me?"

She glanced in the direction of Jonathan's office, wondering, not for the first time, why he kept an emotional distance between himself and the people who truly cared about him. Then she reminded herself it was none of her business, no matter how much she wanted it to be.

CHAPTER ELEVEN

Jonathan stood off to the side and scanned the crowd mingling about his parents' large family room. People were clustered together in small groups, laughing, smiling, discussing their lives, jobs and kids, holding plates loaded with his mom's amazing food. Beck, his very pregnant wife, Gwen, and their daughter, Alice, were here. Caleb and his wife, Dawn, and her sister, Luna, had all flown in for the party as well. Everyone was here to celebrate Ashling's six-month clean bill of health checkup.

Ashling had passed all the required milestones. She was beautiful, healthy, happy and growing like a weed. It was the great news he'd been waiting for—they'd all been waiting for. Then why the hell wasn't he happy? Why did it still feel like razor blades tumbled in his gut? Why did he feel like he wanted to punch something ... all the damn time?

He downed the last of his drink, turned to head to the bar set up in the dining room and stopped short when he came face to face with all six foot four and a half inches of his father.

"Wonderful news, isn't it, son?" His dad spoke to him, but

his eyes were on Ashling. Jonathan's daughter wiggled in his mom's arms and held court in the middle of the crowd with her adorable coos and gurgles.

His little girl truly was the sweetest, most amazing miracle, and he loved her more than life. Yet he couldn't seem to let himself get too close to her.

"Yeah, great news, Dad." He gave the closest thing to a smile he could muster, then tried to move around him.

His dad matched his move, effectively blocking his path.

"You sure you need another one?" His father's brow lifted, and concerned eyes fell to the glass in his hand before tracking back up to his face. "I have to say, I thought you'd be happier when this day came."

Yeah. So did I.

Jonathan's jaw clenched and his free hand fisted at his sides as he glared at his dad. How fucked up was it that he was itching for a fight with the most important man in his life? Maybe he was hoping to get his ass whooped, because his dad could still do it.

He shoved past him and grabbed a bottle from the sideboard. Halfway to the front door, he locked eyes with Andi where she stood, alone, on the other side of the room. She looked away, but not before he saw the look of ... pity?

Oh, hell no. Without thought, and driven by a churning, gut-deep rage that had nothing to do with her, he worked his way across the room.

Her back stiffened, and her eyes darted side to side. She stepped into the hallway, out of sight. He caught up to her just as she was about to slip into the bathroom.

"What the hell are you doing here?" He kept his voice low, each harsh word ground out between clenched teeth. "I thought I told you to stay away from my sister. My agreeing to work with you isn't an all-access pass to my family."

As usual, she didn't back down. Just the opposite. She got

in his face the same way she had many times during the past few weeks they'd worked together.

"Your mother invited me. I couldn't say no to her, you a —" She closed her eyes, took a deep breath, then slowly released it. "Listen, I know this must be difficult for you, but—"

"You have no fucking idea what the hell you're talking about." He turned, took a few steps, then rounded on her again.

She faltered back against the wall between two old family photos.

He leaned in, nose to nose, and growled at her. "Stay away from my family."

A flash of something zipped across her features, then quickly disappeared behind her much-practiced mask of aloofness. Maybe he was so wasted he'd imagined it, but it looked a lot like the hurt he'd seen there before.

There was a time when Jonathan never would've treated anyone the way he'd just treated Andréa, let alone a guest in his parents' home. Michaleen and Molly O'Halleran had taught him better. Yet, since the day he'd found out about Marilyn's deception, his anger had grown and festered. Which, in turn, fed and nurtured a dark, acidic guilt. With each day that passed, the man he used to be seemed to disappear little by little. The worst part was, he didn't know how to stop it from happening.

"Screw this." Jonathan turned and stormed off. The look of concern on his beloved mother's face was the last thing he saw as he slammed the front door.

ON A BLUFF HIGH above Bowman Bay, battered by grief from the inside out, Jonathan collapsed to his knees. The dark, turbulent waters of Puget Sound stretched out before him in the distance, mirroring the darkness in his heart. The cold that had taken up residence in every crevice and corner of his soul had nothing to do with the freezing rain that lashed his face and drizzled down the back of his collar.

He'd staggered up to this spot behind his folks' place about an hour ago. No matter how long he stood there and railed to the heavens, no matter how much alcohol he dumped into his system, Marilyn was still dead. His wife would never have the chance to see their beautiful baby girl or to look into Ashling's adoring eyes. He would never have the chance to ask her why she didn't tell him the truth.

A twig snapped behind him. He didn't have to look to know who it was.

"Why are you here?" His words slurred, and he shoved up to his feet, unconcerned about the mud coating his pants legs.

"I could ask you the same thing." Hands buried in his raincoat pockets, shoulders hunched against the elements, Michaleen O'Halleran strolled across the muddy overlook.

Jonathan stared out at the storm.

The patter of rain against his father's coat sounded like the unsteady beat of a far-off drum.

"Mom know you're out here?" Their mother was very protective of their father. Almost as much as she was her children and grandchildren. She would be worried about him getting sick. Hell, there was a time when Jonathan would've worried about that, too. Anymore, he resisted caring too much about anyone.

"Who do you think sent me after you?" His father stood shoulder to shoulder with him, not saying a word about the bottle dangling from Jonathan's fingers, his silence louder than any reprimand.

Jonathan continued to watch the storm rumble its way across Puget Sound. "How'd you know where to find me?"

"When you were a kid, you always came up here when you had something on your mind." His father squinted, blinked up through the rain at a lone gull. It cried and keened, swooped and lifted, struggling valiantly against the swirling winds.

"I come here to be *alone,*" Jonathan growled.

"Want to talk about it?" His father ignored his surliness.

Not wanting to do this with his dad now—or ever—he turned to walk away but was stopped when a big, rugged hand wrapped around his upper arm.

Jonathan stared at the ground. He couldn't stand the thought of the hurt, or worse, the disappointment he might see in his father's eyes.

"You're keeping an awful lot of anger trapped inside you, son. You need to find a way to deal with it." He hesitated. "Before it destroys you."

Too late, he thought.

Fueled by too much scotch and too little sleep, the rage Jonathan had managed to fight off all these months finally clawed its way up from the bowels of his despair.

He turned and lashed out at his father.

"Then you tell me, Dad, how do I *deal with it?* Where do I focus my anger? Huh?" He jerked his arm from his father's grip and stumbled. "At Marilyn, for not giving me a say in our future? For lying to me? Or maybe Ashling, for being here instead of her mother? And Christ ... " He clenched his fingers in his hair until he felt the sting. "What kind of father, what kind of man does it make me for even having thoughts like that?"

One hand fell to his side. The other brought the bottle to his lips for a long swallow. The amber liquid no longer burned as it traveled to his gut. He tipped it back for another drink and discovered it was empty. His arm drew back and, with a frustrated roar, he hurled it across the open field. A clap of thunder drowned out the sound of the glass crashing against a massive jagged rock.

His arms hung limp, his shoulders slumped under the weight of utter defeat. He swayed and gazed blindly into the thick woods, oblivious to his soaked clothing or the rain dripping from the end of his nose.

"There are no words to describe how much I love my baby girl. And yet, all I want to do is run from it—from her—because it scares the hell out of me." God knows he'd felt fear before, but it didn't come close to the soul-crushing terror that strangled him at the thought of something happening to his daughter. He would never survive it.

"My heart physically hurts when I think of Ashling growing up without her mother." Jonathan pressed his fist to his chest. "Or that Marilyn will never experience our daughter's wonder at each new day."

His father, ever patient, remained silent.

Jonathan ground the heels of his hands into his eyes.

"You have no idea what it feels like knowing I couldn't have one without losing the other and wondering why." He turned imploring, desolate eyes to his father. "Why couldn't I have both, Dad? Why?" Anguished words scraped their way past the painful lump in his throat, ushering in tears he'd long held at bay.

His father moved closer, wrapped his burly arms around Jonathan and pulled him close, anchoring him.

"You are a damn fine man *and* father, and I'll not have you questioning that. Ever." He tightened his embrace. His words held the earnest steel of a man defending his child. "Jonathan ... " His dad held him at arm's length and looked him in the eyes. "Every time you deployed, your mother and I and Marilyn worried about you out there slaying dragons in whatever hell on earth you were sent to, doing your part to keep us all safe. Hoping and praying you'd come back to us. But we came to accept that life holds no guarantees. Marilyn knew that when she made her decision. But it was worth it to her to at least *try* to slay her own dragon."

"I am just so fucking mad at her, dad. And how messed up is that?" His raspy words barely carried over the harsh wind as the tortured admission burned like hellish flames in his throat.

"It's okay for you to be angry." His father tightened his hold. "Hell, I'm angry she was taken from us too soon. We *all* are. But then I look at that perfect baby girl who has her mother's smile and her grandmother's beautiful green eyes, and I thank Marilyn every single day for her courage."

His father's burly chest rose and fell.

"Ashling needs you. She needs her daddy." His dad gave Jonathan a quick shake. "Don't let your anger or your fear of loss keep you from embracing the one precious thing that can save you from your despair and give you a reason to go on."

Having said his piece, his father gave Jonathan's shoulders one last squeeze, tucked his hands in his coat pockets, then turned toward the trail and disappeared into the woods.

CHAPTER TWELVE

Breaths visible in the cold air, clothing soaked to the skin, Andi pumped her arms and legs as she tore through the woods. The call of a bird, the rustle of leaves as a chipmunk skittered through the underbrush, and the crunch of pine needles underfoot all blended together to create a familiar, soothing chorus.

High overhead, wind blew through the ancient fir, pine and evergreen trees. Like mammoth dancers, they swayed and brushed against each other. Thanks to the relentless Pacific Northwest drizzle, water cascaded down from moisture-laden branches with each gust.

She'd started coming out to the new OSI obstacle course deep in the woods whenever she felt frustrated or needed to work something out in her head. What did it say about her state of mind that she'd memorized every turn, every twist, each dip and climb of the rough terrain?

Like she knew that up around the next curve, a large tree lay across the trail. Her palms still held the evidence of the first time the rough bark had torn through her skin. Today, when she vaulted over it, gloves protected her. Beyond that, a ten-foot wall was the last remaining barrier between her and the finish.

She ducked to avoid a large, broken branch—*that's new*—increased her speed and, with a grunt, leaped up and grabbed the knot at the end of the rope. Her body swung, and her shoulder slammed against the rough surface. Her biceps and glutes burned, and the toes of her boots scrabbled against the wood until one found purchase on a small gouge. With a grunt, she heaved up and dragged herself over. Breath exploded from her chest when she landed in a crouch on the other side. A patch of wet leaves tried to drop her on her ass. She righted herself and kept charging forward.

Cold air searing her throat, heart pounding in her ears, legs burning, she put on a last burst of speed and leaned into the finish. A quick glance at her wrist told her she'd cut almost two minutes off her best time. Hands on her knees, she smiled, then straightened and gave herself a mental high five. Fingers locked together, hands resting atop her head, she walked back and forth, sucking deep breaths in through the nose and out through the mouth.

"Looks like you've done that a time or two."

She whirled around in a crouch, legs planted apart, fists up and ready to strike.

"Whoa, take it easy, killer." Hands held in mock surrender, Jonathan leaned one big shoulder against a tree at the edge of the woods. The corner of his mouth lifted in what was the closest thing to a smile he'd ever directed her way.

Andi lowered her hands and relaxed. He wasn't a threat to her. Not physically, anyway.

"I'm sorry I startled you," he said.

"Didn't know anyone else was out here." She walked over, tugged off her gloves and tossed them in her duffle bag before grabbing her water bottle.

"Emily told me I might find you out here." He shoved off

the tree and walked slowly toward her. Even in the midst of towering trees, Jonathan O'Halleran commanded the space around him.

"I like being out here." She scanned the woods around the small clearing. "Going through the course helps me clear my head. Gives me the chance to think through things."

Jesus, Andi, shut up. Why was she suddenly so chatty with him? *Oxygen debt*, she thought. That's it. Her brain wasn't getting enough oxygen. She took a few gulps of water to keep herself from saying more.

Pine cones crunched under his large boots as he closed the space between them.

"Look." She held up her hand, and he stopped several feet away. "If you came out here to warn me off your family again, save it. You made your point quite effectively the other night."

She snatched up her bag, jammed her water bottle into it and stormed past him.

"Andréa, just ... give me a minute, will you? Please."

The gentle "please" stopped her cold.

Her head fell back, and she stared up at the sky, perhaps hoping some sort of magical winged savior would swoop down and whisk her away from this awkward encounter. Knowing it wouldn't happen, she dropped her chin and heaved a sigh before turning back to him.

He moved a few steps closer. "I know we got off on the wrong foot, and that's my fault."

She looped the strap of her duffle over her shoulder, crossed her arms and cocked out her hip. If he thought she was going to make this easier for him, he was dead wrong. The same way he was about so many other things where she was concerned.

Ever since he tore into her at his parents' house, she was never sure what to expect from him. Not taking any chances,

Andi reinforced her emotional walls and neutralized her expression.

He gave a sad shake of his head and gripped the back of his neck. "You feel like you have to do that whenever you're around me, don't you?"

"Do what?" She stiffened her spine.

"You ... close yourself off." He took another step closer. "Protect yourself."

Shit.

"I have no idea what you're talking about." Throat suddenly bone-dry, she took another long swallow from her bottle.

"I think you do." Heated eyes lifted from where they'd been watching her neck. "But that's not why I'm here."

He came closer.

She took a step back, then instantly wanted to kick her own ass.

"I came looking for you because ... I wanted to apologize." Steam rose from his wet shoulders. Waves of heat poured off him and wrapped around her. "You didn't deserve the way I spoke to you."

"It's fine. You don't owe me anything." Andi dug for her towel to avoid his intense gaze.

There was something different about his eyes. The usual storm in their deep blue depths was gone, replaced by a new kind of serenity. As if some sort of personal demon had been purged from within.

"Yeah, yeah, I do. I want ... need you to understand why I've been acting like such an ass." Jonathan took a deep breath, blew it out. "See ... the thing is ... I've been in a very dark place since, Marilyn ... since my wife died."

He stared off into the woods as he spoke.

"One minute I'm at the FOB, planning a pretty straightforward operation to take out a small group of fighters giving us some trouble in the hills nearby. Just another day at the office, ya know? Next thing I know, I'm in a sterile, neonatal intensive care unit, helpless to do anything but watch and pray as my baby girl fights with everything in her little body to survive. Knowing that the only reason she exists is because her mother purposely kept a dangerous preexisting condition from me."

Jonathan bent, swiped up a twig from the ground at his feet and straightened. He broke off small pieces and, one by one, tossed them aside.

"Other than her doctor, her folks were the only ones who knew. They'd wanted to tell me, but she'd sworn them to secrecy. Anyway, scarring caused by uterine tumors she had as a kid increased her risk for placenta previa. As a result, the placenta tore away from her uterine wall. She started hemorrhaging and went into shock. Ashling's heart rate plummeted, and they had no choice but to perform an emergency C-section. Marilyn died as they were airlifting our daughter to a hospital in Seattle."

Her heart broke for him and for Ashling. A loss of that magnitude would be hard enough to navigate without the conflict of anger and guilt muddying the waters.

He scrubbed his hand over his face and scanned the woods before he looked up at her.

"I've been angry at the world and took it out on you. It was a shitty thing to do, and I apologize."

Andi didn't say anything. What *could* she say? Emotions were strange and impossible things to predict. Hell, a longing for a mother she'd never known had hung over her entire life like a dark shadow seeping into every crevice of her soul.

Anytime she'd asked her father about her mother, he would dismiss Andi with, "I will not discuss Bethany with you" or "Bethany is none of your concern." Always "Bethany," never "your mother" or "your mom." The intentionally callous distinction had robbed Andi of any meaningful connection to the woman who'd given birth to her.

"What is it that makes you so sad, Andréa?" Jonathan's quiet question forced away her untimely stroll down her broken-glass-strewn memory lane.

Nope, not going there.

"We're not talking about me." She draped the short towel over the back of her neck.

"Andréa." He stepped closer—*too close*—and wrapped a powerful hand around each end of the towel, his knuckles resting against her collarbone.

A betraying shiver whispered down her spine, even as heat from his touch seeped through her shirt to the skin beneath.

"You're freezing." His deep, rumbly voice rolled over her, through her, took hold of her, as surely as his hands held her in place. "Please tell me you have a coat or something in that magical duffle of yours."

She looked up at him, and he gifted her with a genuine smile. His manicured beard was no match for the dimple in his left cheek. The sight of it almost knocked her on her ass. *A fucking dimple? Seriously?*

This was not good. The weird, mysteriously gooey way she often felt around him was difficult enough to understand when he was being a dick. What the hell was going to happen if he started being nice to her? How was she expected to cope with such a dramatic shift in their ... what? Relationship wasn't the right word, exactly. More like their interactions?

"I'm—" Andi cleared her throat and tried again. "I'm fine."

He tilted his head and gave her an assessing look. "You're always fine, aren't you?"

Her mouth opened and closed, and she looked away. No way did she trust him enough to tell the truth—that being *fine* was easier than admitting to old insecurities that always left her feeling hollowed-out and needy. Unacceptable emotions for the offspring of Colonel Hampton Swain.

"So, tell me. Is it what happened to Marconi that troubles you?" he asked.

Brows pinched together, her eyes shot back to his.

"I know better than most what it's like when people's lives are on the line," Jonathan said. "You had pressure coming at you from every side. It's understandable how you could've overlooked some things."

His words were like a punch to the gut. Not a day went by that Andi didn't replay the moment she'd been notified about Marconi's death. Wondering if she could've done something, *anything,* to prevent what happened. Instead of telling him that, she wrapped her emotions in barbed wire and fell back on sarcasm.

"Oh, well, thank you so much for your abundant benevolence and understanding. Your absolution means so very much to me." Which was uncomfortably close to the truth.

"Anyway"—he pointedly ignored her snarkiness—"I just ... well, I wanted to apologize. My jackass behavior lately had nothing to do with you and everything to do with me."

"Look, Jonathan—" She held up her hand and took a step back. He released the towel and wedged his hands in his front pockets. "I accept your apology, okay. But let's not pretend that changes anything between us."

"And why is that?" he asked, as eyes that did funny things to her insides never left hers.

"Because you still believe I'm responsible for Marconi's death. And as long as even one cell in your body believes that, then it does have something to do with me."

This time, nothing he could've said would've stopped her from walking away.

CHAPTER THIRTEEN

Disappointment flicked across Andi's features before she left Jonathan standing there wondering what the hell just happened. He'd seen it once before, in his office, when he'd gotten in her face about Marconi.

What the hell was he missing? He scratched his thumb along his jaw. The damn woman was so guarded, he wondered if anyone had ever managed to get behind her barriers.

He followed her—only close enough to make sure she made it back safely. It bothered him that she'd been coming out to these woods alone. Ridiculous, considering she was beyond capable of defending herself.

Jonathan stepped out of the woods and onto the gravel parking lot just as she tossed her duffle onto the backseat of her car.

The sound of a zipper being dragged open floated across the lot, then she peeled her shirt over her head. She tugged her hands from the long sleeves, which gave him a nice view of a black workout bra that shouldn't have been sexy, yet on her, it fucking was. Her tight, creamy-white abs practically glowed in the waning daylight. Then she bent over to tuck the shirt in her bag. Black leggings clung to the curve of her heart-shaped, very toned ass and emphasized the strength of her long, lean legs. She stepped into a loose-fitting pair of sweats and dragged them up and over the leggings. All that gloriousness was covered when she pulled on a giant Jacksonville State University sweatshirt. Slender fingers speared through her wet hair and drew it back from her face.

His mind a scrambled mess, Jonathan stood there as if someone had bolted his feet to the ground. Before he could get his shit together and stop staring, she slipped behind the wheel, fired up the car, then pulled away. Without so much as a quick peek in his direction.

If it had been another woman, he might think she'd been putting on a show for him. Not Andi. From what little he knew of her, he couldn't see her bothering with games like that. His guess? She, like him, viewed her body from a purely practical standpoint—if she took of care of it, it would take care of her. Simple as that.

Why was he suddenly so enthralled by the tough, stubborn woman? And what the fuck had he been thinking, telling her about Marilyn? He'd only come out here to apologize. All it had taken was one look in those big brown eyes of hers and, next thing he knew, he was gutting himself in front of a woman who seemed to enjoy getting under his skin. A woman night-and-day different from his wife.

Jonathan stared until her taillights disappeared around the main building. A quick shake of his head helped dislodge his feet, and he jogged to his truck. After a quick cruise to check the compound, he headed home, the comparison between Andi and his wife now rolling around in his brain.

Marilyn had been a popular, pretty cheerleader with blond hair, big blue eyes and a knack for making people feel like they were the most important person in the room. Everyone adored her. From the outside, her life appeared to be perfect. In reality, nothing could have been further from the truth.

Unlike Andi, she'd never been comfortable in her own skin. Her lack of confidence was the byproduct of being raised by a mother who transferred her own body image issues to her only child, and a clueless father who allowed it to happen. They loved her, but even the best parents could fuck up their kid without meaning to.

She constantly referred to herself as a "big fatty" and weighed herself every single day. Fad diets and crazy exercise programs came and went. Still, there were always "a couple more pounds" to lose before she would be satisfied. Hell, at one point, she'd even started taking dangerous over-the-counter weight-loss remedies. She'd stopped taking them after he told her he was worried about their dangerous side effects.

Not once when they'd made love had Marilyn allowed him to leave the lights on. And she wouldn't have dreamt of sleeping in the buff—which had always nettled him, since he enjoyed sleeping skin to skin. The one time he'd mentioned it, she'd pouted for days. Finally, he gave up, hoping things would change.

Whenever he returned from a deployment, it took them both time to adjust: him to being home where he was expected to instantly jump back into a *normal* life and her learning how to share the life she'd built in his absence.

They were like old friends who knew everything and nothing about each other. Maybe she'd hoped the pregnancy would change all that, and perhaps it would have. They would never know.

Jonathan braced himself against the onslaught of grief, anger and guilt that always slammed into him whenever he thought about her. They were there, whispering deep within his heart—probably always would be. After all, he and

Marilyn had known each other most of their lives. But those dark feelings had begun to fade the night his father stood in the freezing rain and slapped him with some hard realities.

His love for Marilyn had been comfortable, familiar, and he would've spent the rest of his life trying to make her happy. Instead, in the blink of an eye, his life's path had been mercilessly rerouted. He could either move forward and build a new one or let the shattered plans of the old one destroy him.

CHAPTER FOURTEEN

Andi slid the disc from the laptop and snapped it into the case. The sound of the fan in the projector was loud against the silence of the late hour. She clicked it off, and light from the open doorway spilled into the dark conference room. Most folks had already left for the day, but Andi was in no hurry to head home. Her townhouse had suddenly begun to feel too damned empty.

She tapped the plastic case against her thigh—the interviews conducted with the guys assigned to the team the day Caleb was shot. Their statements contained no anomalies, but she was still going to fly back to Quantico to do her own interviews. Unless there were dramatic inconsistencies in their statements, she felt confident eliminating them as suspects. That left Jeffrey Burke, Nancy Raymond, and Isaac Andrews, as well as Dylan Renquist and Frank Morgan, two guys from the team who left shortly before the op was scheduled to go down. Renquist put in for a personal leave of absence two days prior, and Morgan resigned from the Bureau around the same time to take a job as head of security for a major corporation.

Andi leaned back in the chair and stretched her arms high overhead. A huge yawn cracked her jaw.

"What are you still doing here?" Jonathan seemed to appear from nowhere. For such a large guy, he moved with the stealth of a cat.

His presence at the office this late wasn't much of a surprise. He was typically the last to leave. Though recently, that seemed to be changing.

She squinted and blinked a few times when he flipped on the overhead light.

"Eliminating suspects." She stood and started organizing everything on the table. Anything to keep her from noticing how much she liked the way his hair looked all tousled from running his hands through it. "I've cleared the last of the guys who were on the team that day. That leaves us with Burke, Nancy Raymond, Isaac Andrews, and two former Hostage Rescue Team guys—Dylan Renquist and Frank Morgan. They were never interviewed because they'd left the HRT right before the op."

Jonathan cursed under his breath. "I've heard Caleb mention both of those guys before. I really don't want to have to tell him that one of his buddies is a traitor."

"Hopefully, you won't have to." Andi had spent her adult life exposing the slimy underbelly of human beings, but betrayal of this kind was a whole other kind of evil.

"Who's Isaac Andrews?" He moved into the room like a big bear entering its cave.

"He's the comms guy who worked the op from the NSA headquarters." Andi had only met the guy once—her first day, when Nancy was introducing her around.

She gathered up her notes and tapped the edge of the stack on the table.

"What do we know about him?" He shifted his backpack up on one massive shoulder and crossed his arms.

Man, those are some industrial-strength seams in that shirt. His shirt was unbuttoned at the neck, allowing her a peek at the dark hair on his chest.

"Andi?"

"What?" She gave a quick shake of her head. "Oh, I don't know much about him yet. I'll start digging into all of them tomorrow."

"I think it's safe to say we can eliminate Burke. Wouldn't you agree?" He raised a dark brow.

"I agree. He has nothing to gain. Besides, I know Jeffrey, and the last thing he would do is betray someone he trusts, and he trusts your family." Andi loaded up her arms.

"Can I help you with that?" He moved to the table and held out a hand.

"I'm fine." She slipped past him, careful not to touch him. Unfortunately, it didn't prevent her from getting a whiff of his scent. A combination of pine, sandalwood and something else. Something sensuous and uniquely Jonathan.

Keep moving. Keep moving. She repeated the words over and over in her head.

Jonathan sighed and mumbled, "Again with the *fine.*"

Warm light fanned out from the custom-made, blown-glass sconces and glowed across the rich, wood walls lining the hallway leading to her small office, tucked away at the end. A large conference room and supply closet separated her from everyone else. A metaphor for her not being *one of them,* perhaps? Andi couldn't seem to convince herself that it didn't matter she wasn't really one of them. But, hey, at least she had windows.

"Just exactly how well do you know Burke?" he asked as they reached her office.

Only a small lamp on her credenza lit the space. Much too intimate for her pseudo-boss, a man she'd been fighting off some serious fantasies about. She flipped on the overheads and circled behind her desk. Putting space between them was critical. Being near him, even knowing he didn't much like her, did weird things to her concentration.

"Is there something going on between the two of you?" he asked.

"Two of who?" She set the DVDs down, then pivoted to grab her backpack off the credenza.

"You and Burke."

With great deliberation, she set her backpack on her desk. It was that or throw it at his head. Not smart, considering he had the power to boot her ass off the property.

"You actually think I'm screwing my boss?" Eyes narrowed, she fought the urge to deck him. Instead, she flattened her hands on the desk and leaned forward. Because, again, not a good idea to punch the guy you're working for. Even if it was only temporary.

"Are you?"

"Who the hell do you—" She forced a deep breath and straightened. "I've known Jeffrey Burke since he recruited me right out of college."

"That wasn't a no." One thick brow lifted in challenge.

"It's not really any of your damn business. And why the hell do you care who I'm sleeping with?" Andi wasn't sure why she just didn't tell him the truth. Maybe a small part of her hoped his questions were rooted in jealousy.

"It's my business if it interferes with your ability to find the person responsible for getting my brother shot and Power killed."

Nope. Not jealousy. Hope fizzled, crash and burned.

"This from the guy who just wasted a week of my damn time," she muttered under her breath.

"Your voice is different whenever you talk about him." He tried to look relaxed, but tension radiated from him.

"What?" she scoffed, picking up a pen and pencil, then yanking open the middle drawer. "No, it isn't."

He just stood there like a big, gorgeous, pig-headed statue.

"Jeffrey is like a father to me." Andi tossed the pen and pencil inside and shoved the drawer shut a bit too forcefully. "He's always believed in me, been there for me. Unlike my real father," she muttered as she twisted to grab something from her credenza.

"What do you mean?" he pressed.

She sighed, knowing she was about to divulge something he could possibly use as ammunition against her. And yes, she realized that was a sad statement about her view of the world in general.

"Let's just say I wasn't my father's favorite person." Understatement much?

He remained silent, waited for her to continue.

Blame it on the late hour or on the weighty loneliness she'd been feeling lately, but she wanted to share with him.

"I never knew my mother. She died while giving birth to me."

His mouth opened slightly. He dropped his arms and took a step forward.

Oh, yeah, that surprised him.

"My father always blamed me for her death." After all, it made perfect sense to blame the newborn for the death of her mother during childbirth. Right? "On top of that, I had the audacity to be born a girl instead of a boy."

Andi chuffed out a humorless laugh. Unfortunately, by the time she figured out it was her father's problem and not hers, the seed of guilt had already grown deep roots.

She wound the cord around her laptop and thrust it into her backpack. Her mind dragged back to when she was eight or nine years old. In the middle of one of their customary silent meals, she'd mustered up enough guts to ask him what had happened to her mother. All she ever knew was that she'd died during childbirth, and her father blamed Andi. He'd shot the most hateful glare across the table at her, tossed his napkin on his plate, then shoved back from the table and left without saying a word. There were times Andi could still hear the chair scraping across the linoleum and the low click from the heels of his shiny, uniform shoes as he stalked away.

"There was no way to bring my mom back. So my child's brain decided, that's okay, I'll just be the son he wants instead. Easy, right?"

God, she hated talking about this stuff. It made her sound like a pitiful little girl always seeking her daddy's approval. Pretty apt description, unfortunately.

"When other little girls were playing with their Barbies or having sleepovers with their friends, I was learning how to field strip weapons, set bear traps, or sitting alone in a tree blind for hours in the freezing rain waiting to take down a deer with a bow."

At first, she'd busted her ass to learn all she could, thinking it would help her to gain favor with her father. Ultimately, after becoming pretty damn accomplished, she'd ended up enjoying them for herself. She also realized efforts to *win over* her father were futile.

"I bagged my first buck at the ripe old age of nine, then spent hours schlepping it out of the woods on my back." She'd been so proud. Certain her father would be, too.

The moment she arrived back at the hunting cabin was as clear in her mind today as when it happened all those years ago.

Her father and two of his buddies were sitting on the porch shootin' the shit when she finally managed to haul the large buck up over the hill. By then, the sun was almost straight up in the sky.

His friends jumped up to help.

Her dad raised a hand to stop them, looked her straight in the eye and said, "It's her kill. She has to get it to the barn."

They wanted to argue with him, but no one argued with Colonel Hampton Swain.

She clenched her jaw and locked eyes with the old bastard. *Challenge accepted.*

Wet to her bones, cold and hot at the same time, covered in blood, with the stench of deer urine soaked into her clothes, she hauled that buck the entire fifty-plus feet. His friends followed and applauded her achievement.

"Would you like to know what my sweet, doting dad said?" She didn't wait for an answer. "'Had she been a boy, it wouldn't have taken so long to get back.'"

She chuckled and shook her head.

Nine years old and, courtesy of her own father, she'd gotten her first glimpse of what a chauvinist asshole looked like. She never saw those two other guys again, but the look of pity on their faces was burned into her brain to this day.

"Is that why you drive yourself so hard?" Jonathan's head slanted as he assessed her. She hated when he did that. He was far too intuitive. "So you can measure up to some sort of bullshit expectation set by your dead father?"

"Maybe." Of course it was. "My brain knows it's bullshit, but when you're a little kid and the one person in the world who is supposed to support you, protect you—"

"Love you," Jonathan added.

She was going to say *believe in you,* but, yeah, that worked. Love was supposed to be unconditional, especially coming from a parent. Right?

"Ashling is a lucky little girl. She's growing up surrounded by people who love her. You, your parents, her aunts and uncles." She smiled. "Hell, the entire town of Whidbey Cove. There will be times when she'll miss her mother and not even understand why." *Like a part of her was missing*. "But it'll be okay, because she'll always know she has a safe place to land."

Andi would've given anything to have that growing up.

"Just ... don't you ever make her feel like she is anything less than perfect exactly the way she is." There was no hiding the hint of threat in her voice. How different would her life have been if someone had said that to her father? "Anyway ..." She mentally shook off the tension that always settled in her shoulders whenever she discussed her father. "That's my whole sad story."

"Andi—"

"I'll start with Nancy, then move on to the others." Having bared her soul enough for one decade, she wanted off this topic.

He hesitated, then took the hint. "I think you'd be wasting your time looking for something to connect Nancy to this." No surprise there. Research showed that the majority of men had a hard time believing a nice, mild-mannered, middle-aged woman could do something as heinous as betray her country.

"You're probably right, but my job is to eliminate all likely suspects. Even if it makes some people uncomfortable." Nancy's behavior had been strange the last few times she'd been around Andi. She wanted to dig a little deeper to find out why. If Burke found out he had a traitor working for him, he wouldn't hesitate to bring the full weight of his considerable power down them.

"That may be, but I'm still instructing you to focus your efforts on Andrews, Renquist, and Morgan." He waited, as if anticipating further argument.

"You're the boss." She busied herself with locking up the DVDs in the cabinet.

"That's it? 'I'm the boss'?" He cocked his head to the side. "You're not going to argue with me?"

"Nope." Not like it would matter if she did. She would investigate Nancy on her own time and hope she didn't find anything.

CHAPTER FIFTEEN

Jonathan tossed his pen on his desk and lounged back in his chair with a sigh. Eyes closed, he pinched the bridge of his nose and rubbed it. He'd spent the past few hours enduring his own personal brand of hell. Reviewing budget sheets, deployment and manpower reports, payroll, and reading reviews on some high-tech equipment they were considering adding to OSI's inventory. Okay, so that last one had been pretty enjoyable. After all, what red-blooded male didn't love gadgets?

As much as this aspect of his new career sucked, it was still a hell of an improvement over what he'd been doing this time last year. He and his team were holed up in a cave colder than a coal miner's asshole in the Klondike, sleeping with one eye open, nothing but MREs to eat. The Meals Ready to Eat were tolerable, but only if you added ample amounts of hot sauce. Better than the grubs and beetles he'd had to eat during one especially hellacious deployment.

The phone on his desk buzzed.

He touched a button to put Christina on speaker. "Yeah?"

"There's a gentleman here to see you." Her voice held a hint of humor. "Said he wanted to surprise you."

"Send him in." Jonathan didn't even care who it was. At this point, it could be someone selling time-shares and he would welcome the reprieve.

The door opened, and his eyes widened as all six-foot-five inches of Tyrone "Sherm" Jefferson lumbered into his office.

"Well, I'll be a son of a—" Jonathan shoved up out of his chair, walked around his desk and met his former senior chief halfway. "Look what the cat dragged in."

"How's it hangin', L.T.?" Sherm's eyes held a mischievous twinkle, and a huge shit-eating grin lit his face.

They shook each other's hand, and Jonathan pulled him into an aggressive, back-slapping hug, then shoved him away.

His former senior chief's head looked freshly shaved and polished to a mirrorlike shine. He had on faded jeans and a brand-new T-shirt from Brew-Ha-Ha, one of their favorite places in Pacific Beach. Jonathan, his teammates and their significant others would hit up the combination microbrew pub and comedy club whenever they were stateside.

He looked good, *really* good, happy and relaxed.

"What the hell are you doing here?" He hadn't seen his old friend since the day he'd found out about Marilyn.

"I was in the area. Thought I'd stop by." He whistled low as he scanned Jonathan's office. "Nice digs."

"What can I say? Benefits of being the boss." His arm swept toward the sofa on the other side of the room. "Have a seat, man."

Jonathan slapped his friend on his very solid back as they made their way to where a couch and two chairs were set up on the opposite side of the room from the fireplace. The dark leather of the large armchair groaned as he sat across from where Tyrone lowered his large frame onto an equally robust leather sofa.

"No way in hell you were in the area." A Southern boy through and through, his friend hated the cold. "So what really brought you here?"

"I'm out," Sherm said.

"Out of what?" No way he was saying what Jonathan thought he was.

"The Navy." He leaned forward, forearms on his knees, fingers loosely laced together. "I retired a month ago."

Jonathan blinked a couple of times. If a spaceship had landed in the middle of his office and a little green man stepped out, he wouldn't have been more shocked.

"I can see you're surprised." One corner of Sherm's mouth lifted, and deep chuckles rolled out of his barrel chest.

At the sound, Jonathan was struck by how much he'd missed the big lug. You didn't go through what they did together without forming an indelible bond. A bond that was hard to explain and went beyond anything else, including marriage.

"Well ... yeah, I'm surprised." He'd always pegged Sherm as a lifer, one of those guys you just *knew* would die in service to his country.

"After what happened to you ... and Marilyn ... " He looked down at the carpet. His thumbs lazily circled each other. "It was sort of ... a wake-up call."

Sherm sat back on a heavy sigh, his long arm draped across the back of the couch. "I'm almost thirty-nine years old, and I suddenly realized I want what you had. A wife who loves me, a family of my own."

Jonathan didn't bother telling his friend that the marriage he'd thought was so ideal had been fraying at the edges—held together by the promise of an unborn child. As if the birth of their baby would have the power to bring about the rebirth of their relationship. An awful lot of responsibility to heap on the shoulders of one so small.

"That's not going to happen if I'm chasing after a bunch of assholes in the middle of Afghanistan." Sherm's body tensed slightly. "But that's not the only reason." Sherm hesitated. Something he never did.

"What?"

"A month or so after you left, some shit went down in the Kunar province. Seven was called in to provide support." He hesitated. "One night, we dropped in about ten klicks to the east of the Korangal Valley, where a group of Brotherhood motherfuckers was supposed to have some of our boys pinned down. Or so we thought."

Unlike so much of the region, the Korangal Valley was lushly forested with pine trees. Nighttime drops into that area could be extremely risky. It didn't help that it was also the birthplace of the Brotherhood, making it one of the single most dangerous territories in the region. Thanks to the years-long efforts of a multinational fighting force, their numbers were declining. As a result, they'd become desperate and had resorted to using their own followers—the disabled, the elderly, even children—as bait and cover. There was no limit to the evil they possessed.

The hairs on the back of Jonathan's neck prickled. He wasn't going to like what he was about to hear.

"Wasn't till we hit the ground we realized the intel was off by about, ohhhh, eight klicks."

"Son of a bitch," Jonathan cursed under his breath.

"You got that right. We practically landed right on top of those goat fuckers. Milky took a round to the thigh that nicked his femoral artery." Sherm rubbed his hand back and forth over his slick head. "We almost lost the kid, L.T."

Scotty Foreman, nicknamed Milky because he grew up on a dairy farm in Michigan, was the youngest guy on the team, but he was a hell of a warrior.

"The entire time I had my fingers in that kid's leg,

pinching off that artery to keep him from bleeding to death, I just kept thinking, *I am too fuckin' old for this shit.*" One shoulder lifted and fell. "When we finally made it back to base and I knew the kid was going to make it, I showered his blood off me, ate some real food for the first time in months, then sat down and filled out my retirement papers."

Guilt, heavy and oppressive, swamped Jonathan. He should've been there with his men.

"Give me a break, Homer." Sherm shook his head and smiled. "I can tell you're over there blaming yourself like a damn fool. Knock that shit off."

"If I'd been there ... "

"Nothing would've changed. Bad intel is bad intel, doesn't matter who's leading the charge. Besides, your wife dying and leaving you with a tiny little human to raise trumps everything. You feel me?"

Jonathan took a deep breath, then nodded. Leave it to Sherm to blast him with the hard truth.

"Good." His friend leaned forward and clapped his hands together. "So, you finished up here for the day?"

Jonathan looked at his watch.

"I can be." Hell with it. He was playing the boss card and leaving early for a change. "What did you have in mind?"

"There a place in this hick town where you can buy me a beer?" he asked as they both stood.

Jonathan walked to his desk, shoved his laptop in his bag and looped it over his shoulder.

"I have just the place. You'll love it." He clapped his friend on the back, then grabbed his cell phone. "You'll especially love the music. I think it's from your childhood. The forties, right?"

Sherm gave him a playful shove that would've knocked most people on their ass.

"This your little angel?" He picked up the framed picture on the corner of Jonathan's desk.

"Yep, that's my Ashling." It was a candid shot of Jonathan looking down at her as she smiled up at him. He hadn't known about it until his mom gave it to him as a gift.

"She's a beauty, Homer." His friend gave him a questioning look. "Actually, instead of getting that beer, I'd love to meet your little one. That is, if you're cool with it."

"Am I cool with it? Man, I'd love for you to meet her. Come on. I'm sure my folks have beer in the fridge." His friend handed him the picture. Jonathan smiled at it, then placed it back on his desk. He hit the switch to douse his office in darkness, shut the door and walked out to Christina's desk.

"You heading out, Boss Man?" She yanked a pencil from her messy bun and waggled it between her fingers.

"Yeah." He clamped his hand on Sherm's shoulder. "Christina, I'd like to introduce you to Tyrone Jefferson, the toughest Navy SEAL ever to come out of BUDs and the best senior chief any man could work with. Tyrone, Christina Lambert, Queen of OSI."

She rolled her eyes and reached up to shake his hand. "Nice to meet you, Tyrone."

"The pleasure is certainly all mine, Miss Christina." He winked at her and kissed the back of her hand. "And call me Ty."

"Ty?" Jonathan slowly turned to look at his friend. "Since when has anyone ever called you Ty?"

"Only pretty women get to call me that." He puffed out his massive chest, and a confident, toothy grin split his face.

Christina blushed and giggled.

"Okay, okay, that's enough of that, Romeo." Jonathan shook his head, grabbed his arm and dragged him to the elevator.

He reached for the button just as the door slid open and out stepped Andi. She was wearing her standard leather boots, skin-tight black jeans, and long-sleeved T-shirt. It shouldn't set his heart to racing, yet it did. Every. Damned. Time.

Their eyes met and held.

Sherm looked back and forth between them.

"Oh ... um, Andréa Swain, meet Tyrone Jefferson." Jonathan shook off thoughts of what was under all the black clothing she always wore.

"Nice to meet you, Mr. Jefferson. Call me *Andi."* She emphasized the name as she gave Jonathan a murderous side-eye, then snapped her arm out to shake hands.

"Call me Ty." One side of his mouth lifted flirtatiously.

"Call him Sherm," Jonathan corrected.

Her brows furrowed.

"My nickname. You know ... 'cause I'm big. Like a Sherman tank."

"Ah, got it." She chuckled, and her eyes twinkled.

Why did it bother Jonathan that she gave his friend a genuine smile?

"What is it you do here at OSI, Andi?" Sherm asked.

"Andréa doesn't work for OSI." His friend turned to Jonathan. "She's here temporarily doing some consulting work."

There was a definite tightening of her shoulders at his ardent clarification. Honestly, he couldn't say why he felt the distinction was necessary.

"Yeah, I'm just here doing what Jonathan can't seem to manage on his own." She sent a snarky look his way before turning back to Sherm. "It was nice to meet you, *Ty."*

And with that little barb, she turned and walked away.

He pushed the button to call the elevator as Sherm stared at her. She stood chatting with Christina about something.

Probably about what an asshole I am.

"You got a problem with her or something?" His friend waited until they stepped into the elevator to ask.

Hell, yeah, he had a problem with her. He couldn't stop thinking about her. Wondering what she did when she left the office every night.

"Don't be ridiculous." He pressed the button, and the doors whispered shut.

"Right. Sure." Sherm's reflection in the doors smiled back at them. "Whatever you say."

"Fuck you," Jonathan grumbled.

Sherm—the dick—laughed as the elevator began to move.

An hour later, the two hardened warriors sat cross-legged on the floor, making baby sounds like a couple of goobers. Ashling drooled all over her favorite toy—a plastic water bottle with two old bolts from his dad's shop secured inside. A poor man's rattle, his dad called it. His daughter was enthralled by the jingly, crackly noise it made whenever she shook it. Made you wonder why people spent so much money on toys. Hell, she was only six months old and already had a trunk fool of them.

"She really is beautiful, man." Sherm said.

"So, do you know what you'd like to do next?" Jonathan was already hatching a plan, but he wanted to see where his buddy's head was at.

"I've been fighting wars so long, I'm not sure I'm qualified to do anything else." The gentleness with which he stroked his dark, calloused hand over Ashling's head belied his mammoth size. You'd expect him to be clumsy, brutish. Yet his ability at stealth was the thing of legends among the teams.

"We could use someone with your experience and leadership here at OSI." Beck had given him latitude to expand the northwest operation as he deemed necessary. "We're looking to build a couple more teams. You'd be perfect to lead one."

The more he rolled the idea around in his head, the more perfect it became. A guy like Sherm could hit the ground running, which meant less work for Jonathan.

"I'd let you pick your own team. Train them. And I can assure you, the money is a crap-load better than what the Navy was paying you." Now the bad news. "You'd have to work out of this office, though."

"Wow." In one smooth motion, Sherm stood, gazed out the window, then back down at Jonathan. "I didn't come up here to hit you up for a job, man."

"Then it's a happy bonus for both of us." Jonathan never thought he'd be lucky enough to work with him again.

"Come on, Sherm." Jonathan also rose, careful not to jostle his now-sleeping daughter. "I'm finally excited about spending time with Ashling, and I'm up to my backside in work."

At the sound of her name, Ashling looked up at him with drowsy green eyes. He snuggled her against his chest and slowly pivoted side to side as he shared what had happened to Caleb.

"As you can imagine, finding the person responsible is one of our priorities. Because knowing the son of a—gun is still out there, walking around free, is unacceptable." He untangled little fingers from his beard to kiss each one. "OSI could really use your help. *I* could really use your help."

"Do you have any leads?" Sherm folded his thick forearms on the table.

"Andréa's working on narrowing down our list of possible suspects." Jonathan rubbed his hand up and down his daughter's back.

"Speaking of... what's really going on with you two?" The

corner of Sherm's mouth kicked up. "There were some pretty serious sparks flying between you two earlier."

"So? Will you at least consider my offer?" Jonathan disregarded his friend's fishing expedition.

Sherm recognized what he was doing and a deep chuckle rumbled up from his massive chest. Instead of pressing the issue, he said, "When do I start?"

"Listen, before you say *yes* and dive into the middle of this, you need to know there could be some pretty powerful players involved with what went down with Caleb. It could get ugly ... and dangerous."

"Nothin' I'm not used to." Sherm held out his hand. "I'm in."

"Fuck, yeah." Jonathan grabbed his friend's hand and welcomed him to the OSI family.

CHAPTER SIXTEEN

Andi's molars ground together as she bumped her way along the bone-rattling private road leading to the O'Hallerans' home. One of her front and rear tires dropped into potholes at the same time, forcing an involuntary grunt that lodged in her throat. Mud splashed up the sides, and rocks pinged off the undercarriage. Her choice of rental car was proving to be a horrible idea. Good thing she'd paid extra for the insurance.

"Wonder if it'll cover kidney damage?" she muttered to the plant on the seat next to her.

The higher she went, the more beautiful their property became. As she rounded a bend, the house slowly came into view. Gravel crunched under tires as she slowed to a stop and rolled down her window. Her eyes widened and her mouth dropped open.

"Ho-ly shit balls." Her only other time here had been at night, for the baby's party. The darkness had concealed the magnificence of the O'Hallerans' home and property.

Today, there wasn't a cloud in the sky, yet the damp, crisp air served as a reminder that winter's talons still clung to the northwest. Gold sunlight reflected off the soaring plate-glass windows that made up the entire front of the very large house. They offered stunning, unfettered views of a strip of valley below, with Puget Sound and the San Juan Islands off in the distance. Hefty cedar pillars supported the roof over a wide wooden porch running the expanse of the home. Between the big windows, the entire first floor was wrapped in stacked stone, reminiscent of the executive reception area at OSI. Cedar siding covered the entire second story below a slate-shingled roof. Majestic evergreens surrounded it on three sides. It was, in a word, spectacular.

Their home was more than a mass of timber, stone, metal and wires. It was alive, breathing with the essence of every living thing surrounding it and warmed by every living thing within in it. It seemed to melt into the woods yet somehow had the power to dominate mother nature's miracles.

Emily said her father designed and built it for their mother years ago. What a remarkable testament to a man's love for his wife and family. Not one of the eleven homes Andi shared with her father growing up exuded warmth and welcome the way this one did. If it was any indication of Michaleen's skill and quality of workmanship, it was no wonder he was a successful builder.

She wedged her rental car between two huge, four-door pickup trucks, then reached over and grabbed her gifts. Why hadn't she rented a truck? She opened the door, sucked in a breath and managed to squeeze through the narrow opening without losing so much as one leaf from the small Japanese red maple or dropping the pouch of antique woodworking tools in the muddy grass.

Emily once mentioned how much her mother loved trees —any kind of tree. And she'd radiated a daughter's pride when she bragged, rightfully so, about her dad's amazing woodworking skills. *A daughter's pride.* Quite the foreign concept to Andi.

The O'Hallerans were such a remarkable couple. They'd managed to raise six incredible kids, and their love for each other was like a tangible presence in any room they occupied. You could *feel* it. And the relationship they had with each of their children and grandchildren ...

What must that be like? To have both parents in your life and to know they love you unconditionally?

Andi's offerings were her little way of saying *thank you* for inviting her to their barbecue and for always being so kind to her.

She navigated the wide flagstone walkway that led to the front porch. Laughter and lively conversation flowed from inside and out. Her steps faltered and her stomach clenched at the sound of one particular voice.

Since her little confessional last week, she'd managed to avoid her temporary boss. First, she flew back to Quantico for a few days to do her interviews. After her return, she'd managed to miss seeing him at the office, too. Her plan, less than mature as it might be, was to continue doing so.

Her strategy had been working, until Mrs. O'Halleran ... Molly ... had thrown a wrench in the works. Andi couldn't help smiling when she thought back to how Jonathan's mother had marched into her office two days ago like a miniature Patton headed to address his troops.

"Hello, Andi." She'd plunked herself down in one of Andi's guest chairs—so much like her daughter.

"Good morning, Mrs. O'Halleran." She'd quickly been reminded to call her Molly.

"How are you settling in? I know our winters can be a bit dreary."

"I don't mind them at all." Honestly, she loved it. "It's a nice change from where I've been the past few years."

Thankfully, Molly hadn't asked for more details. No way would Andi discuss that hellhole with this sweet woman.

"And your new place—are you happy there? Are you getting settled in?" Molly grabbed a tissue from her purse and dabbed her nose.

"My new ... ? Oh, well, I guess it's okay." Andi never gave much thought to the small townhouse. It had a bathroom, a kitchen where she could cook, a bed she could sleep on, and a small living room where she could chill out. What more did a person need? "I'm staying in a place that's furnished, so it was really just a matter of unpacking a couple suitcases."

"Well, that's nice." Molly's eyes traveled over the files stacked everywhere. "It sure looks like my son is keeping you pretty busy."

"Actually, I'm finished with these. They just need to be refiled." She crossed her arms on her desk. "Things have actually leveled off a bit for me right now."

"Oh, that's wonderful!" Molly clapped her little hands. "That means you can come to the house for the barbecue Saturday."

Andi's mouth dropped open. Words escaped her as she stared at the not-so-innocent smile on the older woman's face. She'd just been played by a master.

"It'll be fun!" Molly stood. "Jeffrey and his assistant, Nancy, will be there, too."

One corner of Andi's mouth lifted. She shook her finger. "You are a sly one, aren't you, Molly O'Halleran?"

Molly leaned close and whispered. "You don't raise six children without learning a thing or two." She patted Andi's cheek. "You have a nice day, Andi, and we'll see you Saturday, any time after two."

And just like that, she'd turned and walked out, leaving her invitation and the light scent of roses swirling in her wake.

The pleasant memory eased some of the tightness in Andi's shoulders. She forced a deep breath and marched up the steps to the front porch.

JONATHAN TIPPED BACK his beer as he listened to Mathias and Killian drone on and on about the latest Seahawks game. His younger, twin brothers had been fans since they were kids. Football was okay, but he'd always preferred exploring the surrounding woods or plowing through books about military history.

His gaze traveled to where Burke and Nancy Raymond stood near one of the picnic tables. He was casually dressed in jeans and a dark blue, long-sleeved Henley, his phone to his ear. She held a plate of food in one hand, a full glass of wine in the other, and was dressed like she'd just come from the office. Nancy didn't look uncomfortable, so much as she looked like she didn't know how to relax.

And speaking of wine, a few feet from them, his dad demonstrated his fly-fishing technique to Darby English, their friend and favorite vintner. The two of them loved to regale each other with stories of their latest special fishing spot.

A low whistle filtered between Killian's teeth. "Who. Is. That?" He stared over Jonathan's shoulder.

A familiar sort of electric current crackled and buzzed through him. Jonathan didn't have to look to know who it was. He did anyway, and holy hell, his heart damn near stopped.

Andi stood at the base of the patio steps. She had one arm looped around a clay pot holding a small tree of some kind. Tucked under the other was something rolled up in canvas.

Skinny black jeans hugged her ass and covered those long legs to where they tucked into black, calf-high hiking boots with fur circling the top. A weathered, brown leather bomber jacket with the collar popped up in back protected her from the chilly fall air. Add to that the choppy bangs and short, wavy dark hair, and she gave off a sort of deadly, sexy-as-hell, badass pixie look. Her slightly crooked nose was pinkened by the cold, yet somehow the imperfection only enhanced her looks. Large, assessing brown eyes were prominent in a classically beautiful face.

He was happy to see her, had missed her even, but damned if he knew why.

"Her name's Andi. Beck brought her in to do some consulting work for the company. We met at Ashling's party," Mathias said as he flashed Jonathan a hard, sideways look. Apparently, his brother witnessed his atrocious treatment of her that night. Since Mathias wasn't one to stick his nose in other people's business, he didn't call him out on it.

"How in the hell did I miss seeing *her?* She is *smokin'* hot. And it appears I'm not the only one who thinks so." Killian circled the air with the mouth of his bottle.

Jonathan stopped mid-swallow, lowered his beer and glanced around. Almost every guy was watching her—even a few of the married ones. Not that he could blame them. Andi moved with an unintentional sexiness, an ease borne of confidence. She didn't set out to capture attention; it just happened. You couldn't help but notice her.

Emily grabbed the crook of her arm and maneuvered her through the crowd of people cluttering his parents' large flagstone patio. His mother smiled and bounced a happy Ashling on her hip as they approached.

Andi said something, then thrust the plant toward her.

His mom handed Ashling off to Emily and accepted Andi's gift. She fussed over her new tree-baby, then set it down. Jonathan knew what was coming next. She raised up on her tiptoes and wrapped Andi in one of her awesome Molly O'Halleran hugs.

Even this far away, he could tell Andi's entire body tensed up. She shot his sister a look of complete confusion laced with desperation. The words *help me* practically poured from her eyes.

Emily gave her a sweet smile and rocked side to side as she kissed Ashling on the temple.

Finally realizing she wasn't going to be set free until his mom got what she wanted, Andi reached around with her free arm and patted her back in an awkward, is-this-how-it's-done kinda way. A serene smile settled on her face, then her eyes drifted shut, and her head rested on his mother's shoulder.

Given what he knew of her tough childhood, the small smile conveyed so much. Jonathan still couldn't believe she'd opened up to him the way she had.

She straightened, stepped back and did a quick scan of the yard.

Their eyes locked for a split second before she quickly looked away. Long enough for him to detect an uneasiness that had nothing to do with the emotional moment with his mother.

Can you blame her, you idiot? From the beginning, he'd done nothing to make her feel welcome. On the contrary, he'd done everything he could to chase her off.

"You've been holding out on me, dude." Killian slowly turned back to him, a crooked grin on his face.

"You're an idiot." Jonathan shifted so his back was to Andi and took a swig of beer, as if he didn't want to stare at her as much as every other guy there. "We work together. That's it."

Liar. His efforts not to care about her had turned out to be futile. There was just *something* that drew him to her.

Perhaps it was the contradiction between her outward take-shit-from-no-one approach to life and the haunting sadness in her eyes.

"If you say so." Killian chuckled, then went right back to gawking at her, his tongue practically hanging out. "Please tell me she's single."

Jonathan tugged on his earlobe and tried to ignore how much he wanted to smash his brother in the face. *Ridiculous.*

"I think so, but Jonathan can probably tell you more about her than I can." Mathias tilted his head toward him.

"What I *can* tell you is you might want to tread lightly. She actually works for Burke, and I doubt he'd appreciate you hitting on one of his people." What he really wanted to tell him was to roll his tongue back into his mouth and back the hell off.

Jeffrey Burke was one of the most intense, dangerous men he'd ever met, and he seemed to have a strong protective streak where Andi was concerned. Jonathan's initial resistance to her had been duly noted, right before he'd been warned to treat her with respect. Of course, now, thanks to a few private moments with Andi, he understood why.

"Is that a set of antique tools?" Jonathan turned at the awe in Mathias's voice.

Their dad stared down at woodworking implements tucked into individual pockets of a canvas tool roll, spread out across the picnic table. Mouth agape, eyes wide, he looked at Andi, then back at the table. With the reverence only a man who'd spent his life working with tools would exhibit, he slowly skimmed work-worn fingers across the contents. One big hand curved over his mouth, and their mother leaned into his side and rubbed her hand up and down his back.

Jonathan could not believe his eyes.

Big, tough Michaleen O'Halleran, the guy who could still

scare the crap out of them without uttering a word, was doing his best not to cry. His throat moved up and down, and he scrubbed his hand back and forth over his mouth. He turned to Andi, wrapped her in a bear hug and lifted her right up off the patio.

Jonathan almost felt sorry for her.

As soon as her feet hit the ground, his mother gave a stunned Andi another hug, kissed Ashling on the cheek, then followed his dad to where he'd started showing off his new *old* tools to Burke.

"Dad is going to love her forever for that," Mathias said under his breath.

"And to think, you've been keeping her all to yourself." Killian continued checking her out. "Pretty selfish, don't you think?"

"What kind of consulting is she doing for OSI?" Mathias slipped seamlessly into his role as family diplomat and tried to steer the conversation in a less annoying direction.

"She's an interrogations tactics specialist." Jonathan finished off his beer. "Burke thought she might bring some value-added to OSI."

"Well, she can interrogate me any time she wants." Killian nudged him with his elbow.

Jonathan shook his head. "You are a child. You know that, right?"

His obnoxious brother just grinned, then chugged the last of his beer.

"Well, will you look at that. I need another beer." Killian tossed the empty into the nearby recycling bin. "Wish me luck." He waggled his eyebrows, rubbed his hands together and headed toward the cooler of beer. Which just happened to be right behind Andi.

Mathias called out to his twin. "Hang on. I'll grab one,

too." He glanced at Jonathan. "I'll make sure he doesn't do anything stupid."

"Good luck with that," Jonathan quipped.

"Not that she needs my help. I got the distinct impression Andi can take care of herself." His youngest brother—by two and a half minutes—grinned, then jogged over to where she stood shaking Killian's hand.

Andi gave his brothers a warm, genuine smile. Far cry from the tight, forced ones directed his way. She was such a loner, he had never seen her interact on a personal level with anyone other than Emily and Christina. Even then, she typically listened as his baby sister steamrolled her way through the conversation.

"How are you, son?" A large hand landed on his shoulder, interrupting his thoughts.

Jonathan and his father hadn't spoken much since their little exchange on the bluff.

"I'm ... better, dad." True statement. "Thanks to you."

"You'll get there." He gave him a last squeeze and dropped his hand. "Give it time. And always remember, you have people who love you."

Jonathan nodded. After having his head up his ass for a while, it was nice to hear.

He looked around at all the friends and family spread across the property.

"Nice turnout." His eyes stopped on Andi, as they so often did these days.

His dad followed his gaze. "She's quite a gal, isn't she?"

"She's good at what she does." He glanced over at his dad and shoved his hand in his front pocket.

"I'm sure that's true, but that's not what I meant." His dad partially unrolled the pouch. "Look at this amazing gift she brought me."

"Very nice." Old tools in such great shape weren't easy to

come by. Andi had gone to a lot of trouble and expense to find just the right thing for his dad. The woman was an enigma, and he suddenly needed to be close to her.

"Can I get you a beer, dad?"

"Thanks, but I've still got some grilling left to do." He carefully secured the tools with the leather strap. "First, I'm going to put these someplace safe."

"Probably a good idea. Give me a minute to check on my daughter, then I'll come over and help."

"Jonathan ... " His dad laid a hand on his bicep. "Take it easy on her, will ya? Poor thing just seems so ... alone. Know what I mean?"

Yeah, and Jonathan knew why.

"Let me grab another beer, and I'll be right over to help." He started toward Andi, just as Emily handed the baby to her.

Andi opened her mouth to protest, but his sister was already jogging up the steps to the back door. Andi held Ashling at arm's length and frantically looked around the yard. You'd think she'd been passed a fragile container loaded with nitroglycerin. Her uneasiness at getting a hug didn't come close to the discomfort she exhibited holding his daughter.

Not one to be ignored, Ashling flailed her chubby legs about, flashed a slobbery, toothless grin and blew bubbles.

Andi slowly turned back to the wiggling bundle. Her eyes softened with an uncharacteristic warmth as they traveled over the baby's face. Slowly, a stunning smile relaxed her customary guarded expression. She tucked Ashling close and brushed their noses together, eliciting a stream of throaty baby giggles. Her nose to the top of Ashling's head, she closed her eyes and took a deep breath.

Jonathan froze, riveted by the scene before him. He swallowed hard, then forced himself to move toward them.

"Best smell in the world, isn't it?" he said. "If I could figure out a way to bottle it, I'd make a mint."

Her body visibly tightened. Large, earnest eyes the color of his favorite coffee stared back at him. Her heart-shaped face was pink from the cold and completely makeup-free. *Damn, but she's beautiful.*

"How's my giggly girl?" His hand smoothed down his daughter's back.

Ashling was oblivious to the tension flowing between the two adults. Her only interest was the chain hanging from Andi's neck.

"What's this?" Jonathan's fingertips accidentally brushed her smooth skin as he lifted the small ring hanging from the chain.

A near-silent gasp filtered from her, and her throat moved as she swallowed.

"It was my mother's. I found it when I was going through my dad's stuff." Her voice was low, husky, and he could've sworn he felt it brush over his dick.

Down, boy.

"It's nice you have something of hers." He thought of his own baby girl growing up without her mom. Unlike Andi, she would always know who her mom was and how much she'd wanted to have a baby.

He got pissed every time he thought about Andi's father. As difficult as it had been for Jonathan to embrace fatherhood and everything that went with it, he could never imagine doing to Ashling what Hampton Swain had done to his daughter.

He patted his baby girl's back and smiled.

"Oh ... I ... I'm sorry." Andi worked to untangle the little fingers from their stranglehold, then started to hand the baby to him. Which did not make his daughter happy. "Your sister gave her to me and sort of ... took off. And your brothers were called inside to help your mom. So I—"

"Andi, relax." His hand smoothed over Ashling's dark hair. "She likes you."

And I like seeing you hold her. Wait ... where the hell had that come from?

"Well, let's be honest. I'm not exactly your favorite per—"

"Listen ..." He held up a hand, halting her from saying the words that would remind him of what a dick he'd been. "I was—"

"Okay, Mom's all squared away inside." Killian interrupted with a smile, robbing Jonathan of the chance to reiterate she'd done nothing wrong. "How 'bout a tour of the property?"

She looked at Jonathan as if waiting for him to finish what he was going to say. He remained silent, unwilling to discuss this in front of his brother.

"Sure, sounds great." She grinned down at the happy bundle in her arms. "But I seem to be on baby duty at the moment."

"Well, lucky for us, her daddy is right here." Killian scooped Ashling from Andi's arms and held her high overhead. "Isn't that right, little Appleseed?"

He made airplane sounds, and she squealed and kicked her chubby little legs as he *flew* her to Jonathan.

"Appleseed?" Andi's brow pinched, and she looked back and forth between them.

Mathias ambled up just in time to answer.

"When each of us kids were born, our dad planted a tree." He pointed at six trees clustered together right at the cusp of where the hill began to slope down into the valley.

"The five evergreen trees represent each of us boys." He tucked his hands in his back pockets. "When they found out they were having a girl, they decided to mix it up by planting an oak tree."

Andi's head tipped back and, squinting against the hazy sunlight, she took in the grouping of trees. They were each at different stages of growth. The smallest, Emily's, was up to about twenty-five to thirty feet.

"They wanted to continue the tradition with their grandchildren. So over there"—Killian pointed to a clearing with one small tree in the middle—"they planted an apple tree when this little squirt was born." He gently tapped the end of Ashling's nose.

"You are one lucky little Appleseed," Andi leaned in and whispered near his daughter's ear.

"So, you ready for your private tour now?" Killian, the family's biggest flirt now that Caleb had found the love of his life, flashed her his trademark smile.

Oh, hell, no, he did not just wink at her, too.

Her eyes on Jonathan, Andi stroked her hand down Ashling's arm, and tiny, chubby fingers grabbed hold of her. She smoothed her thumb over his daughter's knuckles.

He opened his mouth to tell her not to go, that he wanted to do whatever it would take to earn a smile like the one she'd given his daughter. Nothing came out.

She kissed his daughter's little fist, wiggled her fingers free from her grip and turned to Killian. "Sounds like fun."

"Excellent!" He took Andi's hand and led her to a waiting four-wheeler, where he handed her a helmet.

She tightened the strap under her chin, threw her leg over the seat, then tucked in close behind his brother.

"You ready?" Killian finished securing his own helmet.

"Yep." She leaned into his brother and wrapped her arms around his waist.

Jonathan's jaw clenched tight, and he stifled a growl.

"Let's do it." Killian cranked up the engine, revved it with a couple of twists of the throttle, then took off across the field.

"You really just going to stand there while Killian takes off with her?" Mathias asked as they watched them disappear into the woods.

"Like you said before, Andi can take care of herself." He kissed one of his daughter's chubby cheeks. "Come on, honey. Let's go help grandpa."

"It's okay for you to be happy, ya know," the "quiet twin" called out to him as he walked away. "She would want you to be happy." Meaning, Marilyn.

Jonathan smiled down at the beautiful child now asleep in his arms.

"I'm working on it."

CHAPTER SEVENTEEN

Killian stopped about ten feet from the edge of a bluff and powered down the four-wheeler. Andi tugged off her helmet and ruffled her short bangs back into place. She climbed off and worked her way toward the edge. The sudden lack of engine noise amplified the sound of the rustling evergreens and the waves rolling and lapping against rocks.

"Wow." Her eyes scanned the horizon, where the dark, imposing sea touched a crystal-clear, azure sky. Six large Canadian geese honked as they flew overhead in a lopsided vee formation. "It's beautiful up here."

She leaned forward to peek down at the rocky shoreline. Murky water churned and foamed around large, smooth boulders. Sunlight flashed like diamonds strewn across its undulating surface. Sea kelp swayed and tangled around piles of driftwood bleached of all color.

"Isn't it?" Killian set his helmet on the seat and joined her. "It's Jonathan's favorite place. Well, here and in those woods back there."

He indicated the trees behind them. Lips pursed, he gave her a sideways look.

"What?" She frowned. "What's that look for?"

Did she have something on her face? Or maybe a bug between her teeth?

"No look." He lifted one shoulder and gazed out over the water. "Just thought you might like it, too."

"Oh, well, I do." A person could really get lost in their own thoughts up here. "It's peaceful, but in a rugged kind of way."

"Yeah, kinda like Jonathan." Killian picked up a couple of rocks, shook them in his big hand.

Didn't matter that he and Mathias were identical twins. Andi could easily tell them apart. Mathias seemed more reserved. A real cards-close-to-the-vest kind of guy. Killian was a charming flirt with a perpetual wink ready to be let loose on unsuspecting women. The day he ever truly set his sights on *the one*, the poor girl would be in deep trouble.

"He's different from the rest of us kids. Always has been." He hurled a rock. The *plunk* when it hit the water carried up the cliff face. "I don't know if you know this, but he's crazy smart. Like, Mensa smart." Another rock thrown. This time he bounced it off a waterlogged hunk of wood. "Because of his size, people often underestimate that about him." Sounded like Killian might have a slight case of hero-worship for his older brother.

She could certainly understand why. Jonathan was an impressive guy.

"They quickly learn what a mistake that is." He turned, a knowing smile on his face.

Andi had been guilty of the same hasty judgement. She'd shown up at OSI expecting Jonathan to be another knuckle-dragging meathead. How wrong she'd been. He had depths to him that would take forever to plumb.

"Killian, why are you telling me all this?" Her hand across her forehead shielded her eyes.

"What do you mean?" Killian looked at her with playful eyes the same deep, almost royal blue bestowed upon all the O'Halleran men. Emily, Molly and Ashling were equally blessed, but their eyes were a frosty emerald green, unlike anything Andi had ever seen.

"I don't know. I guess I just assumed since you—"

"Since I asked you to join me that I was hitting on you?" A sly smile played across his face, and he winked. She wasn't even sure he knew he was doing it.

"Well, yeah." Andi chuckled at his directness.

She was flattered, but like it or not, she was too wrapped up in her complicated feelings for his brother.

"It's obvious he has a thing for you, and I just wanted to needle him a little." A gust of wind blew his hair away from his face. "The opportunity to do that seldom presents itself, so I had to take advantage."

She snorted. "Trust me. The only *thing* your brother has for me is restrained contempt." As much as it pained her to say the words out loud, she couldn't deny the truth in them. "I'm pretty sure he has a calendar somewhere with X's on it, just counting down the days until I'm gone."

"I disagree." He opened his mouth as if to say something, then snapped it shut.

"What?" she pressed. "Spill it."

"See ... " Killian's devil-may-care attitude fell away, replaced by genuine concern. "Jonathan's been through unimaginable hell the past few months."

"He told me how his wife died." She still questioned why he'd shared something so deeply personal. With her, of all people.

"He did?" He turned, a look of surprise on his face.

She nodded.

"Wow. I'm amazed. He's hardly talked to any of us about it." He rubbed the back of his neck, looked down as he dug the toe of his boot into the dirt. So much like his brother.

"Not being here when she died tore him up inside. He blamed himself." He shook his head. "Before he had time to process that, he had to watch Appleseed struggle to survive. In case you couldn't guess, being helpless is not something a guy like my brother is used to."

Andi understood all too well. She'd spent a good part of her childhood feeling like her world was beyond her control and swore she would never feel that way again. It's why she spent so much time training, shooting, and training some more. And, yes, keeping herself closed off.

"Staring down the barrel of raising his daughter alone, right after finding out his wife kept something so big from him ... " His troubled gaze locked on the strip of small, rocky islands in the distance.

"Killian." She placed her hand on his arm, and he dragged his eyes from the horizon back to her. "I didn't know Marilyn, but for her to take a risk like that, she must've desperately wanted a child."

"Jonathan had a right to know." He rolled his shoulders back, took a deep breath and blew it out. "It's going to take some time for him to come to terms with it."

She agreed. He should've been given a voice in a decision that would have such a profound effect on his life. Andi never considered having a child of her own. Because seriously? What the hell did she know about being a mother? But after holding Ashling in her arms, hearing her giggle and seeing the joy she brought to everyone, even she could understand Marilyn's desperate need to roll the dice. Even with the slimmest hope, the leap of faith would be worth it, if it meant being blessed with a life spent watching her precious little girl grow up.

A heartbreakingly beautiful sacrifice.

"Will you tell me about her?" What kind of woman captured the heart of a man like Jonathan O'Halleran? She felt petty for being jealous of a dead woman.

"Marilyn?" He smiled. "She was ... sweet. Bubbly and light. A real people-pleaser."

Vastly different from Andi. The opposite, actually.

"Thing is, as long as we all knew her, I don't think we ever really knew *her*. Know what I mean?"

"No." Her brows drew together. "I don't think I do."

"That doesn't surprise me." He chuckled and bumped his shoulder against hers. "You're a strong woman, Andi. And you're very sure of yourself."

Ha! If he only knew what a fraud she was. She didn't bother to correct him.

"Marilyn would always adapt who she was to fit in with whoever she happened to be with. If they liked tennis, suddenly, she loved tennis." He rolled his eyes.

"She hated camping. Bugs, sleeping on the ground, peeing in the woods—she hated all of it. Yet she would go every damn time. All because she wanted to be a part of what everyone else was doing. If they wanted to go for sushi, she would happily go along. Not because she liked sushi—I know for a fact she didn't—but because she desperately wanted to fit in."

Desperately wanted to fit in.

Huh. Maybe she and Marilyn *did* have at least one thing in common. Difference was, Andi had learned to disguise it behind a contrived self-assuredness.

"Yes, but Jonathan must've known that about her and loved her anyway."

"Maybe. But here's the thing you need to understand. She set her hooks in Jonathan back in elementary school. Used to tell everyone they were going to get married someday. He just sorta went along." He threw the last rock, brushed his hands on his jeans and talked as he walked back to the four-wheeler.

"Don't get me wrong. He loved her, but ... " He gave Andi a long, meaningful look. "I'm not so sure she was his *great* love."

Andi chided herself the whole way back to the house for the flicker of hope his words ignited.

CHAPTER EIGHTEEN

Jonathan looked toward the woods and checked his watch for what had to be the hundredth time.

Where the hell are they? The property wasn't that big. And why the hell did it matter so much to him?

"Wouldn't you agree, Jonathan?"

"What?" His head snapped around at the sound of his name.

Beck, Caleb and Jeffrey Burke, along with Caleb's best friend, Mason Croft, stared at him. Sherm would've fit right in with this bunch, but he'd gone back home to Georgia to spend some time with his mom before relocating to Whidbey Cove.

"Sorry." He forced his mind away from the fact his brother and Andi had been gone for almost two hours, searched for a thread of the conversation. "Wouldn't I agree about what?"

"I was just saying how much we've benefited from having Andi at OSI." One side of Beck's mouth hitched up, and he tipped his head in Burke's direction. "I threatened to woo her away from Mr. NSA here with a permanent job offer."

"Permanent?" They now had his full attention. "I'm not sure that's such a great idea."

Burke crossed his arms. "Not that I'm in any hurry to get rid of her, but why exactly would it not be such a great idea?"

Jonathan took in the four men standing before him. No way would he divulge the real reason he didn't want her here. That she made him want things he couldn't have. Or that the feelings he had for her scared the shit out of him and threatened the well-ordered life he wanted everyone to think he was rebuilding. He definitely wasn't going to admit he was a chickenshit coward when it came to Andi.

"I'm not sure she'll fit in here." A ridiculous response if there ever was one, but it was the best he could come up with.

"I don't know about that," Mason chimed in. "Seems like everyone here really likes her."

He was right. She seemed to be getting along with everyone. Well, everyone *except* him.

"That's not what I mean. She ... well, she just seems to be the kind of person who needs to be in the middle of the action." True enough, yet he remembered the way she'd methodically scrutinized every single file he'd dump on her. Andi was confident in her skills and passionate about her work. He smiled to himself. She was also stubborn as all hell and would do anything to prove him wrong.

"Okay, so give her what she wants." Beck looked across the patio and gave his wife a warm smile and a wink. She blew him a kiss with one hand as she rubbed her rounded belly with the other.

Jonathan envied his brother for getting to witness his wife's body grow and change as their baby developed inside her. Beck and Gwen's feelings for each other were deep, like, DNA-level deep. The nightmare they'd endured had only made them stronger, individually and as a couple. He could admit, if only to himself, that he was a bit jealous of what they had together.

He'd loved Marilyn, but theirs had been a sweeter, more innocent kind of love. Certainly less intense than the feelings shared between his brothers and their wives. Seeing them together showed Jonathan there could be more to loving someone.

"She's better trained than some of our operatives." Mason continued his defense of Andi. "And her expertise would be an asset in the field. Hell, I'd team up with her any day."

Didn't seem to matter she was as tough as a lot of men he'd worked with and that she could shoot better than most. The idea of putting her in harm's way churned in his gut like rocks in a tumbler.

"You have a problem with her?" Burke pressed.

Having the full power of the NSA director's glare directed at you was not something anyone wanted to experience, but Jonathan refused to back down.

"Personally? No. Professionally? Yes. Due to an incident in the past, I have reason to believe some of her methods may be flawed."

"Let me guess. Marconi?" Burke asked.

Jonathan nodded.

The NSA director checked their surroundings, then turned his attention back on the four men.

"You all have TS clearances, so you're authorized to hear this. But it goes no further." Burke looked from one man to the next in question. "Am I understood?"

He waited for acknowledgment, looked around once more, then continued.

"A formal investigation was conducted after the incident occurred."

Jonathan perked up. Finally, he would get some answers. At the time, he'd tried to get details up the chain of command. He'd been told information was being provided on a need-to-know basis. Apparently, they didn't feel he needed to know.

"The official findings of the inquiry determined that only a few hours had elapsed between the time Andi started her questioning to the time her report was relayed forward." Fatherly pride suffused Burke's voice. Was she aware Burke returned her affection? She, more than most, needed to know there were people who cared about her.

Members of the Brotherhood were known to be more educated and better trained than your garden-variety do-as-they're-told terrorist. For Andi to have garnered that kind of detailed intelligence in such a short time, from men who considered women nothing more than property, was unprecedented. They probably thought they were so much smarter than a mere woman. She'd proven them wrong.

"Had Marconi waited for the intelligence she gathered, he would've known one of the Brotherhood's highest-ranking leaders had not only taken control of the region, but that the sect had set up his newest training camp there. Instead, he led his team into an ambush, got himself killed and three of his men wounded."

Heads shook, and a colorful variety of expletives were grumbled by their small group. Each of these men served their country in one way or another. They understood the dangers faced on a mission and the importance of timely intelligence coupled with solid teamwork.

"They managed to make their way up into the hills. Hell of a feat, considering one guy was carrying Marconi's body over his shoulder and the others were helping their injured buddies up and over some of the most punishing terrain in Afghanistan. They eventually found cover and called in an airstrike that took out the majority of the village. Several hours later, they were airlifted out."

All this time, he'd been blaming Andi, when in reality, she'd done a stellar job. He needed to see her, to apologize for being such an ass.

"Let me nutshell it for you," Burke continued. "In her three-plus years in theater, Andi questioned over two hundred people, including some of the most devout leaders and members of the Al Mu'min Brotherhood. And when I say devout, I mean sacrifice-their-own-children level of devotion. The information she garnered saved untold numbers of lives, both military and civilian. For one particular incident, she was awarded the Secretary of the Army Award for Valor."

Caleb whistled between his teeth. "Impressive."

As hell. The award was only given to a civilian who exhibited great courage or sacrifice involving heroism or bravery voluntarily and beyond the call of duty.

Before he could ask Burke for details, the growl of a four-wheeler breaking through the tree line captured their attention.

Andi smiled, and her arms were still wrapped around Killian. They stopped about twenty-five feet away, in front of the large storage shed where all the motorized *toys* were kept. She rose from the seat, pulled off her helmet and dragged her fingers through her hair in that sexy way of hers. At some point, she'd zipped her coat to the top and wrapped a scarf around her neck. Killian's scarf.

His brother smiled up at her and said something. She laughed and gave his shoulder a playful shove.

Jonathan's teeth ground together.

What the ever-loving fuck? Was she flirting with his kid brother?

She slowly turned as if sensing Jonathan's eyes on her. The laughter stopped, and her smile fell. In typical Andi fashion, she cocked up a brow the same time she lifted her chin and looked him square in the eye. As if daring him to ... what? Say something? Confront her?

What could he say? That the idea of another man touching her made him want to put his fist through a wall? Even if it was his brother? Or maybe he should tell her that he wanted to be the one to make her laugh, to be the person she turned to when she was feeling lonely or troubled.

He'd never felt this type of inexplicable jealousy before. Not even with Marilyn. He wasn't sure what to do about it, and it pissed him off more than he had a right to be. Fair or not, he blamed her.

"Looks like those two are getting along." Caleb spoke around a last mouthful of hot dog. He swiped a napkin across his mouth and swallowed. "I had a chance to chat with her while I was tweaking the alarm system in her rental. She's pretty friggin' cool."

Jonathan turned back to the group. "What would your wife think of you being alone with her?"

Caleb snarled and took an aggressive step forward, hands fisted at his sides. "And just what the fuck is that supposed to mean?"

The rest of the guys looked at Jonathan like he'd lost his damned mind.

He cursed under his breath. Maybe he had.

"Sorry, man." He put his hands up in surrender, sighed and gripped the back of his neck. "That was outta line."

At one time, Caleb had been quite the ladies' man. All that ended the first time he spotted Dawn across the room at a fundraiser. He would never do anything to disrespect his wife or jeopardize what they had together. It had been a shitty thing to say, and Jonathan deserved the beat-down his second oldest brother looked anxious to dish out.

"You're damn lucky Mom's standing over there talking to

Nancy, or I'd have to kick your ass." He kept his voice low, not wanting her to hear.

Everyone was afraid of their tiny mother. Rightfully so.

"What's going on between you and Andi?" Beck asked.

Burke, who'd stood by quietly as the family drama unfolded before him, crossed his arms over his chest. "You have some other kind of problem with her?"

"I'd like to hear the answer to that one myself." Andi and an angry-looking Killian stood behind him.

Fuuuuck. Jonathan's head fell forward on a sigh.

"You know what?" She held up her hand and shook her head. "Never mind. I already know the answer." She unwound the scarf from her neck and handed it to Killian. "Thank you for this and for the tour. The property is beautiful."

She turned to the group, and Killian shot Jonathan a dirty look over her shoulder.

"Gentlemen." She gave each of them a tight smile. "If you'll excuse me, I've got some work to finish up."

Unlike most women, Andi didn't stomp away in a pout. She looked him square in the eye when she said, "Jonathan, as always, so good to see you." Then she turned and headed toward the back steps.

Beck, Caleb, Mason, Burke and now Killian stood shoulder to shoulder.

Ignoring the muscled wall of crossed arms and glaring hostility, Jonathan jogged after Andi. He caught up to her in the hallway—the one she'd retreated to when he'd ripped into her at Ashling's party.

"Andi ... " His fingers wrapped gently around her elbow to stop her.

"Christ," she whispered under her breath. Her shoulders drooped. "Do you mind?" Keeping her back to him, she jerked her arm free. "I just wanted to use the damn bathroom before I go."

"I need to talk to you." He kept his voice gentle, low.

"There's nothing ... Look, I just want to go home." Something in her voice seemed different.

Jonathan leaned in to cradle her chin with his fingers and gently drew her face around to him. Tears pooled in her big, brown eyes. Tears he'd put there and that, surely, pissed her off. She blinked, and the sight of a lone tear streaming down her rosy cheek flayed him wide open.

"Satisfied? This *is* what you wanted, isn't it?" She jerked her chin free of his grasp. "Now, if you don't mind—"

"I do mind." He closed in on her, and she shuffled backward until she was flush against the wall. "And that's not at all what I wanted."

"Please, just ... let me go," she whispered, her quiet plea making him feel like the world's biggest asshole.

Andi's tough-as-nails exterior was like armor she used to protect the deeply sensitive woman inside, the lonely child whose father never showed her an ounce of affection, let alone love. Jonathan's callousness had ripped through it, baring the part of her she kept sheltered from the severe hurts of her past.

"I can't do that, Andi." The backs of his fingers stroked down the dewy-soft skin of her cheek, wiping away the trace of moisture. "I know the truth about what happened to Marconi and his team."

"What?" Confused eyes flew up to meet his. "How ... ?"

"Burke." He pressed his forehead to hers. "Why did you let me go on thinking it was your fault?"

"I ... I can't do this right now." She tried to sidestep him, but Jonathan flattened a hand against the wall on either side of her head and pressed his body against hers from chest to hips.

He stifled a groan. God, she felt good.

She sucked in a breath. Her pupils expanded, crowding

out the deep brown of her irises. Her heart hammered against his chest and pulsed at the base of her slender neck.

Yeah, she noticed the way his body reacted to her. Hell, his dick was doing everything in its power to burst through his zipper.

Andi was skilled enough to evade him, but he was counting on her insatiable curiosity to keep her in place.

"What if I had told you the truth? Would you have believed me? And what difference would it have made?" Uncertainty or anger tinged her words. He couldn't be sure which. "Let's face it, Jonathan, you hate m—"

His mouth crashed down on hers, keeping her from completing that sentence.

Andi's body stiffened, and her hands flattened against his chest as if to push him away. Undeterred, Jonathan tilted his head and took the kiss deeper. A split second later, a small moan hummed in her throat, and she relaxed into him. Her hands smoothed up and over his shoulders until she wrapped her arms around his neck. Magnificent breasts, their nipples beaded, pressed against his chest.

Fingers splayed through her short hair, he cradled her head in his big hands and held on as he explored the hidden secrets of her mouth. Salvation. Redemption. Hope.

Andi lifted to her toes and fisted her hand in the back of his hair. As with everything, she gave as good as she got.

"She wouldn't leave without saying goodbye." Emily's voice managed to filter its way through the thick haze of lust.

"Of course she wouldn't." And that was his mother's voice.

The screen door screeched open, then banged shut. "I'm pretty sure I saw her come inside."

Andi pulled her lips away with a *smack,* flattened her hands to his chest and shoved him away. Wide, confused eyes stared at him across the few feet between them. Her chest heaved with each stuttered breath, and she lifted shaky fingers to her puffy, shiny lips.

Emily and his mother rounded the corner and came to an abrupt halt. Two sets of inquisitive green eyes looked from Andi to Jonathan, then back to Andi.

"Everything okay?" His sister dragged out each word as she continued to look between them.

"What? Oh, um, yeah." Andi hesitated. Her eyes darted around, then she blurted out the most ridiculous response. "Jonathan was just showing me where the bathroom is."

She skirted around him, putting as much space between them as the hallway would allow. As if afraid he might reach out and grab her. *Smart girl.*

"I was just going to ... um ... Well, you know ... Before I head home."

He rubbed his mouth to hide a grin and watched with fascination as she fumbled for words. This less-in-control side of her was sweetly endearing.

She dashed into the bathroom, turned and stuck her head back out the door. "I'll come say goodbye before I leave."

"You sure everything's okay?" Emily narrowed suspicious eyes at him and dropped her hands to her hips. "He didn't say something stupid, did he?"

"Knock it off, squirt." Jonathan's eyes remained on Andi.

"No. We were just ... " Andi's face turned an adorable shade of pink. She groaned, rolled her eyes and slammed the door.

In unison, Emily and his mother turned to glower at him.

"What?" He shifted his stance and tried to hide the bulge in his jeans.

"She's a very nice girl, isn't she?" his mother asked, a bit of a scary smile on her face.

"Sure. I guess." He tried to step between them, but his mother's next words stopped him cold.

"You should ask her out." *Shit.* Last thing he needed was his mother in matchmaker mode.

"She works for me, Mom." Well, not really, but sort of. Either way, she was leaving in a couple of months. Earlier, if they figured out who the mole was. Besides, he was a married man. *Not anymore,* a little voice reminded him.

"Ashling really seems to adore her. Don't you agree?" Emily turned to his mother and spoke about his life as if he wasn't standing a foot away. "I've never seen her take to someone the way she did Andi."

"You know, Emily, you are so right." His mom looped her arm through his sister's as a conspiratorial smile lit her face. "Even your dad noticed it."

Oh, dear God. He didn't stand a chance if these two busybodies ganged up on him.

"Listen, I'm not looking for anything permanent. And I'm certainly not going to allow just anyone to be a part of Ashling's life. Especially someone who lives out of a suitcase and doesn't know the first thing about kids."

Emily and his mom's eyes widened as they looked over his shoulder. His sister gave a near-indiscernible shake of her head.

Jonathan turned to find Andi standing just outside the bathroom. *Christ.* He really needed to brush up on his situational awareness. Twice in the span of a few minutes, she'd managed to catch him off guard.

"Excuse me." She fashioned what looked to be a forced smile and scooched by him.

"Molly, I had a wonderful time. Thank you so much for having me." She reached out as if to shake his mother's hand.

Yeah, that wasn't going to work. Molly O'Halleran wouldn't be satisfied with a handshake. Proving his point, she pulled Andi into a hug and kept her there for a moment or two as if she sensed Andi's need to be comforted.

"You are welcome here anytime, Andi." She held her at arm's length, a reassuring smile on her face. "Whether you like it or not, you're as good as family now."

His mom wasn't just being polite, either. She was the most nurturing, loving woman he'd ever known, and she never said anything she didn't mean. Once she added you to her circle, there was no escape.

Andi gave a quick nod, then turned to his sister. "Emily, I'll see you at the office Monday."

Jonathan could tell she was struggling to keep it together, desperate to escape the barrage of emotions clogging the hallway. What he wouldn't give to walk over there, take her in his arms and tell her he hadn't meant what he said. But why deny the truth? They weren't a good fit.

"Are you sure you have to go?" Emily raised up on her tiptoes to glare over Andi's shoulder at him.

"Yeah, I've got some more work to get done." After a quick sideways look in his direction, she said her goodbyes and walked out the back door.

"What the hell, Jonathan?" Emily marched right into his personal space. Growing up with five older, much bigger brothers, she'd learned to hold her own. His baby sister never let her diminutive stature stand in the way of getting in someone's face. He worried it would get her into trouble one day.

"Language, young lady," his mother scolded. As kids, if they got caught cussing, she would make them bite into a bar of soap. "Why don't you go check on your dad. Make sure he's not sneaking another piece of pie."

Emily pursed her lips and squinted up at him, then turned and stomped off, muttering "jerk" under her breath.

"Shit." He squeezed the back of his neck and looked down at the floor.

"What is it with my children and their language?" His mother watched Emily leave, then swung back to him.

He started to make a move, but she inserted herself between him and freedom.

"Huh-uh." She flattened her small hand to the middle of his chest. "I'm not done with you, young man."

Young man? He flashed back to when he was seven years old and she discovered his plan to live in his treehouse deep in the woods and survive off the land. He could've done it but had been secretly relieved and happy when she came looking for him.

"Jonathan." Her short, deceptively strong fingers took hold of his hand. "Honey, you do not have to spend the rest of your life alone."

He opened his mouth, and she lifted her hand to silence him.

"Please, let me finish. For whatever reason, you're punishing yourself. Maybe it's because you were gone when Marilyn died. Or maybe you feel you have to pay some sort of penance for being angry at her about not telling you the truth. Whatever it is, it's dumb and you need to stop it, right this minute."

Jonathan tucked his chin and blinked a few times. He scowled down at her.

"Don't look at me like that." She released his hand. "You're a smart guy. Why don't you step back and look at this objectively, like you do everything else? What would you do if one of your brothers or Emily went through what you've been through?" Her hands landed on her hips. "Would you expect them to give up on finding some kind of happiness?"

"Of course not," he said. *But this is different.* Wasn't it?

"Maybe Andi isn't the right fit for you. Maybe someone else is. What makes me sad is that you're not even willing to find out."

"But Marilyn—"

"Is gone, honey." Her tone softened, and she grabbed hold

of his hand the way she did when they were little and had to cross the street. "But you're here, and you have Ashling and all the rest of us. Who does she have?" Her head tipped toward the screen door. Andi stood on the other side with his dad as he thanked her again for the tools.

"What makes you so sure she *wants* anybody, Mom?" Not everyone was interested in being surrounded by a loud, nosy family.

"Just because being alone is all she's ever known doesn't mean it's all she's ever wanted." Having dropped one of her Molly O'Halleran wisdom bombs, she curled her hands over his shoulders, tugged him down to kiss his cheek, then walked away.

CHAPTER NINETEEN

Matt's heart knocked in his chest when he looked down at the caller ID on his phone. It had been weeks since he first spoke to the man on the phone. Two young interns gabbing about their weekend plans glanced at him as they walked by. He forced a smile, nodded and looked at his watch. After the conversation faded down the marble hallway, he ducked into a small alcove on the second-floor rotunda and swiped his finger across his phone.

"Yes." Voice hushed, he turned to face the wall. Who the hell knew if there were listening devices planted all over this damned building or not? He'd already made a mental note of where the cameras were. The ones he could easily spot, anyway. Some might accuse him of being paranoid. He liked to think of himself as vigilant. In this city, it was one of the things that separated the successful from the failures.

He slipped a pen and small notebook from his breast pocket and took notes as his investigator filled him in on what he'd learned.

"I want to see everything. E-mail it to the account I set up for you." Matt hung up and tapped the notebook against his leg. He smirked, tucked the pen and pad away, then headed to his office.

Smile firmly in place, he pushed open the door and greeted the senator's support staff. "Good morning, everyone."

Six individuals of varying ages and ethnicities smiled back at him. They'd all undergone an extensive background check to ensure they were squeaky-clean. More importantly, every single one of them would walk through fire for their boss. None of them believed a word they read about the senator's ... extracurricular activities. Or if they did, they were smart enough not to discuss it.

"How are you this morning, Margaret?" Margaret was his boss's executive secretary. A real character. Middle-aged, crotchety, and a lock-jawed pit bull when it came to protecting the senator's time.

"Well, let's see now." She appeared to give it some thought. "My son's oldest child is still an idiot. Lord, I love him to death, but if that boy had a brain, he'd take it out and play with it." Her voice had the raspy growl of a lifelong smoker. Made sense—her family had been in the tobacco business for generations. "And my daughter is pregnant. Again. I guess six kids wasn't enough. Why not have one more?"

An aggrieved sigh rattled from her chest.

"Oh ... " She snapped her fingers. "And then there's my husband. He refuses to accept that he is no longer thirty years old. As a result, he is currently lyin' on the sofa whinin' about his back after tryin' something called cyclo-cross. A ridiculous kind of bicycle race. Sorta like steeplechase, but with bikes instead of horses." Her eyes rolled as she shook her head. "Damn fool." She crossed her hands on her desk and looked up at him. "And how is your morning?"

"Well, boring compared to yours." Matt chuckled.

"I'd sell my husband for boring right now," she said under her breath as she reached for her jumbo-size thermos full of diet soda—her caffeine of choice. Ice clattered when she took a swig and set it down with a *thunk*.

"Is he in?" He glanced toward the large carved door behind her.

"He's on the phone but said for you to go on in when you get here." She swiveled back to her computer and began clicking away on the keyboard.

"Thanks."

She flicked a wave over her shoulder without missing a keystroke.

Matt headed to his office, located adjacent the senator's. He shut his door, rushed behind his desk and set his messenger bag on top. Fingers shaking, heart racing, he dug out his personal laptop. His knee bobbed up and down, and his palms were damp as he waited for it to boot up. What seemed an eternity later, he logged into the e-mail account he'd set up for his investigator. The only one listed was the one they'd discussed earlier. He printed the attachments and viewed each one as it slid from the machine, his satisfaction mounting. He slipped them into a manila folder and tucked it under his arm. A couple of keystrokes later, his computer went dark. He wrapped himself in his usual unperturbed attitude, gave a quick tap on the adjoining door, then swept into his boss's office.

"Yes, Gerald, I understand our agreement completely, but the director of the NSA has my budgetary nuts in a vise." The senator waved Matt in and pointed to the chair in front of his desk.

Matt unbuttoned his suit jacket and sat down. He flattened the folder on his lap, scanned through his phone and pretended not to listen.

"I have no idea how long. All I can do is keep pressing

forward." His boss crossed his ankle over his knee and reclined in his chair. He stared up at the ceiling, listened and nodded his head in silent agreement. "Absolutely. It's my number one priority." More listening. "I will, and you tell that beautiful wife of yours I said hello. Yes. Talk to you soon."

He sat forward, slammed the phone down and cursed under his breath.

"Trouble, sir?" Rhetorical question. Matt made it a point to stay on top of anything and everything relative to the man seething across from him.

"Davenport is pissed. He's threatening to pull his support for the next campaign." Etheridge tugged on his lower lip.

Gerald Davenport owned a company located in the senator's district that created state-of-the-art military drones. He'd already made one sizable donation to the senator's campaign coffers. A second, larger one had been guaranteed after an implied promise to move his company to the top of the list when the military started shopping for drones. The guy was well-liked and had serious political juice that could sway a great many voters for or against a candidate.

Burke had gotten wind of their deal and, suspicious of the terms, jumped into the fray. Things had been stuck in limbo ever since. The senator was left with egg on his face—like he couldn't deliver on his promises. A very bad thing to have shadowing you in a town where promises were traded like currency. One broken promise to the wrong person could sink the senator's chances of going any further in his political journey. And he'd made some pretty lofty promises to a lot of important people.

Matt's boss stood and walked over to the window. He'd finally made it to the much-coveted third floor of the Russell Building, which afforded him a spectacular view of the Capitol.

"Fucking Burke." The senator thumped his fist on the windowsill. "Always standing in my way."

"Well, sir, I have an update on the other *matter of concern*." Matt grinned as he pulled a printout from the folder on his lap.

"You finally found him?" The senator stalked over and snatched it from his hand. He stared down at the photo of a man sitting in a car, then shot a look his way. "You sure this is the guy?"

Matt nodded.

"How? Where?" Etheridge's voice held a mixture of alarm and disbelief.

"I managed to get the first two letters of his license plate as he was pulling away from the hotel that night. I gave that, a description of the car and the driver to my investigator. He worked his magic and got a copy of the guy's driver's license. Once he had that, he was able to find out where he works, lives, everything." His boss wasn't the only one who knew how to leverage secrets.

Matt tipped his chin toward the photo. "That picture was taken while he was waiting for his next passenger."

"Passenger?"

"Yes, sir. The guy drives for one of those hired car services." Matt still couldn't believe it. They had been trying for weeks to locate this guy. All the while, he'd been cruising around the capital picking up riders. If it wasn't for the damage he could cause the senator, the whole thing would be laughable.

"You have got to be shittin' me." His boss propped his hand on his hip.

"I shit you not, Senator."

"Who the hell is he?" The senator handed him back the picture and sat behind his desk. "And what are you doing about him?"

Matt walked over and checked both doors were closed. Having this conversation in this particular building was a risk.

He moved back to the front of his boss's desk and set a copy of the driver's license in the center. "Right now, I'm not willing to risk doing anything about him. For now, I've instructed my guy to watch him."

"What do you mean, you're not willing to risk it?" Etheridge asked.

"Because his name is Jared Raymond, and his mother is Nancy Raymond, the—"

"Personal assistant to Jeffrey Burke." Etheridge exploded out of his chair and began pacing. "Goddamn it."

"Apparently, her son had a bit of a drug problem. He took off for The Farm to get clean." Matt kept his voice calm as he read through his notes. He didn't have the luxury of losing his shit. How nice it must be to know someone was always around to clean up your messes.

"Who the hell cares why he was there? He *saw* me!" Etheridge's voice elevated with each word spoken.

"Sir." Matt pointedly looked over his shoulder. The entire goddamned office did not need to know their boss was losing his shit.

The senator took the hint and lowered his voice. "Now you're tellin' me his mother works for the man determined to not only keep me from becoming president but to destroy me while he's at it?"

"I think there's more to this than just a guy trying to get clean." Matt kept his voice low, encouraging his boss to do the same.

"Well, if there is, it sure would be nice if you'd share it with me, Matt." Etheridge continued his efforts to wear a hole in the carpet.

"Sir, why don't you have a seat, and I'll tell you everything

I know," Matt said, just as the phone buzzed. Etheridge stormed over and snatched it up.

"Yes?" He checked his watch. "Son of a— Please call him and make my apologies. I'm running a few minutes behind." He slammed the phone down.

"I am about to be late for a meeting with my father-in-law." Etheridge lowered his sleeves with a few rough jerks, then clipped on his cufflinks. The senator's father-in-law was not a man who liked to be kept waiting.

Matt continued his report as his boss got ready.

"According to my source, Raymond somehow ended up being a runner for Nikolai Radoslav." No need to explain who the Russian mobster was. His face had been all over the news after he was killed during a raid on his compound. "Speculation is, he skimmed some of the product or saw something he shouldn't have—not sure which—and decided it was time to disappear and get clean. One of the other dopers who worked for Radoslav told him about that place in Montana."

Probably thought he could hide out up at that commune while he kicked his habit. Dumbass obviously had no idea how easy it was for a guy like Radoslav to get the answers he needed from a druggie or how far his reach extended.

Etheridge being seen at The Farm wasn't the only fire Matt had to extinguish. Thanks to this newest discovery, the senator's connection to Nikolai Radoslav was in jeopardy of being exposed as well. A connection Etheridge knew nothing about. It was critical to Matt's future it stayed that way.

"Anyway, a few weeks later, a tactical K9 handler with the FBI's Hostage Rescue Team was shot and his K9 partner killed. They were ambushed when they showed up for a meeting with a confidential informant from The Farm."

Coincidence? Doubtful.

"My guy is still digging, but, what we know so far is, other than the CI, who was already dead when they got there, and the HRT guys assigned to the operation, there were only three other people who knew about that meeting."

The senator slowly turned from the mirror where he'd been adjusting his tie.

Matt flipped to the next page.

"Jeffrey Burke, Nancy Raymond and a tech specialist named Isaac Andrews. Andrews was in charge of electronically monitoring the meet-up with the CI, and ... wait for it ... there just happened to be a dramatic increase in his savings account balance shortly after this all went down."

"You're telling me one of them gave up details to the meeting?" His boss practically salivated at the thought Burke might somehow be involved, even peripherally, in the shooting of an FBI operator.

"At this time, there's no proof any of them are responsible for what happened." But Matt didn't believe in coincidences, especially in this town.

The head of the NSA wasn't involved—the man was too damn smart. Not to mention, he was conducting his own investigation into the leak. Nancy Raymond was a lonely, middle-aged woman who was too fucking loyal to her boss to do anything that would jeopardize her position. No, Matt's money was on Andrews. And all of it happened right under Jeffrey Burke's nose.

"I'm still trying to track down where the extra cash in Andrews's account came from." Best to have all the information before making a move.

"Is that everything?" Etheridge spoke as he slid his arms in his jacket and tugged the cuffs down.

"A couple more items you might find interesting. The woman rescued from Radoslav's compound is Beckett O'Halleran's wife. And the FBI operator who was shot?" He tucked his notebook in his pocket and stood. "Just happens to be his younger brother."

Probably unrelated, but another set of startling coincidences.

"Where's all this information coming from?" His boss grabbed his cell phone and tucked it in his breast pocket.

"For your own sake, senator, I think it's best you not know." Matt buttoned his jacket.

"Is this *source* of yours credible?" Etheridge pinched a piece of fuzz from his lapel, tightened his American flag lapel pin and straightened his pocket square. Though his boss would deny it, he was always a fidgety mess before meeting his father-in-law.

"One hundred percent."

"Damn fine job, Matt." His mood improved. His boss gripped his shoulder and gave it a little shake. "You just keep pullin' that string."

"Will do, sir." He pulled open the door and followed him into the busy front office area. Phones rang, staffers' voices mingled, copiers hummed, and a coffee pot spit and sputtered. The tedium that fueled the engine of democracy.

"Here are your messages, Senator." Margaret handed him a stack of pink notes. She refused to use the high-tech calendar software. "If it ain't broke, don't fix it," she'd said.

"Why, thank you, Margaret." He gave her one of his patented Preston Etheridge swoon-worthy smiles. "What would I do without you?"

Margaret's cheeks creased in a smile and, if he was able to see through her thick makeup, Matt would guess she actually blushed. Proof no woman was immune to his boss's southern charm.

Except for one ... Matt reflected on the enigmatic woman at the fundraiser. Burke's warning about her had piqued his curiosity. On his own, he'd delicately tried finding out what he could about the statuesque brunette. He'd finally given up, unwilling to risk Burke getting wind of his snooping. She was like a damn ghost. Time to task his investigator with solving that little mystery.

Etheridge swept by his staff, blessing each of them with a smile.

Margaret sighed. “The senator is a great man.”

“Yes, yes he is,” Matt said, then headed into his office, determined to do whatever was necessary to ensure people continued to believe that.

CHAPTER TWENTY

Andi stood at the O'Hallerans' front door, admiring the impressive door knocker—a large, metal cluster of four oak leaves. Polished by years of use, brass shone through certain parts of the lovely green patina. She thought back to the story Michaleen told her about the elaborate piece.

"I had it made by a local artist and hung it the day we moved in. The oak leaf cluster represents great strength. And my greatest strength comes from those who dwell within this home—Molly and my children and now their families, too." His long fingers reverently traced over the ornate decoration, then he flattened his hand on the door, as if feeling the love that pulsed from inside.

It had been the sweetest, most moving thing she'd ever heard in her life. And she'd desperately wanted to be included in that list.

Enough of that, she scolded herself, then gave four solid knocks. A deep, warm sound resonated through the heavy wood, amplified under the overhang of the large porch.

A moment later, the massive door swung open.

"Andi!" Molly's face lit up. "It's so good to see you again."

The older woman rushed out onto the porch and threw her arms around her. She had an amazing way of making people feel important, like they really mattered.

"It's great to see you, too, Molly." Instead of balking at the display of affection, as she typically would, Andi heartily leaned into it, absorbed all the joy, acceptance and, most of all, love Molly's embrace offered.

Holding her this way reminded Andi how tiny the O'Halleran matriarch was. Yet her life force, like her daughter's, was bigger than that of anyone she'd ever encountered.

"I wanted to drop this off." Andi slid an envelope from her coat pocket and held it out to her.

"Come on in." Molly tugged her inside, then shut the door. "Can I get you something to drink? A soda? Tea? Water?"

She strolled into the front room, expecting her guest to follow.

"Oh, well ... " Andi hurriedly toed off her boots and went after her. Folks in the northwest had a thing about leaving shoes at the door. "That's very sweet, but—"

Just then, a persistent beeping started in the general direction of the kitchen that was immediately overlapped by giggles, coos and burbles filtering through the baby monitor on the coffee table.

"Wouldn't you just know it." Molly picked up the monitor and smiled down at the screen. "Looks like someone is done with her nap, right when I need to check my muffins."

"Oh, well, I'll just leave this here." Not wanting to get in the way, Andi set the envelope containing the certificate of authenticity for Michaleen's woodworking tools on the end table and made a move to go. She'd been so on edge about coming to the barbecue, she'd completely forgotten to bring it with her.

"Andi, would you be a dear and run upstairs and grab Ashling for me?" Molly grabbed Andi's hand, plunked the monitor in it and actually started to walk away.

"Oh ... I don't ... I'm not really qualified ..." Andi shook her head and took a few steps forward, trying to hand it back to her.

"All you have to do his pick her up and keep her busy until I get there." Molly gave her a patient smile and rushed to reassure her. "At the top of the stairs, turn left, and her room is the last door on the right." She patted Andi's hand, which was suddenly clammy. "I promise, I'll just be a few minutes. I have to make sure the muffins are just right."

The annoying beep continued unabated as Ashling's demands to be noticed grew louder. Not in a cranky way, just enough to ensure anyone listening knew she was awake and ready to get the heck out of that crib.

"Don't worry." Molly leaned close. "I won't make you change her this time."

Then she winked—*winked!*—and dashed off to the kitchen.

Andi's back stiffened. *This time?* What the hell did she mean by that?

She stared wide-eyed down at the small screen and whipped her head toward the kitchen. Was the woman crazy? Trusting a clearly freaked-out novice with her grandchild? She looked at the screen again, not sure what to expect. The camera was pointed directly into the crib, and she could swear the little cutie smiled up at her. Not for a million bucks could she have stopped herself from smiling back.

"Okay, kid. Ready or not, here I come," Andi muttered to herself. She set the monitor down, hung her coat on a hook by the door, then took a deep breath and jogged up the steps.

As instructed, she made a left at the top, her thick socks silent on the wood floor as she walked slowly down the wide corridor. Andi hesitated in front of the door with the *Baby Is Sleeping* sign dangling from a hook, then cast a last hopeful look to the foyer below. A minute passed, then two, and still no grandma cavalry to the rescue. Damn it, she was on her own.

You've driven over IED-infested roads knowing snipers perched overhead. Surely, one small child had to be easier than that, right? She swiped her hands down her pants legs and took a moment to collect herself, the same way she did before heading into an especially grueling interrogation.

With a slow twist of her wrist, she turned the knob. The door was silent as it swung open. She peered over at the crib on the far side of the room like it contained a snarling tiger.

Ashling's dark hair stood out against the pastel pink bedding. She rolled her head toward Andi and, the second her green eyes caught sight of her visitor, arms began to flail about, pudgy little legs kicked wildly against the mattress, then she stuck her tongue out and gave a very loud, very slobbery Bronx cheer.

Andi laughed, and all her trepidation vanished—she felt lighter, more at ease. Drawn by the precious creature smiling out at her through the slats in the crib, she made her way across the room.

"Hey there, sweetie. Do you remember me?" Not wanting to frighten her, she kept her voice gentle as she leaned over and picked her up. Andi supported the baby's bottom on her forearm and splayed a hand across her back.

Ashling stuck two fingers in her mouth and, with the trust only an innocent child could possess, nestled her head on Andi's chest. Busy little fingers on her other hand opened and closed against her neck.

Andi cuddled the tiny, warm child close, smoothing her hand up and down her back as she slowly rocked side to side. Eyes closed, she filled her lungs with the baby's soft, powdery smell and locked it away, knowing this was the exact moment she lost her heart to this child.

In no hurry to end this peaceful post-nap bonding moment between them, she remained there, letting her eyes travel around the room. Puffy clouds and unicorns danced and floated across one wall. A cushy rocking chair sat in one corner next to a stack of books. A handcrafted wooden toybox with her name lovingly carved in the side overflowed with what looked like a thousand different species of stuffed animals. Beside it stood a tall chest of drawers with a small lamp, a couple more books, and a framed photo perched on top. She took the few steps necessary for a closer look.

A young, pregnant woman with light blue eyes, long hair the color of sun shining through fresh honey, and perfect teeth smiled out at her from where she leaned against a split-rail fence.

Marilyn.

Andi leaned in close, tilting her head as she took in all the details, then straightened.

Most people would look at the picture and think, *hey, that person seems really happy,* but she had years of experience observing and studying human micro-expressions. Everything Marilyn must've been going through at the time was all right there—in the slight tension of her features and the way her smile never quite reached her eyes. Pregnant and knowing she might die because of it. The burden of keeping such a heavy secret. Worry and fear that her husband would be killed in some nightmarish part of the world.

As she held Marilyn's daughter to her chest—the daughter she would never know—a wave of sadness washed over Andi, even as her respect for the woman grew.

"You are a very lucky little girl, Ashling. Someday you'll hear how brave and strong your mommy was and how she loved you very, *very* much." A whisper was all she could manage around the invisible fist gripping her throat. "If you were mine, I would tell you every day. All the time. You would never, not for one single minute, wonder about that."

Andi instinctively snuggled Ashling closer and pressed a lingering kiss atop her head. Poor little thing had experienced so much loss and suffering for one so young.

"Okay, enough of that." Tears threatened. She sniffled and blinked them away. "Let's go find your grandma. Sound good?" She turned toward the door and froze.

Molly's face was soft as she padded across the carpet and picked up the photo.

"Marilyn was a wonderful girl." She looked down at the smiling face of her daughter-in-law, then looked over at Andi. "Did you know that she and Jonathan met in the second grade?"

Andi didn't have the heart to tell her that her third child wasn't big on sharing. Especially with her. *That's not really true. He shared with you how she died.*

"Who am I kidding?" Molly rolled her eyes and shook her head. "Of course he didn't. Jonathan has always been my independent, solitary child. He's not big on sharing his feelings or what's going through that complicated brain of his. He prefers to work through things on his own." She set the picture on the dresser and walked over to the changing table. "Marilyn's family moved in about a mile up the road." She grabbed a fresh diaper from a basket.

"She rode the same school bus as our kids and, as fate would have it, ended up sitting next to Jonathan her first day. Growing up, all the kids played together, but she would tag along after him. And though he wasn't much of a talker, she would hang on his every word like it was a nugget of golden wisdom." She chuckled, lost in her recollections.

"It must've driven him crazy, but he was too polite to tell her to leave him alone. Instead, he kept doing the things he loved—building tree houses or forts, traipsing through the woods playing war with his brothers or practicing his survival skills. After a while, Marilyn lost interest in being outside and getting all dirty. But she never lost interest in Jonathan."

"I can't imagine how difficult it must've been for you all to lose her." *Who will care when I'm gone?* Andi's heart squeezed at the thought, and she quickly shoved it aside. "And then to be faced with the possibility of losing Ash—" Her throat squeezed, and she couldn't bring herself to say it aloud. She tightened her hold around Ashling.

"Yeah, those months were horrific, a nightmare. Jonathan pretty much lived at the hospital. He refused to leave. We had to force him to eat, to shower, to change clothes." Molly lifted Ashling's hand from Andi's neck and stroked her thumb over the little fingers. "He was dealing with the terror of possibly losing his daughter at the same time he was blaming himself for not being there for his wife. As rigid as he seems on the outside, he's deeply sensitive on the inside. Anyway, to protect that part of himself, he just ... shut down emotionally."

Ashling gurgled and blew bubbles, effectively breaking through the heavy moment.

"Are we not paying enough attention to you?" Andi bent her knees and bounced her gently.

"You're very good with her." Molly tilted her head to the side.

"It's not me. It's her." Andi popped a tissue from the box on the table and swiped up the drool from the baby's chin. "She makes it easy."

Ashling took that as her cue and let loose a muffled fart against Andi's forearm, then filled her diaper. Loudly and with a great deal of fanfare.

Molly laughed.

Andi looked down at the little poop factory in her arms, then at the other woman.

Ashling's eyes sparkled with mischief. She giggled, blew bubbles, then farted again.

"You know what? I changed my mind." Molly clapped her hands once, which her granddaughter happily copied. "This seems like the perfect time for you to learn how to change a diaper."

Andi groaned.

The older woman chuckled.

"Go ahead and lay her down here." She patted the thick pad on the changing table.

"I'm afraid to move." Andi continued to gaze down cautiously at the bundle in her arms.

Molly laughed harder, and Ashling joined in.

JONATHAN SLOWED to a stop and leaned a shoulder against the wall next to Ashling's bedroom door. One corner of his mouth lifted as he listened to his mother instruct Andi on the proper method for diapering his daughter.

When the sound of Velcro tabs being pulled apart accompanied the baby's typical sounds of contentment, he waited ... *Three. Two. One ...*

"Holy mother of ... ?" Andi exclaimed with disgust.

There it is. He pressed his hand over his mouth to cover his laughter.

"I have to say, Molly, I've seen some scary things in my day. But that ... that is just ... disturbing."

His mom laughed.

"I'm serious." Andi sounded worried. "You might want to get her checked."

Rather than get busted eavesdropping, he turned and

silently made his way back downstairs. He rounded the corner to the kitchen just as his dad was coming through the back door.

"Hey, son." His dad hesitated, glanced up at the clock on the wall above Jonathan's head. "Thought you were working today. Everything okay?"

"Yeah, everything's fine." He'd gotten into the habit of going in to the office on Saturdays—like a big fucking coward. But those days were in the past. "Just needed to grab some paperwork I left in my office. Thought I'd take Ashling for a hike through the woods after she has her snack."

Jonathan looked over his shoulder as voices filtered into the room from the stairs.

"Who's that with your mom?" His dad leaned to see around Jonathan.

Before he could answer, his mom entered the kitchen and headed straight over to give his dad a kiss. "Hello, handsome."

"Hi, yourself." His arm rested across her shoulders, and he tucked her into his side.

"Guess who stopped by." She swept her arm toward the large opening between the kitchen and family room, and they all turned to Andi.

She came to an abrupt halt, eyes wide, and looked from one to the other, stopping on Jonathan. Ashling hadn't noticed them. She was too busy chewing on Andi's necklace.

"Um, hi." Like a pro, she gently freed the chain from his daughter's grip and shifted her to her other hip. "I, um, I only came out to drop something off for your dad."

Jonathan hoped someday she wouldn't get so defensive whenever he saw her holding his daughter. *Wait. Someday* implied she would be coming around more in the future. Not gonna happen, since she would be leaving soon.

"Andi, you're welcome anytime," his dad said over his shoulder from where he stood at the sink, washing his hands.

"Absolutely." His mom bustled past him and patted Andi on the cheek, then tapped Ashling's nose with a "boop."

"You know, you don't have to explain why you're here." Jonathan forced himself not to move closer to her.

Upon hearing his voice, his daughter finally turned, and her face lit up when she saw him. And to think he'd spent weeks denying himself that smile.

"Hey, you." He stepped up to them, hunched down and kissed Ashling's cheek. Which put him smack dab in front of Andi's chest.

Her shoulders tensed, and she stretched her neck back to give him room. He glanced up at her, and one side of his mouth lifted. Maybe he was being a dick, slipping into her personal space that way, but seeing how happy his daughter was in her arms combined with how comfortable Andi was holding her did strange things to his insides. Not to mention, the woman smelled damn good. Not perfume—she didn't seem the perfume type. He'd guess it was her soap or shampoo. Whatever it was, it floated around her like a scented halo.

Jonathan straightened and took a step back.

Andi's entire body seemed to loosen, and he could've sworn she blew out a relieved breath. Would she ever be as comfortable around him as she was around his folks? She responded totally differently to him when they were at the office. Not that she was ever truly relaxed around anybody. He got the impression Andi just didn't have it in her to let her guard down. Understandable, considering her bizarre upbringing. Then again ...

Jonathan thought back to something he'd overheard upstairs, the genuine sadness he'd picked up in her voice when she talked about how hard it must've been for everyone after Marilyn died. The way her voice broke ever so slightly at the thought of Ashling not being here. It was a side of her he never would've imagined.

"Why don't you go see your daddy, sweetie?" She tilted her face to drop a kiss atop Ashling's head. "I really should get going."

Andi held Ashling up to look her in the eye. She hesitated, smiled, gave his daughter a peck on the cheek, then handed her to him.

"Michaleen, I left an envelope for you on the table in there." She pointed her thumb over her shoulder. "It's the certificate for your tools."

"Ah, thanks, honey." His dad stepped up and wrapped her in one of his big bear hugs, then released her, only to have his mother take his place. Jonathan was surprised when Andi didn't even flinch.

"That was sweet of you to bring it all the way out here," his mom said.

"I didn't mind at all. The drive is beautiful, and the view over the water is so relaxing." Her eyes darted to the side as if she might've revealed too much. Then she dipped her chin toward him. "See you Monday."

"Have a good weekend, Andi," he called out as she turned and walked away. All of a sudden, Jonathan was really curious about what she did with her free time. Not that she gave herself much. Between working on Caleb's case, the O-course and the gym, she spent more time at the OSI facility than he did these days.

He turned to catch his parents staring at him with goofy smiles on their faces.

"What?" He walked to the fridge and grabbed a snack for Ashling. "What's that look for?"

"Ya know, it might be nice if someone offered to show her

around." Okay, he could see where his mom was going with this.

"Mom ..." He sighed. "Andi's a grown woman who can more than adequately take care of herself. Besides, I think she's been spending time with Christina and Emily." He'd finally recognized he was being an overprotective ass where his sister was concerned and had decided to back off.

"We can all use another friend, son." His dad clapped him on the shoulder, then he and his mom strolled out to the back porch.

"What do you think, Appleseed?" He tucked his chin to look down at his daughter. "You think Andi needs another friend?"

Ashling smiled up at him, and he could've sworn she nodded her head.

CHAPTER TWENTY-ONE

Jonathan's locker door swung shut with a metallic *bang*. He spun the dial on the lock, grabbed a towel from the closest stack and strolled into the main area of their large workout facility. The massive structure loomed like a boxy giant about a hundred yards behind the main building.

At one time, freshly cut lumber had been stored here before being trucked to lumber yards all over the country, or to ships bound to foreign ports. Unfortunately, the recession hit this part of the country like a hammer's blow, and the mill owners had no choice but to consolidate operations at their main timber mill in Oregon.

OSI bought the structures and as much surrounding land as possible and hired out-of-work locals for various ancillary support positions—administrative, janitorial, grounds maintenance. It didn't make up for the loss of the mill, but it was a step in the right direction.

After a major gut job and renovation—overseen gratis by their father—it now contained state-of-the-art workout equipment, grappling mats, climbing ropes and multiple punching bags. At the back, behind a set of double glass doors, was the pièce de résistance: a fifty-meter-long, eight-lane-wide swimming pool with a separate diving well. Fifteen feet deep, with a seven-and-a-half-meter-high platform, it provided an excellent opportunity for diversified conditioning. Combined with hours spent on the gun range and their three outdoor obstacle courses, training here meant OSI employees were physically and mentally at the top of the private spec ops food chain.

Loud music crashed off the walls and filled the cavernous workout room. High windows surrounding the perimeter of the large open space were fogged over from the frigid air outside clashing with the heat pouring off the bodies inside. Jonathan filled his lungs with the humid air that had already begun to coat his skin. The odor of sweat, rubber mats, and chlorine blended with the lingering scent of cedar.

God, it was great to be back, pushing himself to his physical limits. Crashing into bed each night so damned tired, sometimes even the nightmares couldn't torment him.

Until a few months ago, when a shit-storm tore through and derailed his life, he'd always been physically active. As a kid, he'd ridden bikes all over hell and back, wrestled with his brothers, charged through the woods around their place. He'd cut down trees with his dad and spent more hours than he could count chopping firewood. During his time at the Academy and throughout his career as a SEAL, maintaining peak fitness, both mentally and physically, meant the difference between coming home alive versus inside a flag-draped box.

After six-plus excruciating months, his life had finally begun to take on a new sense of peace. Of rightness. He'd taken huge strides toward settling into civilian life as a single father and had launched himself back into daily workouts.

Jonathan was beginning to feel like a newer, hopefully improved version of his old self.

Ashling played a huge part in that transformation. Each joyous moment spent with her brought him closer to understanding why Marilyn took the chance she did. He still wrestled with occasional bouts of loss, anger, frustration, guilt. Then his baby girl would smile at him, her green eyes flashing with mischief, and all the disquiet he suffered would fade away.

He grinned just thinking about her as his eyes tracked to the boxing ring in the back, right corner.

Mason's deep, lazy Texas drawl could be heard over the scuffing of feet on canvas, the thud of padded gloves connecting with flesh, the occasional grunts or explosive breaths. Arms crossed, feet planted apart, he was laser-focused on the two guys circling each other, maneuvering for an arm bar or choke hold or knee strike, sweat and blood flying when punches connected.

"In the ring, you are not teammates. You are enemies. Your mission, your very *survival* depends on finding your opponent's weaknesses and exploiting them." His ominous directives continued unabated. "Do not hesitate. Do not blink. They will both get you killed."

Beneath the surface of his laid-back, good-old-boy demeanor simmered one of the deadliest men Jonathan had ever met. Mason's skills had an almost mystical quality about them. Lethal as all hell with a blade, he could hit a moving target in pitch-black darkness. He'd been known to shoot the stem off an apple at fifty yards with a bow while running full-out. Oh, and he had the ability to fly just about anything.

Definitely not a guy you wanted for an enemy.

Nearby, cables whirred, weights clanked, and guys grunted through their circuits. Their spotters stood over them, *encouraging* them with "don't be such a pussy" or "my ninety-year-old grandma can lift more than that." Nothing motivated an alpha male more than having his manhood questioned.

Whistles, cheers and clapping drew him over to the corner, opposite the ring, where a crowd gathered around one of the grappling mats. He shouldered his way to the front of the group, and his entire body clenched tight at what he saw.

What the ever-loving fuck?

Andi was laid out flat on her back in the middle of the mat. Sherm sat atop her, knees straddling her midsection, his powerful tree-trunk legs securing her arms against her sides. Red-faced, teeth clenched, she grunted and twisted her body, wriggling her hips as she tried to work her way from beneath him. Finally, she stopped struggling and blew out a defeated puff of air that ruffled her wet bangs.

A hush fell over the group, and Sherm relaxed his posture.

Huge mistake.

Her long legs swung up in one smooth, fluid motion, wrapped around him, then her ankles crossed against his solar plexus. With his arms now trapped and useless at his sides, she pressed her legs forward as she levered her body up at the hips and, with a burst of breath, drove the big man to his back. In a flash of dark hair and spandex, she'd reversed their positions and now straddled his barrel chest. Arm drawn back, she let out a war cry as she drove it down, halting her fist short of his temple. Another half inch would've resulted in a debilitating blow.

There was a second of stunned silence, then cheers erupted. High fives were exchanged to shouts of "pay up" among the assembled group.

"Holy shit. I've never seen anyone move that fast before." This from a guy at the back.

"Dude, you should see her on the O-course. Total badass." Next to him, his buddy sounded equally impressed.

Jonathan couldn't help but be proud of her. Whether

driven by the requirements of a job that demanded she be in top physical condition or by some bullshit standard set by a remote asshole of a father, Andi pushed herself to the limit in everything she did.

"Well, I'll be damned." Sherm blinked a few times, surprised by the power shift. "That was one hell of a sweet move, Swain."

His white teeth flashed in a slow smile, then a laugh rumbled up and shook his barrel chest. She bounced up and down from the reverberations beneath her. He managed to slip his arms free, crossed his hands under his head. Then the big jerk stayed right where he was—with Andi's perfect ass perched atop him.

"Okay, that's enough." Jonathan stepped to the middle of the mat and looked around at the assembled group. "I'm sure you all have something to do."

Smiling and rehashing what they'd just witnessed, the guys all wandered away.

Andi's burst of laughter surprised him—he so rarely heard her laugh. She knuckle-knocked with Sherm, then hopped up and reached her hand down to him. The dick took it, as if he needed her help to get his ass off the floor.

"Care to tell me what the hell is going on here?" Arms crossed over his chest, face scrubbed free of expression, Jonathan hid how aggravated he was about the fact a few thin layers of fabric had been the only thing separating his friend's junk from Andi.

"What's to tell?" She smirked and looked up at Sherm. "Tank here just got his ass kicked."

"It's Sherm, smart-ass." He rolled his eyes and dragged his forearm across his brow.

"Tank. Sherm. Whatever." She held her hand out, palm up, then wiggled her fingers. "You still owe me five bucks."

He smacked his palm to hers, giving her a different sort of five.

"Oof!" The big man stooped over when her elbow connected with his gut. "All right. All right. It's in my locker." He swept his towel up from the floor and wiped it over his bald head. He grimaced as he rubbed his hand on his ripped abs. "Jeez, you're so bloodthirsty."

"Yeah, and don't you forget it." Eyes narrowed, she pointed at his nose before he turned and walked away. "Don't make me hunt you down."

Sherm shook his head, flipped her the bird over his shoulder and moseyed toward the locker room.

Jealousy of their easy camaraderie settled over Jonathan. Didn't seem to matter that it was unwarranted, stupid and, certainly, immature.

Sherm disappeared into the locker room, leaving the two of them on the mat. Andi's chuckle died along with her smile. Then, as if he wasn't there, she pivoted to grab her water bottle from a shelf mounted above the old, disabled, metal radiator. Using her teeth, she popped it open, pursed it between her lips and tipped it up.

A bead of sweat dripped from the damp hair at her temple. Like a radar locked on target, his eyes followed the damn thing as it snaked its way down the side of her face, skimmed along her jawline and meandered down her long, slender throat, where it became trapped in the hollow at the base of her neck. It teetered there until it finally arrowed its way down into her workout tank. He'd never tracked a terrorist with such rapt attention.

His mouth went dry, and his dick took notice. *Breathe, dude. Breathe.*

The torment continued, and he held back a groan when she bent to pick up her towel. Knowing he shouldn't—for his own sanity, and because she'd kick his ass if she caught him—

he looked at her ass anyway. Fucking. Amazing. The high-tech fabric of her workout shorts hugged those perfect globes, and his eyes focused on them like they held the answers to the origin of the universe.

Camel spiders. Sand ticks. Spit-up. Poopy diapers. Jonathan's mind scrambled for anything to keep him from getting a boner in the middle of the gym. Not to mention a charge of sexual harassment.

What the hell was going on with him lately? He'd been a master of impulse control and decorum until Andi. Why was he drawn to her when everything about her screamed *off-limits, back off, not interested, I have baggage?* Hell, who didn't?

"What?" Andi whipped around to glare at him, and her foot hit a wet spot on the mat. Her arms windmilled, the water bottle flew one direction, the towel the other, and she tumbled backward.

"Andréa!" Jonathan lunged forward and wrapped his arms around her in time to halt her descent. Wide, startled eyes stared up at him. The back of her head hovered alarmingly close to the blunt edge of one of the treadmills.

Son of a bitch. If he hadn't caught her in time ... His hold on her instinctively tightened at the disturbing thought, which brought the entire front of his body fully against hers. As if he were dipping her at the end of a bizarre dance number.

She was warm and dewy and, being this close to her, he couldn't help himself. He pressed his nose to her ear, closed his eyes and inhaled a deep breath. Under the light musky scent of hard work, she still managed to smell like spring. How the hell did she do that?

Her quick puffs of warm breath panted across his ear and shot straight to his cock.

Down, boy. His silent command fell on deaf ears and did nothing to stifle his dick's eagerness.

"I've got you." Jonathan drew back his head, their lips only an inch apart.

Their hearts hammered against each other. His eyes dropped to where Andi's pulsed at the base of her neck. Her breasts were flattened against his chest, and each tempting pant of breath feathered across his lips. Her throat moved up and down. Her fingers tensed around his biceps. She gazed up at him with those bottomless, liquid brown eyes of hers.

Oh, yeah. She felt it too—the electricity flashing between them, around them, connecting them.

"You okay?" Desire scratched his voice like sharp rocks grinding together.

One inch closer, and he could have his mouth on hers again. Could eat from those pillow-soft lips and drive her to make those enticing little sounds that proved she was enjoying it, too. Jonathan was afraid to breathe, afraid to flinch a muscle for fear of shattering the moment. As if he were captive to some outside force intent on throwing them together.

His eyes traveled over the beautiful woman currently cradled within the circle of his arms. It would take a man as strong as Andi to be able to look beyond her prickly outer shell and her ball-busting attitude. Someone who could force her to see through all the bullshit from her past to the *real* Andréa Swain just beneath the surface. An equal partner—in her bed and in her life. *Shit. Why did I have to think about a bed?* The word conjured up images of her lying with another man, writhing beneath him as his hands, mouth and everything else roamed over her toned body ...

An aggressive, head-banging song came on overhead and, blessedly, scrubbed away the maddening visuals before they could fully form in his brain.

She blinked a few times, gave a quick shake of her head. She darted a frantic look around the room and, desperate to escape his hold, stumbled as she put some space between them. Jonathan reached out to steady her but lowered his hand when he saw the stiffness of her shoulders and the pleading look in her eyes. Last thing she would want was for these guys to think she had something going on with their boss.

"You okay?" he asked again, then folded his arms to squelch the savage urge to pull her back to him.

"Um, yeah, I'm fine." Her water bottle peeked out from under the radiator. She squatted down, fished it out and stood. "Was there something you wanted to say to me, O'Halleran?"

"Andréa—" He dragged her towel from where it had ended up draped over the treadmill display and held it out to her.

"No ... wait." She snatched it from his grasp. "Let me guess. You want me to keep my distance from your friends, too? Is that it?"

Hell, yes. If it was the only way to keep them from touching her.

"Of course not." Even if imagining another man's hands on her made his skin feel too tight. "You can work out with anyone you want."

"Then?" The towel went onto her shoulder, and her arms crossed over her chest. "What. Is. Your. Problem?" She spoke slowly, enunciated each word, as if he were a simpleton.

"How 'bout you give me a try?" *What the hell?* Where had that come from?

"Excuse me?" Her eyes narrowed, and suspicion coated her words.

"You and me, best of three falls." The more he thought about it, the more he liked the idea. Fuck, he *loved* the idea. "We'll get Mason over here to make sure it's all on the up-

and-up." Jonathan couldn't help himself. He smirked. "Wouldn't want you cheating or anything."

Eyes like molten chocolate made a lazy trip from his feet up to his legs, then slowed at his abs and chest, where they lingered before continuing their visual trek, ending on his face.

He didn't allow so much as a muscle twitch as she sized him up.

Would her common sense override her competitive nature? How would he feel if it did? Since their smokin' hot encounter in his parents' hallway, he'd been burning up with the need to get his hands on her again. Every night, he'd lain awake—hard and wanting—remembering each whimper and moan that came from her. Holding her moments ago had only stoked the fires of his need.

"You sure you're up to it?" One side of her sassy mouth hitched up in challenge. "I know you've been out of the game awhile, just lazing arou— Shit." Eyes squeezed shut, she cursed herself. "I'm ... I'm sorry." She rubbed her forehead and muttered, "Jesus, I am such an insensitive ass."

"Andréa." His fingers curled around her wrist, and he gently lowered her hand. The silkiness of her skin rivaled his daughter's baby-soft cheeks. He waited until she stopped beating herself up long enough to look at him. "It's okay. Really."

"No, it's really not." Her chest rose and fell with a disgusted sigh. "I spend so much time knocking egos with guys, I don't seem to know when to lay off. Still adapting to being back in civilized society, I guess. Not sure I ever will."

Jonathan often wondered the same about himself.

There were nights—fewer now than when he'd first come back—when thoughts of war ripped through his subconscious and tormented him as he slept. He'd jolt awake and, soaked in sweat, heart racing painfully, he'd lain there, still and silent as a stone. As if anticipating the next attack, the next firefight. Focusing on his surroundings, his deep breaths would fill the silence of his room until, eventually, the ghosts of war would slither away. When the quiet and stillness threatened to close in around him—suffocate him—he would throw back the covers and head downstairs to satisfy his craving for the peace and openness of the backyard. He'd stand there in his boxer briefs and gaze up at the stars dotting the inky black sky, the very same stars he'd stared at while in Afghanistan as he prayed for his team to make it home again. The low, droning, white noise of the night always soothed him, calmed his racing heart and anchored him to his surroundings, reminding him where he was. And where he wasn't.

"Jonathan?" The concern on her face suggested she'd said his name more than once.

"Do you ever miss being over there?" he asked. Unless you'd spent a chunk of your life living and working in a war zone, it would sound like a ridiculous question. Because, seriously? What the hell kind of masochist missed dodging IEDs or being shot at while continuously pushing their body to the edge of physical oblivion?

Horrible existence, right? Thing was ... before you knew it, the body and mind craved, no, it *demanded* the constant adrenaline rush. Losing both required a period of adjustment.

"Frequently." Andi's one-word answer came without hesitation. Her eyes traveled to the high windows, as if the hellhole of the Middle East loomed on the other side. "That world, over there ... as fucked up as it was, it made sense to me. I had a job to do, I did it, and that was it. And, conveniently enough, all the crazy shit I learned growing up—weapons, tactics, the hunter mindset, depending on my own wits for survival—would finally serve a purpose. I fit in there more than I ever did stateside."

As if realizing she'd disclosed too much, she shot him a quick side-eye.

"I don't know about that. You seem to be fitting in here just fine." Jonathan recalled what Mason said at the barbecue about how all the guys got along with her, respected her, treated her like one of them.

Why, then, did he have such a bug up his ass about her?

Because you're attracted to her, dumbass. Which made him feel disloyal to Marilyn, as if he was cheating on her by even thinking about another woman.

Like a gnat buzzing around his head, a pesky voice asked, *But why?*

With his back-to-back deployments and her untimely death, it had been over a year—thirteen months, three weeks and two days—since he and Marilyn were in the same room together. Even then, things felt ... different between them. Awkward. Too much time and distance had changed the dynamic of their relationship. Had changed them. He'd become hardened, more remote, sullen. She'd become independent and learned to thrive without him.

Despite all that, they'd remained committed to each other, to their marriage, and decided to start a family of their own. A short time later, he was in Kandahar, two days away from bugging out in search of their next set of targets, when he'd found out she was pregnant.

He abruptly brushed the timeline rationalizations aside as immaterial. Between growing OSI's operation and raising Ashling, he had enough shit on his plate to deal with. His daughter was his life now, the only thing that mattered. Andi would leave for DC, and his attraction for her would fade—an anomalous blip on his emotional radar—and he could focus on his future.

"*If* I am fitting in here, it's because I've spent my entire life surrounded by guys," she said.

"Maybe so, but Christina's mentioned how much fun she has when she hangs out with you and my sister." More than most, his office manager deserved to have some carefree fun in her life.

"But that didn't sit too well with you, did it?" She smirked. "Don't worry, I'll be gone soon, and the two of them can go on with their lives"—she curved her shoulders inward and wiggled her fingers like a witch over a cauldron—"safe from my wicked influence."

"About that ... " Jonathan gripped the back of his neck. "I was being an overprotective dick when I warned you off my sister. What can I say? Force of habit. Or maybe it's that whole being-back-in-civilization thing we just talked about." Except, that wasn't all it was. The woman standing in front of him, looking at him as if waiting for the other shoe to drop, pushed his buttons in a way no one ever had.

He looked down at the mat as he scratched his jaw.

"Emily let me know in her very special way that I was out of line, and she's right." His eyes met hers. "I apologize."

"Thanks." One brow lifted. "That caused you a great deal of discomfort, didn't it?"

"I will admit, it was a bitter pill to swallow." He chuckled, loving this atypical lighthearted banter between them, a welcome and refreshing change from their normal sniping.

She rolled her eyes and laughed, and damned if his heart didn't expand in his chest. He memorized the sound, knowing it would end with what he was about to say.

"Andréa, about what happened at my folks' place, during the barbecue ... " Sexual chemistry, that was all they had between them.

"What about it?" Her smile faltered.

"I know I—"

"Hey, Andi, you ready to work on your punches?" Mason

strolled up behind him, then looked back and forth between them. "Shit, did I interrupt?"

She looked from Mason to Jonathan, hesitated, then said, "Nope. I think we're done here. Let me just get my gloves from my locker." She gave Jonathan a last long look, then swept past him and vanished into the women's locker room.

CHAPTER TWENTY-TWO

Matt cast a quick glance at the manila envelope on the passenger seat next to him. He thought back to what his private investigator discovered about Isaac Andrews, the guy who worked for Burke and who did the comms for that failed op.

Apparently, Andrews had been living paycheck to paycheck until, one day, his bank account was suddenly busting at the seams. Like, one hundred fifty thousand dollars' worth, to be exact. Of course, Matt had known all this already. What he hadn't known until this morning was where the money came from. And that information changed everything. He now possessed an invaluable commodity. Leverage.

The all-powerful, self-righteous Jeffrey Burke had a traitor working for him, right under his nose. And if they were willing to share secrets once, Matt would convince them it was in their best interests to do it again. Only this time, he would be the one calling the shots. *Damn.* He could practically *feel* the power shifting, and it was fucking awesome.

The female voice of his GPS cut into his thoughts,

instructing him to take the next exit. He made a last-minute dive into the right lane, narrowly squeezing between two cars. The sound of their honking horns faded behind him as he turned off the exit.

The timing couldn't be better. He'd started hearing whispers about the senator being involved in something dirty, but no one seemed to know what. Fucking gossips and rumormongers. DC was filthy with them. They were like cockroaches, scurrying away when you shined a light on them.

Cleaning up the senator's messes was monopolizing way too much of Matt's time these days. Decisive action was required. He had more important things to tend to. Like the senator's upcoming presidential campaign.

He was prepared to do whatever it took to ensure he achieved his goal. Which is why, at great risk to himself, he was making this surprise visit to one of Jeffrey Burke's exalted employees. Tonight, he would set the wheels in motion to destroy the esteemed NSA director.

Matt turned onto the dark, quiet street, leaned forward and squinted to see the numbers on the mailboxes. Rather than announce his arrival by pulling into the driveway, he parked at the curb a couple of houses down. He locked up his car and made his way down the sidewalk and up the short path to the front door. A moth buzzed around the porch light as he gave three sharp knocks to the door.

A shadow passed by the large front window. He could swear he felt eyes on him through the peephole.

The door swung open about three inches, the chain still in place. "What are you doing here?"

CHAPTER TWENTY-THREE

Andi looked around the Don't Know Pub. She was going to miss this quirky place, from the walls covered with old black and white World War II-era photos to the giant, top-hat-wearing stuffed bear greeting people as they walked in the door. Even the barstools made from old metal tractor seats and the ridiculous pull-chain toilets in the ladies' room. And where else could a person go to hear music from the forties and fifties playing on a constant loop from an antique jukebox next to a small wooden dance floor?

The pub wasn't the only thing she was going to miss when she left Whidbey Cove in a couple of weeks. She would miss how everyone, from the lady at the small grocery store to the kid that pumped her gas, always had a smile and remembered her name. And yes, here in Whidbey Cove, someone still pumped your gas for you. No one had ever done that for her.

The nagging ache in her chest when she thought about leaving had less to do with this open-hearted little town and more to do with leaving a certain aggravating widower and his beautiful baby girl.

You're a hopeless idiot, Andi.

She sorely regretted gutting herself in front of him by divulging her fucked-up daddy issues. She'd locked that taboo subject down, good and tight, a long time ago. *Apparently not.* Five measly minutes alone with Jonathan in a dimly lit room, and she'd dropped her guard. Whether he'd meant to or not, he'd somehow snuck past the snarling beasts and scaled the high stone walls she'd carefully put in place years ago to protect her mangled heart.

And the make-out session in the hallway? What the hell kind of colossal mistake had that been? Sure, he might have kissed her first, but she'd happily, and with great enthusiasm, kissed him back. Her fingers brushed across her lips. Damn things still tingled from the feel of Jonathan's mouth moving against hers, devouring her. What would've happened had they not been interrupted? What did she want to have happened?

Years of training helped her recognize Jonathan's little proclamation in the gym for what it was—he was afraid, terrified, actually. Afraid to disrespect the memory of his dead wife. Afraid to disappoint his family. Terrified of screwing up with his daughter. They were all excuses he used to keep from having to face those fears. Until he allowed himself to let go and be truly happy, there was no place in his or his daughter's life for Andi. Or anyone.

Thankfully, she'd been out of town interviewing Dylan Renquist and Frank Morgan, and he'd spent the past week in California for some kind of strategic meeting at OSI's main compound. It had given her the time she needed to clear her head and get her feet back under her.

Liar, her inner voice scolded.

"Earth to Andi." Emily waved her hand in front of Andi's face. "Come in, Andi."

"Oh, sorry." She blinked and muzzled her inner voice with a *shut the hell up*. "I was just ... thinking."

"Well, stop that. We're here to have fun, and that's easier to do if you don't think too much." The youngest O'Halleran sibling let loose one of her bigger-than-life laughs. "Am I right, Christina?"

"You are absolutely right." Christina's smile lit up their little corner of the bar. Not once, in all the time she'd been consulting at OSI, had Andi seen the woman anything but happy. How was that even possible?

"Okay, let's get some drinks." Emily grabbed the laminated menu and flipped it open. "We should get something to nosh on, too."

"What can I get you guys?" Devlin Masters's deep voice rumbled down over them like a far-off thunderstorm. He glanced back over his shoulder at the big clock set in the middle of an old wagon wheel. "Happy hour has officially started."

Devlin ran the place for his uncle. A tall, way-too-good-looking guy, he was friendly enough, but still waters ran deep with that one. Andi sensed it in the way he scanned the large room, as if expecting a threat to present itself at any given moment. Yeah, there was definitely something there. Too bad she wasn't going to be here longer. She would enjoy trying to figure out what it was.

"Oooo, goody." Emily wiggled her hips in her chair and clapped like a little kid. "We'll have a pitcher of margaritas." She pointed up at him. "And don't skimp on the tequila. It's been one of those kinds of weeks. Know what I mean?"

"No problem." He chuckled.

"Does that work for you guys?" She looked at Andi and Christina.

Andi nodded.

Christina stared dreamily up at Devlin.

He looked down at her from his six-foot-plus height. One corner of his mouth kicked up.

"Christina ... " Emily nudged her with her shoulder. "Sheesh. What is it with you two tonight?"

"Oh ... yeah, margaritas sound great." A blush poured across Christina's face, and she suddenly became fascinated by something in her purse.

"Cool. We'll also have an order of chili cheese fries, jalapeno poppers and, what the hell." She snapped her menu shut and set it aside. "Give us a large order of wings, too."

Typical of Emily to take charge and decide for everyone else. Fortunately, Andi perceived food as fuel, so she'd eat pretty much anything. Except sautéed goat intestines. That shit was nasty.

"You got it." Devlin nodded, then headed back to the kitchen to turn in their order.

They all tilted their heads and watched him walk away. Old, faded jeans enhanced the quality of his butt, and narrow hips emphasized the width of his shoulders. The way he moved affirmed to Andi he was far more than just a bartender.

"That is a whole lotta yummy right there." Christina leaned her elbow on the table, rested her chin in her hand and sighed like a lovelorn teenager. "And seriously? Devlin? Even his name is sexy."

"Why don't you ask him out?" Andi suggested, recognizing the irony of her giving dating advice, considering her innate cynicism regarding the viability of long-lasting interpersonal relationships. She wasn't exactly overflowing with experience in that area, either. Most of the guys she'd been with—and there hadn't been that many—understood and were totally on board with her lack of interest in any serious involvement.

"Yeah, you've been moony-eyed over him since the first

time he looked at you." Emily nudged her with her elbow. "And I'll never forget the look on your face the first time you saw him bend over to pick up a case of beer."

She crooked her finger at Andi as if she wanted to share a secret. Andi played along and leaned close.

"Christina almost fell out of her chair trying to get a better look. And I'm pretty sure there was drool coming out of her mouth."

They all laughed at Emily's outrageous observation.

Who would've ever thought Andi would be sitting here, hanging out with two women who were her total opposites and loving every damn minute of it? She'd never had girlfriends before and had let herself get used to it. God, she was going to miss them.

Dusky, early evening light spilled through the door, into the room. Killian, Mathias, Mason, Sherm, and Golden Bailey stepped inside and glanced around. People couldn't help but turn and stare at the new arrivals. Each of them over six feet tall, they exuded power and strength. Didn't hurt that they were all easy on the eyes.

Killian's smile when he spotted them softened the don't-fuck-with-me vibe they threw off, and they all headed toward their table.

"Well, howdy-do, ladies. Mind if we join you?" The guy was such a goofball.

In a perfect world, they would stay in touch and their friendship would continue to grow. Realistically, and because the world was far from perfect, it was highly doubtful. Especially if she managed to convince Jeffrey to send her back overseas. Maybe immersing herself in her old work would be enough of a distraction to allay the sense of loss she was already beginning to feel.

"Only if you agree to buy our first round of margaritas and two of our appetizers." Emily, ever their ruthless negotiator.

No doubt a survival skill learned being the only girl growing up surrounded by five alpha-male older brothers.

"You really think you're going to need a second round?" Mason curled one hand around the back of her chair and flattened the other on the table in front of her, then leaned in close. Like, nose-to-nose close. Voice softened by concern, his eyes traveled over her face. "You know what a lightweight you are, Em."

"Is it a deal, or are you guys going to find someplace else to sit?" Undaunted, she crossed her arms.

"I'll get your first round of drinks," Mathias interjected as he dragged a table over next to theirs. "Killian will cover two of your appetizers."

"What the hell?" Killian smacked his twin's arm with the back of his hand.

Mathias shrugged.

"Don't be so cheap, Kill." One side of Golden Bailey's mouth lifted. At six feet eight inches tall, Golden towered over most everyone. Add to that his long, dark blond hair hanging past his shoulders, and he looked like a modern-day Norse god. You could easily imagine him storming ashore on his Viking longboat, axe held high, ready to pillage and plunder. His unique light-gold eyes served him well as one of the world's best snipers, and he also happened to be one of the genuinely nicest guys she'd ever met.

"Yeah, ya cheap bastard." Sherm chimed in. Obviously, he was assimilating with the group just fine.

He and Golden plopped into their chairs and the poor things popped and creaked, threatening to collapse.

"Fine," Killian grumbled and held up two fingers. "But I'm only paying for two of them."

Mason lifted Emily, chair and all, and set her down on the opposite side of the table.

"Hey! I know you guys have a thing about sitting with

your back to the wall, but you could've asked me to move." Emily glowered across the table at him. "And you could've hurt your shoulder, you big ape."

"My shoulder is fine, Em, but it's sweet that you're worried about me."

She snorted. "As if. I just don't want to have to hassle with re-doing your deployment paperwork if you reinjure yourself."

A laugh rumbled low in Mason's chest. "If you say so."

Andi watched them—their body language, eye contact, even the tone of their voices as they spoke to each other. Serious sparks crackled between those two. If they ever acknowledged it, the world better hold on tight.

She wondered if Jonathan knew his little sister had a thing for his brother's best friend.

From what Andi had heard, Emily's concern for Mason's shoulder was warranted. One day at the gym, Mason had been giving her some pointers on the heavy bag. When he'd demonstrated a more efficient way to get power from her left hook, she'd spotted the ugly scar on the front of his left shoulder.

"Nice, huh." He'd glanced down at it and said, "I got in the way of a bullet." Then he'd told her how he'd been shot when OSI went in after Caleb's wife, who wasn't his wife at the time, and her younger sister when they were being held captive in a commune in Montana.

"Looks like it must've been pretty bad." The scar was still fresh.

He'd dismissed her concern with a wave of the hand —"Eh, no biggie"—then he focused back on her technique, effectively changing the subject.

"How's it going?" Killian settled into the chair next to Andi.

"Good." She crossed her forearms on the table. "It's taken

me several weeks, but I've watched all the statement videos, flew back to Quantico for a couple of follow-up, face-to-face interviews, then to Detroit and Maryland to talk to a couple of Caleb's former teammates. I have a couple other ideas I'm still looking into."

What she *had* learned troubled her enough to keep her awake nights.

"Here ya go." The waitress set a hefty pitcher of margaritas and three salt-rimmed glasses on the table. "Your food will be up in a couple minutes. Do you need a few more glasses here?" She pointed at the pitcher, then the guys.

"Nah, we'll let the gals have their margaritas," Mathias said. "And go ahead and put that one on my tab, please."

"Sure." She tucked her tray under one arm, then fished out her order pad and pencil from a pocket in her black apron. "What can I get you guys?"

They each ordered a locally brewed beer and variations on the pub's popular gourmet burgers, which came with unlimited hand-cut fries. Andi looked from one big guy to the next. The Don't Know would likely lose money on this bunch tonight.

"Excellent choices. I'll put your food orders in and grab those drinks for you." She tucked her pencil behind her ear, picked up the discarded straw wrappers and headed to the back.

To their credit, not one of the guys watched her ass as she walked away. Guess that made them better humans than her, Emily and Christina.

"I wasn't asking about work." Killian lowered his voice. "I was asking about the other thing we discussed."

The other *thing* being Jonathan.

"Nothing to discuss." Andi made sure her tone indicated she was less than interested in pursuing this line of questioning.

As tempted as she was to confide in him, he was Jonathan's brother. Putting him in the middle would be unfair. Her plan was to hurry up and find the person responsible for what happened to Caleb and his partner, then get the hell out of Dodge.

"Okay." Killian nodded. "But if you ever want to talk about it ... "

"Thanks." Andi forced a smile, grabbed the pitcher and filled the glasses.

He nodded once and started sharing a few ideas he had for enhancing one of the obstacle courses. They were pretty ingenious, allowing for modifications between each use, which would make them a hell of a lot tougher. She was bummed they wouldn't be done until after she was gone. She would've loved the challenge.

Andi snuck a small sip of her drink. The Cointreau mellowed the tartness of the lime, while the tequila loitered among them. She relaxed into her seat and tuned in to the conversations swirling around her.

About an hour later, the waitress set the second pitcher of margaritas on the table. Andi had allowed herself one, then switched to water. She was a big fan of being in control. Alcohol tended to mess with that.

Thanks to the guys, all that was left of the appetizers were a few inedible remnants of nachos and a bunch of small plates stacked with chicken bones and balled-up napkins. Golden and Mathias were still working their way through the bottomless fries in their apparent effort to bankrupt the pub.

Their server—defying the laws of gravity—managed to pile it all up and carry it to the back in one trip. *Amazing*.

Andi's gaze traveled over the room. The place had gotten a lot more crowded, the music a little louder. Two couples were trying their best to swing-dance, hunching and twisting, mostly just laughing and bumping into each other.

"I'll be damned." Killian lowered his beer from his mouth.

Her eyes skimmed from the dance floor to the new arrivals.

Jonathan, Jeffrey Burke and Nancy Raymond stood just inside the door. The two men checked their surroundings, the way everyone who made a living working in the shadows was conditioned to do.

Andi's vision tunneled and focused on Jonathan as the rest of the room and its occupants blurred and faded from sight. Her stomach flip-flopped, and her breath caught. *Shit.* She couldn't blame it on the tequila. She hadn't had that much. Maybe the fried food? Nah, it was all him.

Okay, so maybe I need more time away from him.

"I don't think he's been in here since he got back." Killian popped a peanut in his mouth.

With a slight lift of his chin, Jonathan acknowledged Devlin behind the bar, then glanced around the room until he landed on their group—her, specifically. Then his gaze dropped to where Killian's arm was now stretched across the back of her chair.

CHAPTER TWENTY-FOUR

Jonathan's jaw clenched tight enough to grind down his molars. *What the fuck?*

He and Andi had practically incinerated each other with the hottest kiss of his life. Not to mention the connection they'd shared in the gym. And now she was, what, flirting with Killian?

Nah, Andi wasn't the type of woman who flirted. *Even if she is, you have no say in who she dates.*

She drew back her shoulders and a sort of you-want-a-piece-of-me look settled over her features.

"Looks like they're all having a good time." Burke dragged his scarf from his neck and tucked it in his pocket, then helped Nancy remove her coat.

The head of the NSA was in town for an in-person update on the status of OSI's investigation into Caleb's case. Burke was conducting his own very hush-hush, lateral investigation and wanted to discuss and share all they'd learned.

Jonathan's plane had landed right behind Burke's at the regional airport. While Burke and his assistant were securing a rental car, Jonathan had called the house to check on his daughter. He'd been disappointed when his mom told him Ashling was already asleep. Her bath and bedtime had become the highlight of his day.

They all decided to stop for a quick drink at the Don't Know before heading to their hotel. Jonathan hadn't been here since before Marilyn died. Strange how his life now fell into two categories—*before* Marilyn died and *after* Marilyn died. He'd begun to reconcile with the former and was slowly adapting to the latter.

Mathias waved them over.

"Jonathan!" Emily popped up out of her chair and threw her arms around his middle and squeezed. "You're here!"

"Hey, squirt." He hugged her back, then held her at arm's length. "How much have you had to drink?"

"Only two." She held up three fingers, then two, then three again. Her eyes crossed as she tried to focus on them.

"Two *pitchers*, she means." Mason pulled her away and plunked her down on his lap.

"Tattletale," she slurred with a scowl as she grazed a punch off his good shoulder.

"Stop it, brat, or I'll bend you over my knee." Mason's lips were close to her ear, but Jonathan still heard him.

His sister giggled, flopping her arm around the back of his neck. Her head lolled until it rested on his shoulder, then her eyes drooped shut.

Jonathan wasn't sure how he felt about all that, but he had other things on his mind right now. Namely, the fact his brother was sitting too damned close to Andi.

"Good evening, Jeffrey." Andi set down her glass of what looked like water and slid it away, leaving a trail of moisture behind. "Jonathan."

"Andréa." He nodded, getting a kick out of the spark in her big brown eyes and the traitorous light pink that snuck across her cheeks. She was too beautiful to carry around a guy's name.

"NANCY, it's nice to see you again." Andi smiled at Jeffrey's assistant.

"It's so great to see you, too, Andi." Nancy's effusive greeting and exaggerated smile was contradicted by the way her white knuckles were wrapped around the purse strap hanging from her shoulder.

Devlin joined them.

"Hey, man. Good to see you again." He shook Jonathan's hand. "I was really sorry to hear about Marilyn."

Jonathan nodded but said nothing.

Her heart hurt for him because what could he say? "Thanks" just didn't seem quite right.

"Dev." Jonathan introduced Jeffrey and Nancy to him as old friends of the family.

"What can I get you folks?"

"You pouring Little Sumpin' Sumpin'?" Jeffrey glanced over Devlin's shoulder at the row of uniquely-shaped beer taps lining the wall behind the bar.

"You bet. I'd lose a lot of business if I ever tried to get rid of it." He chuckled and turned to Nancy. "How about you, ma'am?"

"Nothing for me, thank you." Her smiled remained, though it quivered slightly at the corners as her eyes skipped over the group at the table.

"The usual, Jonathan?" Dark brown bottles clinked together when he snatched the empties off the table with one hand.

"You still got the Macallan Twenty-Five back there?" he asked.

"Always." His friend smiled.

"Yeah, sounds great."

Emily had mentioned that Jonathan and Devlin grew up together. They both left Whidbey Cove to serve their country—Jonathan as a SEAL and his friend as a Marine Recon Sniper.

Tending bar seemed a waste of Devlin's hard-earned skills and instincts. A man with his background would be a great asset to OSI.

"Perfect. Menus are on the table. I'll give you a few minutes to figure out what you want and send one of the servers over to take your orders."

Jeffrey pulled out a chair for Nancy, who now looked a little pale and restless.

"You know, I ... I'm a bit more tired than I realized." Nancy fumbled through her bag for her phone and shot another tight-lipped smile in Andi's direction. "I think I'll just call a cab and head to the hotel."

"Don't be silly. I'll take you." Jeffrey started putting his coat back on.

"I was just leaving, Mr. Burke." Golden stood. "They don't have cabs here, Mrs. Raymond, but I would be happy to give you a lift."

"Oh, well, if you're sure it's no trouble." She struggled with her coat.

He hustled around to help her slip it on. "It's no trouble at all, ma'am."

Golden was raised by his very strict, very religious grandmother, then entered the military right out of high school. He had the manners of an altar boy—a very *large* altar boy.

Andi stood and squeezed between the back of Killian's chair and the wall, then circled the table. She knew from a previous conversation with her, that Nancy wasn't a fan of flying, especially the NSA's smaller jet.

"You sure you're feeling okay?" She bent her knees to bring her face level with the older woman's. "I know how much you dislike flying."

Nancy turned away and spoke as she dug for something in her purse. "Yes, I forgot to take something before we left. Silly, me." She pulled out a bottle of pills and gave them a little shake as she let loose an awkward chuckle. "Here they are."

Anxious eyes raced over the group now watching her. Without a word, she turned and hurried toward the door. Her coat flapped behind her as she weaved through tables. Her purse bumped someone's head, and she tossed a distracted apology over her shoulder.

"Bailey." Burke frowned as he watched his assistant rush away. "When you get there, please make sure to escort Mrs. Raymond inside, will you?"

"Yes, sir." He gave a casual salute, said goodbye to the group, jogged to catch up, then opened the door for her.

JONATHAN SHARED A LOOK WITH ANDI. She lifted a shoulder and sat back down. Next to Killian.

Burke took the seat next to Mason. That left an empty chair next to Andi. Jonathan dropped his coat over the back and sat down.

"Have any idea what that was all about?" He leaned close to her, keeping his voice low, for their ears only.

"No idea." One finger circled the edge of her glass, then tracked down the side, disturbing the condensation.

His dick twitched as if she'd stroked him. *Shit.*

"She's acted squirrelly the last couple times I've been around her." Her eyes narrowed as if contemplating what she'd just said. "Smiling too big, micro-tension around her eyes, focus issues whenever she spoke to me. Just ... different."

Devlin walked up and set a thick-bottomed, crystal glass in front of him. Two fingers of one of the best scotches in the world nestled inside.

"Thanks, man." Jonathan lifted it to his lips and inhaled. The sweetness of the mahogany-colored scotch tickled his nose before he took a sip. Because it would be a sin to toss back Macallan. It was to be savored, appreciated. The intensely full flavor of citrus and dried fruits, combined with a smoky warmth from being matured in sherry casks, glided over his tongue and warmed its way down his throat to where it settled nicely in his belly.

The glass close to his lips, Jonathan spoke in hushed tones. "I've never seen her act that way before."

He took another sip, eyed the people enjoying their Friday night, but spied on Andi with his peripheral vision.

"Maybe I'll try talking to her tomorrow. See if I can find out what's bothering her," she said. "It's the least I can do. When I first started at the NSA, Nancy helped me navigate my way around the administrative crap that I hate so much."

He nodded as he slowly swirled the brown liquid in his glass.

"Andi, ready for another margarita yet?" Killian jiggled the pitcher.

"You tryin' to get me drunk?" They laughed together, and she held up her hand. "No, I'm good, but thanks."

Killian checked with everyone else and headed over to the bar.

"Something going on with you and my brother?" Jonathan cast a quick glance at him chatting with a couple of folks he went to high school with.

"Seriously? After what happened between us, you think I would—" Andi balled up the napkin and tossed it on Golden's abandoned plate. She stood and looked down at him, hesitated for a moment, then said, "You still don't know a damn thing about me. Even after I ... " Strangely enough, she looked more bewildered and sad than angry.

After she what? After she confided in him about the lonely, painful past she'd suffered, thanks to her dick of a father? Yeah, Jonathan was feeling like the world's biggest asshole.

He shoved his chair back and stood.

"Shit, Andréa, I'm sor—" He noticed the table had grown silent as everyone stopped to take in the drama unfolding before them. *Just fucking great.* She would hate being the center of that kind of attention. Hell, he wasn't too thrilled about it either.

"What's going on?" Killian walked up, a bottle in each hand, looking back and forth between them. His smile slowly dropped away.

"Emily and Christina, thanks for including me." Andi tugged some bills from the front pocket of her jeans and threw them down on the table. "The rest of you, have a great night."

She jerked her coat from the back of the chair and walked away. Every guy in the place had their eyes glued to her ass as she effortlessly weaved around tables and chairs on her way to the door.

Killian and Jonathan called out to her simultaneously.

"Andi—"

"Andréa."

"Shit." Jonathan cursed under his breath as he pulled some cash from his wallet and tossed it down next to hers.

"What was that about?" Killian stepped in front of him.

"Move, Kill. It's between Andi and me." Last thing he wanted to do was go toe to toe with his brother.

Killian stared him down for a minute, then pivoted to let him pass.

Burke's fingers wrapped around Jonathan's forearm as he walked by.

For a split second, he thought about shaking him loose. Then remembered who he was dealing with.

Christ, he needed to talk to Andi.

"I know you're both adults and whatever's going on between you two is none of my business." Burke remained seated, a position that in no way diminished his power. "That said, you need to understand something here, O'Halleran."

He paused as if debating how much he wanted to divulge.

"Andi may seem tough on the outside, like she can handle anything, but that's only because she's had to deal with some pretty harsh stuff in her life."

"You mean her father." Jonathan looked up and she was gone.

Goddamn it.

"She told you about the Colonel?" Burke's brows rose in surprise. "Interesting."

"Sounds like the guy was a real son of a bitch." What he wouldn't give to have five minutes alone with the man who made Andi feel like she was anything less than the amazing woman she was. *You mean, kinda like the way you just did?*

Burke nodded.

"So you know the kind of shit I'm talking about." He pierced Jonathan with a warrior's eyes. "I'd hate to see you adding to it."

Message received, Jonathan nodded and raced toward the door. As far as silent threats went, it was a pretty damned good one.

CHAPTER TWENTY-FIVE

"Come on, damn it." Andi wrestled her arm into her coat. Her fight or flight instincts had kicked in and, considering the myriad sets of eyes on them, she'd chosen flight. She was almost to her car when music from inside poured into the parking lot, followed by heavy-booted footsteps crunching over gravel behind her.

"Andréa," Jonathan shouted.

What the hell now?

"Keep walking. Keep walking. Don't turn around." She repeated the words to herself as she quickened her pace.

He cursed. Boy, did she have a knack for bringing out the worst in him or what?

A press of a button on her key fob and the horn beeped; the doors unlocked. She slid in, slammed the door, then reached over her shoulder to tug on the seatbelt. The engine fired up and, illuminated by the headlights, a very determined-looking O'Halleran stomped her way.

Without hesitation, she dropped the car into reverse, stretched her arm across the top of the seat and twisted to look behind her. She backed up several feet, then slammed it into drive. Gravel and mud kicked up, and she turned out of the lot. The back end fishtailed on the shiny, wet pavement until the tires found purchase and the car sped down the street.

A few minutes later, headlights appeared in her rearview mirror. She squinted, recognizing the front end of Jonathan's big four-door pickup.

"Are you fucking kidding me?" Her heart pounded in her chest, and she sped up, hoping the local cops were busy elsewhere. "Just fucking great."

Andi didn't have it in her to survive another confrontation with him tonight. She might do something she regretted, like reveal how his insinuation pierced through her like a hot spike. Or worse, she would spill her guts and expose her true —stupid—feelings for him.

She turned right at the old Ice Cream Palace, then left at the next cross street, then right again. Not the most direct route, but she wanted to shake his tail long enough to make it home. He would have no reason to know where she lived.

After making a sharp turn into her complex, she maneuvered her way around the parking lot to her designated spot. The tires squawked when she hit the brakes, and the car rocked forward. She cut the engine and stared at the rearview mirror, then sat and listened.

No headlights cut through the dark. No massive truck screamed into the lot.

Confident she'd lost him and weirdly disappointed by that, she heaved a deep sigh, yanked her keys from the ignition and hustled down the path toward her townhouse. The sounds of her heavy breaths and boots against cement cut through the cold silence of the night. Her keys jangled on the ring as she shuffled for the right one.

"You really should be more careful when you're walking by yourself at night."

Andi reached for the weapon she usually kept tucked at her hip. *Shit.* She'd left it locked in the safe in the back of the closet because state law prohibited weapons in places like bars and pubs.

Jonathan stood at the base of the steps, silhouetted by the porch light next to the door.

"You should be more careful about sneaking up on someone who's typically armed." She looked around, wondering how he'd beat her here.

"Truck's back there." His chin lifted in the direction of the back lot. Fog blew from his mouth with each word. His long shadow loomed across the small patch of brownish-green grass in the front yard. "And I didn't sneak up on you."

Damn it. He looked ridiculously good standing there, feet braced apart, hands wedged in his pockets like he'd been waiting all night. She was seriously screwed up in the head.

"How the hell did you know where I live?" Her keys bit into her palm, and she forcibly loosened her grip.

"Christina is the one who helped you find this place, right? She works for me, so ... " He lifted one strong, ridiculously big shoulder. "I've known since the day you started working with OSI."

"Whatever." Wanting to put this night behind her, Andi gritted her teeth and stomped up the three steps of the small front stoop.

He slipped his hands from his pockets and angled aside just enough she was forced to squeeze past him.

Ass.

Her back to him, she tried to ignore him as she jammed her key into the deadbolt and unlocked it.

"Andréa." Jonathan's breath heated the shell of her cold ear.

Her eyes drifted shut, and an involuntary shiver zinged

through her. God, the way her name sounded in that baritone of his ...

"You're cold." He closed the space between them, molded his body along the length of hers. His warmth washed over her like he was a goddamned human furnace.

Andi wrapped the memory of his rejection tightly around herself like a suit of armor and jabbed her elbow into his gut.

"Back off." For all the good it did—the big lug didn't so much as flinch.

"Andréa ... " Frustrated impatience edged his voice in the way he dragged out her name.

She turned to confront him but not before plastering her best *I could give a shit* look firmly in place.

"Awww, what's the matter, O'Halleran?" Andi cocked her hip and folded her arms over her chest. "Need to hurl a few more baseless accusations at me before you can head home for a good night's sleep?" Whatever he wanted to say, he could damn well say it to her face. "Well, then, by all means, get on with it. It's been a hell of a day, and I'm tired."

"I want to tell you that I'm sorry."

"Great. Good. Glad to hear it." She spun around, shoved a different key in the doorknob. They rattled against the wooden door as she cursed the temperamental lock. It had nothing to do with her shaking hands.

"Andréa." One big, calloused hand came up to wrap around hers, stilling her futile efforts. His other arm curved around her waist, and he drew her back slowly against him.

Remembering how amazing it felt to be held by him and craving the closeness, she relaxed, even as a small voice inside told her, *Push him away. He'll only hurt you again*.

His chin lowered, and his lips brushed across her ear in a whisper. "I really am sorry for what I said back there. I didn't mean it."

"Then ... why?" She managed to turn in the circle of his

arms and glared up at him. At almost five ten, Andi was taller than most women. Her repressed girlie side liked that Jonathan towered over her.

"I saw you with Killian and, well, I didn't like it." His warm hand rested against her back, just above her butt. "I was jealous."

"Jealous?" She frowned up at him. "That's absurd. We're just friends. He knows I—" Her mouth snapped shut. She looked away.

"Knows you what?" He stepped closer.

Her boots scuffed back until the solid door prevented her retreat.

Jonathan radiated determination as he leaned his forearms on the door on either side of her head. A low groan rumbled in his throat when he nestled his powerful body against hers from thighs to chest.

Andi's breath hitched, and her mind swirled. Her body came alive. Every nerve ending. Every single strand of hair.

"He knows I'm not interested in getting involved with anyone right now." She swallowed hard and choked back the words that would expose too much.

"Why do I feel like you're not being honest with me?" His eyes narrowed on hers, gauging her truthfulness.

"Jesus. What the hell do you want from me?" Andi heaved a frustrated sigh. She was feeling vulnerable and weak, and that pissed her off. She desperately needed alone time to shore up her defenses.

"What I want ... " His brow creased, and he shook his head. "What I *need* is for you to say you accept my apology. For tonight and for all the other times I acted like such an ass to you."

"It's fi—"

"Please." He pressed the pad of his thumb gently against

her mouth and caressed it back and forth across her lower lip. "Please, don't say it's fine."

The cold night conceded to his scorching heat as his thumb brushed against her sensitive flesh.

"It's a hell of a long way from fine." The banked desire in his voice raked over her, stole the breath from her lungs.

"I ... You ... " Was that her, sounding all breathy and wispy? Andi didn't do breathy and wispy. Never.

"What, Andréa?" His eyes pleaded with her to continue. "Tell me."

A painful lump formed in her throat. *Do I dare open myself up to him again?*

Big hands, warm despite the frigid air, gently framed her face. His thumbs skimmed over her cheeks as his eyes seemed set on finding a path to her soul.

He was on to her—had figured out her secret. That deep inside, she was still that little girl desperate for love but burned by rejection over and over. Her emotional survival instincts had kicked in, and she'd programmed herself to believe wanting love was needy, useless, a weakness someone could exploit. She'd buried it deep, walled herself off and become conditioned to ignore the loneliness it created. Thirty years old, and she was still doing it.

Enough. She was done letting her past dictate her future. Andi took a deep breath and released it into the cold air. Heart pounding, she set aside her fear and, yes, her pride, to put voice to her true feelings.

"You hurt me, Jonathan."

"I KNOW. And I am so, so sorry." Her painful confession gouged a trough through Jonathan's heart. A solitary tear streamed down her rosy cheek, and a part of him died inside knowing he'd caused it.

"I promise, I will try my damnedest *never* to hurt you again." His fingers speared into her short hair, and he held her in place. His thumb under her chin, he lifted her face to him. "Andréa?"

Moonlight shimmered in her watery eyes as she searched his for the truth. Her internal struggle was there in the stiffening of her shoulders and the way she yanked up a sort of invisible guard whenever she felt cornered. She was debating whether to put herself out there and trust him or play it safe and turn him away. The latter was not an option. Not anymore. Things had gone too far between them.

A moment later, she blew out a resigned breath and said, "Fine. I forgive you."

His own shoulders relaxed. Relief poured through him.

"But don't do it again, or I'll have to kick your ass." She scrubbed the heel of her hand over her cheek to wipe away the remnants of the offensive tear.

"Thank you." He brushed his lips over her forehead and dragged them down her temple to her chilled cheek, where they lingered. Her skin warmed beneath them, amplifying her light, feminine smell. "That means a lot to me."

Not just her willingness to forgive him, but trusting him enough to reveal her vulnerable truths. He'd suppressed enough of his own to appreciate how difficult that must have been.

Jonathan drew his head back to look down at her.

Her body relaxed against him, and she flattened her hands on his chest. Eyes that would haunt his dreams long after she left gazed at him from a face luminous as silk under the moon's milky glow.

Afraid of severing their fragile connection, he was determined to take it slow. He leaned down and dragged his mouth from one corner of hers to the other, then nibbled her juicy bottom lip. Her quick intake of breath accompanied the squeak of leather as her grip tightened on his jacket. She tugged him close, lifted up on her tiptoes and pressed her lips firmly against his.

Her soft moan blew apart the control he'd worked so hard to keep in check. Weeks of pent-up sexual tension between them roared to the surface. His fingers gripped the hair on the back of her head, and he turned it for a better angle.

She gasped and, seizing the opportunity, his tongue dove between her lips. The kiss went deeper, became wilder with every stroke of one tongue against the other, every whimper, moan and halted breath between them. He wanted to memorize her taste, savor it.

Who knew one woman's kiss could hold such power?

Somewhere between his brain and his body, the message to take it slow vaporized. He couldn't breathe, couldn't think beyond wanting her. His head buzzed, and his dick tried to bust through his zipper. He growled and ground himself against her. Wanted her to feel his body's reaction to her.

After Marilyn died, he'd told himself his love for Ashling and his family would be enough. Then Andréa Swain barged into his life like a stubborn thunderstorm and flipped his well-ordered world upside down. His gut clenched, and he gave himself a good internal shake. No, they were simply two adults scratching an itch after weeks of denying their physical attraction. Nothing more. He'd sworn never to risk his heart by getting close to another woman again, and he'd meant it.

Andi threw her arms around his neck and tried to take charge of the kiss.

He almost chuckled. *Nope. Not how this is going to go.* In this, she would have to give up control. Boy, was this going to be fun.

He drew his lips away from hers, but only a fraction. "Invite me in, Andréa."

Breaths heaving, she looked up at him with foggy, half-closed eyes. Her arms slid from around his neck, and she turned away. Jonathan felt a pang of regret, certain he'd blown it, that she was about to tell him to go to hell. Instead, she pushed the door open, stepped over the threshold and moved aside to let him in.

Hallelujah.

The security system Caleb installed blinked and beeped from the elaborate keypad on the wall. She brushed by him, pressed a few buttons. Silence enfolded them, enhancing the sense of intimacy.

Jonathan leaned against the door and locked the deadbolt behind him with a quiet *snick*.

Her shoulders drew back, then she turned and looked at him.

The blinds on the large front window were closed. But dim light crept into the room from a small bulb above the stove.

"So, um—" She fiddled with her keys.

"Andréa." He shoved off the door and took a step. "Do I make you nervous?"

"Nervous? What?" She snorted, dropping her keys into a bowl on the small entry table. Then pulled off her coat and tossed it over the back of the couch. "Don't be ridiculous."

Yeah, she was nervous. An adorable anomaly for a woman who liked to be in control.

"If I do, just say the word, and I'll go." He took another step.

Eyes locked on him like prey alerted to their hunter, she shuffled back a step.

"After what happened out there"—he tipped his head over

his shoulder toward the front porch—"I would be disappointed, but I would respect your wishes."

He kept his approach slow.

She swallowed. This time when she retreated, her butt ended up against the edge of the small bar separating the kitchen from the main room.

Jonathan's next step brought him to her. He pressed a hand on either side of her on the cool, granite counter, his face inches from hers. "Is that what you want? For me to leave?"

One corner of her mouth lifted, and she shook her head.

"The words, Andréa. I need the words."

"No," she whispered without hesitation. "That's not what I want."

He leaned close, his lips a hair's breadth from hers, and whispered, "Thank God."

Her eyes dropped to his mouth, and a full-fledged smile brightened her face. The corners of her eyes crinkled, and, for the first time, he noticed a slight dimple in her right cheek.

That was it. *Game over*.

Jonathan growled, and his lips crashed down on hers. He cupped a hand over each of her perfect ass checks and yanked her to him. She moaned, and he lifted her up and settled her on the counter, never breaking the kiss.

Andi scooched close to the edge. Long, powerful legs wrapped around his hips at the same time her sinewy arms snaked around under his. She spread her hands across his back and tugged him close. Their mouths met somewhere in the middle, and the battle for control was on.

His hand wedged between her butt and the granite, and he angled her against him. A small sound of pleasure murmured in her chest. He could feel her heat against his crotch, and it was fucking amazing.

Her hands skimmed around his rib cage and slipped under the front of his shirt. She dragged her fingers up his chest and down to his abs, where she seemed to count each ridge.

He left her lips long enough to reach behind him with one hand and drag his T-shirt over his head, then pitched it over his shoulder. His mouth found hers again, then trailed light, sucking kisses along her jaw to a spot just below her ear.

"Your turn." He growled the challenge across the shell of her ear.

As if she couldn't wait a second longer, she yanked her black V-neck T-shirt up and off, then tossed it over his head. It landed somewhere in the small living room behind him. She gave a quick shake of her head. Her short hair settled back into place, and she tucked it over her ears.

Jonathan's mouth dropped open, and his eyes almost popped out of his head. Her perfect breasts were cradled by some sort of light blue lace that seemed to enhance the ivory color of her skin. The fancy, delicate lingerie was a contrast to the toughness she worked so hard to project.

"What?" She looked down at herself. "Did you think I only wore sports bras?"

"That's not why I'm staring, Andréa." His eyes traveled over her. "It's ... you're beautiful."

"Oh ... well, thanks." She smiled and remained still, let him feast his eyes on her.

Jonathan had been right. Andi lacked any kind of body issues. Rightfully so, because she had one hell of a bangin' body. Her shoulders were square and strong, proud, and yet softly feminine compared to his. The long legs currently tightened around him were toned and leanly muscled, as were her arms. He already knew the quality of her ass, having snuck peeks at it. Not to mention cradling it in his hands. Her height might be due to genetics, but everything else was earned through hard work and discipline, which he'd gotten a hint of the day he'd watched her slay the end of the obstacle course. In her line of work, dealing with the people she did, she understood the importance of maintaining a certain fitness level.

As a Navy SEAL, Jonathan could respect that.

He felt her eyes like a touch all over him. She hummed as her inquisitive hands returned to exploring his chest, shoulders, biceps, abs, pretty much anywhere skin was exposed.

Jonathan's eyes were glued to what had to be the most perfect breasts ever created. Anywhere. On the planet. He reached out and, with the tip of one finger, traced one beautifully pert nipple where it poked against the sheer fabric. Goosebumps skittered across her chest as it pebbled beneath his palm. Andi's short nails clenched into the skin just above his hips, not enough to hurt but enough to send his heart rate through the roof. Her mouth fell open on a sigh, her head fell back, and her eyes drooped shut.

Hell. Yeah.

"You must never stop what you're doing." She slowly lifted her head, her eyes locked with his.

He chuckled.

"Your wish is my command, Ms. Swain." His other hand joined in the fun. Each one covered a breast and gave them a slight squeeze.

Not too big. Not too small.

Fucking. Perfect.

Andi gasped, her eyes ever watchful, always on him.

Creamy smooth, soft as an angel's wings, her fair skin was a bit of a surprise, considering she'd just spent three years in the brutally hot Middle East. It begged for his touch, and he was happy to oblige. His fingertips skimmed around the outside of each breast, trickled down each rib until he managed to tuck his hands into the back of the waistband of her skinny black jeans. *Elastic. Best invention ever.*

Not one to sit idly by, she reached out and trailed her hands up his abs, over his pecs, which she gave a squeeze of her own. They traced over his collarbone and around his neck, where she threaded her fingers into the hair at the back of his head.

"You are such a specimen, Jonathan O'Halleran." She leaned forward and pressed a long kiss on his chest, just above his heart. Warmth from her soft lips seeped deep inside him, like a healing balm to his battered soul.

Jonathan gave himself an internal shake. *One-night thing, remember?* Ashling deserved ... *needed* his full and undivided attention. Her unconditional love had filled the cracks in his broken heart. *Andi can be your added layer of protection*, a faint voice whispered from the back of his mind. *Christ.*

"Andi, we—"

She put her hand over his mouth. "Jonathan, listen. You don't have to say anything." Her hand fell away. "I know exactly what this is." She waved her hand back and forth between them. "We're blowing off steam. Releasing the strange sexual tension between us. That's all. We both know this has no shelf life."

Even though she was right, and it was exactly what he needed to hear, Jonathan felt strangely compelled to argue with her. Of course, he didn't.

Her hand cradled his jaw, and she gave him a small smile as her thumb rubbed over his cheek.

"Let's just give ourselves this one night." She tilted her head. "No strings. No promises."

Andi was so matter-of-fact about the whole thing. Like she was totally cool with opening her body to him, then walking away. She also said everything he thought he wanted to hear. Which was great. Right? Then why did it suck so much? Even more confusing, why did he already feel cheated? Man, he was a fucking head case.

"Okay?" She raised her brows and waited.

He nodded, oddly disappointed it was all they would have but willing to take it anyway.

"I'm going to need the words, Jonathan." She deepened her voice and grinned as she threw his own demand back at him.

"Okay." He dropped a soft kiss on her lips.

"Good. Now ... " Nimble fingers began working to undo his belt. "Where were we?"

He placed his hands over hers and looked in her eyes. "I just ... I can't give you anything more right now." It needed to be said, because the last thing he wanted to do was hurt her again. A small part of him hoped she'd back out, because he had genuine concerns that one night might not be enough for him. And even though he knew it was the right thing to do, he wasn't sure he had the strength to turn her away. "I need you to be absolutely certain, Andréa."

"I'm very certain, Jonathan." Voice low, she returned to fiddling with his belt buckle.

Last thing a woman like Andi wanted was to be away from the action, stuck in some small town where she didn't know anyone. Right? A small voice reminded him she'd just come from a girls' night with his sister and Christina. Not to mention, his parents and everyone at OSI absolutely adored her. The smile on Ashling's cherubic face whenever Andi held her flashed through his mind.

"The question is, are *you* sure?" Her voice snapped him back to the moment, and her hands had stilled.

Enough with the doubt. He wanted this. Wanted her.

"Hell, yeah, I'm sure." Jonathan lifted her so he was carrying her over his shoulder. "Where's the bedroom?"

CHAPTER TWENTY-SIX

Andi forced a laugh. An ironic way to cover the sound of her heart shattering into a million pieces. She'd tossed the whole *one night, no strings, no promises* thing out there, hoping maybe, just maybe he'd fight her on it. Silly notion, really. But if one night was all he could give her, she would take it and worry about the ramifications later.

The room spun, and she found herself on her feet, facing a very big, very aroused and powerful male. They gazed across the few inches between them. The only sound in the small space—their combined heavy breaths. Words seemed frivolous.

Not willing to waste a second of their one precious night together, she reached around and unhooked her bra, then tossed it onto the dresser. Expensive lingerie was one of her few concessions to her femininity. She tucked her hand in the front of his waistband and tugged him to her. He let her, and a wicked grin lifted each side of his mouth as he slid his long fingers around her hips and wedged them into the back of her jeans.

She wanted to smack herself when her fingers shook as she finished unhooking his belt, then released the button on his jeans. *Real sexy, Andi.* Mimicking him, she stepped into him, slipped her hands into the back of his jeans, and squeezed his tight ass cheeks. Her tongue snuck out and teased its way all the way across his collar bone, down the middle of his chest.

His jaw jumped and his nostrils flared. Dark blues eyes bored into her. Still, he remained silent. Jonathan O'Halleran was a guy who expected to be in control, so she needed to have her fun while she could.

No sooner had the thought entered her mind than she found herself being picked up and tossed onto the middle of her bed, with his powerful body sprawled out over her. He'd nestled himself between her spread legs, and his weight bore down on her. He held her arms above her head, restrained in the powerful grip of one hand. The other tucked between her butt and the mattress.

"Keep those hands right there." His words vibrated from his chest against hers.

"So ... you think that's how this is going to go, huh?" She shifted her hips beneath him, gave an experimental tug of her hands. Not really trying to break free, but not wanting to concede too easily. Andi had her reputation as a badass bitch to protect, after all.

"Yep." He tilted his head in challenge, then pressed his hardened crotch against her center. "You have a problem with that?"

There it was—that demand for control. Andi shouldn't like it, considering she was as much a control freak as him. But, just this once, she wanted someone else to run the show, to be in charge. For whatever reason and despite their history, she trusted Jonathan enough to give him that.

Andi sucked in a breath at the pressure against her happy spot. All she could manage was a whispered, "No."

A smug grin snuck across the bastard's handsome face just before his mouth crashed down onto hers, stole her breath, sent sparks of heat spiking through her. Ruthless, he took everything she had to give and more. Their tongues tangled and explored the dark recesses of each other's mouths. Frantic, seeking, needing. Remnants of the two sips of scotch he'd had earlier lingered. Lips too soft to belong to a warrior drew back slightly to nip and skim across hers until she writhed beneath him. She could orgasm just from the combined weight of his body and power of his mouth on hers.

His fingers dragged up her side to cup her breast. She moaned and arched into his touch, telling him without words what she wanted. He kneaded the soft flesh, plucked her nipple like the most delicate bloom.

"Jonathan ... " His name poured out on a sigh.

He lifted his head just enough to ask, "What do you want, Andréa?"

"I want ... " Everything. *You, Ashling, your family, this kooky town, my happily ever after.* "Your skin on mine. Now."

Coward.

Jonathan hesitated, his eyes searched hers. For a horrified second, she thought she might've spoken her dreams aloud. Diversion time. She lifted her head and dragged her tongue up the side of his throat, burrowed her nose against his chin.

"I love the way you smell." The words whispered across his ear had the desired effect.

His eyes dragged shut. He pressed up to his knees, then shuffled to stand at the foot of the bed. He kicked off his boots and socks, made quick work of removing her boots, and they hit the floor with a resounding *thud.* Her socks were tugged off and flew through the air, one, then the other. With the finesse of a brain surgeon performing a delicate operation, his rough hand smoothed across her belly, then he unsnapped her jeans and drew down the zipper one damn tooth at a time.

"Lift," he growled.

Andi did as she was told and lifted her hips off the mattress. He peeled her jeans down her legs and unceremoniously dropped them at his feet. She lay there in nothing but her matching lace panties as his eyes slowly caressed every inch of her, his erection pressing against the front of his jeans.

She wanted to shout a *thank you* to the universe when he lowered his zipper, tucked a thumb in each side of his jeans and shoved them and his boxer briefs to the floor. His belt buckle hit the hardwood with a *clank,* and he shoved them aside with his foot.

Jonathan placed a knee on the bed. His long fingers skimmed the top of her feet, circled her ankles and continued their sensual glide up her legs. Another knee dug into the mattress, and his hands traveled over her knees to tickle the delicate flesh of her inner thighs. Instinctively, her knees rubbed together to relieve the ache in her core.

"Open 'em, Andréa." He gave a light slap to her outer thigh and waited, as if knowing she might protest.

Her mouth opened, prepared to do just that. But she'd agreed to give him control. After a tense few seconds, she sighed, and her knees fell open.

"Nice." He planted a soft kiss to each one.

He dragged her panties down her legs much too slowly, and they joined the rest of her clothes on the floor. Jonathan used his shoulders to wedge her knees farther apart. She held her breath as he gave her a last long look, as if expecting her to protest. *Ha!* Not friggin' likely. Instead she gave him a small smile and relaxed. He took that as permission to proceed, then slowly ... so ... damned ... slowly ...

lowered his face to her and ran his warm, soft tongue up her center.

Hallelujah. Her knees drew up, and she pressed her heels into the bed.

He hummed against her as he worked some kind of witchcraft with his tongue, his teeth, one or two fingers. Even his beard seemed to be in on the torment. She couldn't be sure—her brain had turned to mush. Her breasts felt engorged, and her inner muscles pulsed and contracted as her hips pressed up into his face. A large hand, dark against her pale skin, splayed over her lower abs and pressed her into the mattress. *Curse the man!*

A storm built inside her, taking her up and up, and just when she was about to tumble over, Jonathan slowed it down and started all over again. Her heart pounded like a drum in her chest. She had a white-knuckle grip on the bars of the old brass headboard to keep from reaching for him. God, she wanted to reach for him.

She was so close ... almost there, yes, yes ... then he lifted his head. *No!* Andi growled. She wanted to smack him, to cry out in protest, to tell him to get back in there. Until his mouth moved to caress one hip, then the other, up one side of her rib cage and down the other, against the underside of one breast and across to the other, dragging his lips too gently over and around each tight, pert areola. Like her body was some kind of roller-coaster ride for his tongue.

Breathe, Andi, breathe. Yeah, the reminder was necessary. She was about to pass out, because never before had foreplay been this intense.

"You still with me?" He looked up from where his chin rested against her navel with a smug grin.

Barely. A single nod was all she could manage.

He levered up to his knees and rolled a condom onto his very erect, very large penis. Where had he been keeping that?

The condom, not the erection. She'd been acutely aware of its location since he'd pressed it against her while pinning her against the front door.

"What's going through that amazing mind of yours?" A hand on either side of her head, he grinned down at her.

All the things I want to do with your dick.

"Nothing. Nothing's going through my mind," she responded innocently.

Jonathan narrowed his eyes, then must've decided to believe her, because he reached down and took himself in hand. He stroked up and down a couple of times, which was the sexiest thing she'd ever witnessed in her entire thirty years on this planet, then placed the head of his dick at her opening and pressed into her one amazing inch at a time. And, *hoo boy*, there seemed to be a lot of inches.

"Christ, you feel good." Jonathan groaned as he seated himself fully inside her, his beard tickling across her neck. He levered up, held himself on his forearms and stroked his thumbs across her temples. His jaw rippled with restraint as he seemed to be captivated by her features.

What do you see?

"Jonathan, can I touch you? Please, I need to touch you." Okay, so she might be begging a little. No big deal.

"Please do." His head lowered, and he kissed her with so much tenderness, tears burned behind her eyes.

Tears? Really? Jesus, she needed to get control of herself.

Andi released her grip on the bed, flexed her fingers to get the blood circulating through them, and dropped them straight onto his tight, rounded butt cheeks. She smoothed over them, dragged her finger lightly up the cleft between. A breath hissed between his teeth, and he took her mouth in a punishing kiss meant to remind her who was in charge. His dick slid out almost completely, then he slammed himself back home. Over and over, he pounded into her, his tongue jutting in and out of her mouth, his teeth nibbling on the tendon running up the side of her neck.

No matter what they both wanted to believe, this was more than sex. More than two people *scratching an itch*. But they'd made a deal, and she would honor it. Even if it meant she would live the rest of her days hollowed out inside.

Andi closed her eyes, locked her arms around his neck and gave herself over to the sensations bombarding her. He wedged his hand under her butt and tilted her hips up, reaching that special spot deep inside. His hold was tight enough to leave bruises. Those, along with her memories, would be all she had when their night together ended. Her long legs wrapped easily around his hips, and she crossed her ankles and met him stroke for stroke. The sounds of their grunts, moans and skin slapping against skin filled the room. With each slide of flesh against flesh, one more piece of her heart was relinquished to this man. She loved him, and admitting this—if only to herself—gave her the freedom to let go. The split second her guard dropped, a guttural cry escaped from deep within. Her body tightened and bowed as an orgasm of epic proportions blasted through her in relentless waves of pressure and pleasure combined. Endless, commanding, overwhelming, all-encompassing. Her heart nearly exploded with her feelings for him as it was crushed by the reality that he didn't return her love.

He drove into her two, three times, then growled her given name as his own release slammed through him. His hips flexed against her for a moment longer, then relaxed. With a groan, he collapsed atop her. His nose nuzzled that erogenous spot beneath her ear. His soft facial hair sent goosebumps skittering across her entire body. His wide, strong back, damp from exertion, rose and fell, and his heart beat strong against her chest.

Her pulse raced. Andi squeezed her eyes and, damn it, a

betraying tear glided down her temple to soak into her hair. Arms still wrapped around him, she turned to wipe her face across her shoulder. No sense risking their evening being cut short by her inability to get a handle on her stupid emotions and letting on how gone she was for him.

A few moments later, a sudden, weighty silence hung over the room. As if they both held their breath wondering, *what next?*

"Andréa." His muffled voice vibrated against her neck. "I can practically hear the gears in your brain working."

He levered up to his forearms, his hair an unruly, dark mess. Narrowed eyes flashed back and forth between hers, and his thumb stroked the exact same spot her tear has just traveled.

She wasn't crazy about the way he could read her so well.

"Just wondering what happens next." She ran her fingers through his hair, kissed his shoulder, kept an intentional lightness to her words. His skin was salty, incredibly warm.

"Well, first, I ditch this condom." He gave her a quick peck on the lips, rolled away and stood. His eyes scanned her from head to toe and back again. "Then I get another one, and we do that again."

Andi's girlie parts quivered and screamed with joy as she muzzled her vulnerable heart's declarations of love.

She sat up and tilted her head, her eyes locked on his ass like a ballistic missile locked on a target headed downrange. He disappeared into the bathroom and shut the door. Water ran in the sink, and she flopped back on the bed with a heavy sigh, draping an arm over her face, more relieved than she should be over the fact he wasn't leaving yet. A deep breath pulled in the smell of their lovemaking, filled her nose. Andi's arm dropped to the bed.

"Now *that* is a sight to behold." Jonathan stood, legs wide, silhouetted by the bathroom light. He moved to the bed, every tall, muscled, perfect inch of him ratcheting up her desire and her need to have him again.

She turned to her side, propped up on one elbow. Her eyes fell to his crotch and widened. His glorious dick—and it truly was a thing of beauty—stood rigid against his abs, a condom already in place. The guy was a regular magician with the condoms.

"What are you, a machine?" Her tongue slid along her bottom lip.

He growled.

"All right, Andréa. You know the drill." Jonathan approached the bed, his hand wrapped firmly around himself. "Grab the headboard."

And, thank God, it began again.

A FEW VERY BUSY hours later, Jonathan stared up at the unmoving ceiling fan above Andi's bed. His head turned to her. Soft light from the bathroom poured into the room from the partially closed door, casting every curve of her body in sensuous shadows. He hadn't planned to be here this long, but since he was ...

"Why did you let me believe what happened to Marconi was your fault?" He rolled to his side to face her, elbow bent, head resting on his hand.

For months, he'd blamed her for the ambush. Because, like an idiot, he'd jumped to the stupid fucking conclusion that the intel she'd provided Marconi was faulty. When, in reality, his friend was killed and three guys on his team were seriously injured, all because he was an impatient hothead.

"Let's face it." She sighed, then shifted to face him, one hand tucked beneath the pillow, the other to her chest. "You weren't exactly interested in hearing anything I had to say."

"I'm not proud to admit it, but, yeah, you're probably right." No *probably* about it. His finger traced her bare, proud shoulder, down the curve to her waist, then back up and over her hip. Her skin was a satiny, soft shell that masked the tough woman underneath. *But she isn't as tough as she wants people to believe.* "I've spent so many months being mad at the world, feeling sorry for myself. Unfortunately, you ended up in the blast zone."

"I can't imagine what that kind of loss must be like." Andi smoothed her hand down his beard, then laid her hand over his cheek. "Ashling is so lucky to have you and your family."

She hesitated, opened her mouth and closed it.

"What is it?" The woman never hesitated to speak her mind.

"Will you tell me about her?" For the first time since meeting her, Andi's voice was tentative.

Shit. How had they gotten on this topic? A night of tension-relieving sex was all this was supposed to be. No sweeping confessions or quiet conversation about his dead wife. Unwilling to risk the loss of this refreshing closeness between them, he took a bracing breath and charged ahead.

"Think of the stereotypical bubbly, blond, blue-eyed cheerleader type. That was Marilyn. Growing up, she loved to have fun, never took life too seriously." Which, once they were dating, frustrated the hell out of an intense guy like him. "Her lightheartedness was a good balance against my tendency to get too deep into my own head."

Needing her warmth against the chill of memories, Jonathan reached out and drew Andi into him so they were pressed together from chest to hip, their legs entwined, one of her arms trapped between them. She draped the other over him and tightened her hold.

"We knew each other since second grade, which is, apparently, when she decided we were going to get married." She'd always been so sure of it. "She was diagnosed with uterine tumors when she was twelve years old." Jonathan couldn't imagine getting that kind of life-altering news at such a young age.

"In all the years after that, when we officially started dating, got engaged, even after we were married and talked about having a family, she never let on, never said a word." Did she keep silent out of fear it would change the way he felt about her?

Andi smoothed her hand down his back, offering quiet comfort and encouragement.

"After she died, my emotions were all over the place. Grief that she was gone and would never know our daughter. Guilt for not being here when she needed me most. And angry as hell when I found out what she'd hidden from me." Voice low, he shook his head. "Let's just say it was powerful. Which fed right back into that crushing guilt."

He pressed a soft kiss to her forehead, then said, "I spent countless hours thinking back, dragging up every memory. Wondering, *did I miss something?* We were so close, shouldn't I have noticed something was different?"

"Give yourself a break, Jonathan. You're only human." Her voice was a quiet whisper.

A low chuckle rumbled in his chest. Leave it to Andi to cut through all the bullshit.

"After some pretty tough love from my dad, I finally understood why she did it."

"Ashling." She gave him a sweet smile, cupped his cheek with her delicate hand.

"Ashling." He would be forever grateful to Marilyn for the amazing gift she left behind.

"Thank you for sharing." Andi grinned as she pushed him to his back and straddled him, her perfect ass rested on his junk.

"You're welcome." He growled, and his hands smoothed up her thighs, her hips and stopped at her waist. Of course, not wanting to miss an opportunity to be inside Andi, his dick twitched and jumped against her as it became rigid.

"Well, well, well." The little tease shot him a devilish grin and wiggled her butt. "What might that be?"

He pressed up, grinding against that little bundle of nerves. "Turnabout is fair play."

Andi's head fell back, and her mouth opened on a sweet moan. Her nipples tightened into perfect little buds, and her hips shifted.

"Now ... " Without breaking contact, she reached to the nightstand for a condom and tore it open with her teeth. Slowly, and with agonizing deliberation, she rolled it onto his dick. "Where were we?" Her top teeth dug into her bottom lip as she lowered herself, taking every bit of him into the warmth of her body.

CHAPTER TWENTY-SEVEN

Andi stared out the wide window to the city bustling about on the other side. Small groups of tourists, all bundled up in heavy coats and boots, braved the frigid temperature and slushy, filthy snow as they traipsed from one monument to another. Political power brokers—their assistants buzzing around them like bees—hurried to meetings with other power players with their own assistants waiting to do their bidding.

At some point, most of them had arrived in DC pounding podiums and shouting promises to do good work and make a difference, until they were swept up by the soul-sucking Washington political machine. These days, it was nearly impossible to tell the good guys from the bad.

Her appreciation for the amazing architecture and history of DC was overshadowed by her extreme dislike for what took place behind the walls of the very buildings she admired.

Late last night, she'd left a message for Christina that she had personal business to attend to and jumped on a red-eye back to DC. Instincts she'd learned not to ignore screamed there was something going on with Nancy Raymond. Even though Jonathan told her not to worry about Burke's assistant, Andi wouldn't feel satisfied until she eliminated all doubt.

She'd managed to eliminate Dylan Renquist from her suspect list. He had a legitimate reason for taking leave—his son had been seriously injured in a car accident. Frank Morgan was proving to be a bit more slippery to pin down. She'd called his office and was told he was out of the country and unable to be reached. When she'd told them she was conducting an official investigation, they'd given her attitude and referred her to their corporate counsel. Troubling reaction, to say the least.

Jonathan's instructions regarding Nancy played through Andi's mind. She took a bracing gulp of coffee in an effort to squelch the guilt trying to wriggle its way into her subconscious. She would deal with his reaction later. After all, just because they'd slept together didn't mean anything had changed between them.

Yeah, you keep telling yourself that.

Her finger tapped the side of her coffee cup, and she thought back to her one and only night with Jonathan. Or, more accurately, her few hours with him. After sharing about his wife and a couple more rounds of unrestrained, blissed-out sex, she'd fallen asleep, his big arm tucking her back close to his chest.

A short time later, she felt a sudden chill and discovered he'd rolled away from her to sit on the edge of the bed. Elbows on his knees, he dug his fingers into his hair and held them there. His broad back expanded and contracted as he heaved a troubled sigh.

Regret.

Their time together was over.

Not realizing she'd begun to reach for him, she curled her fingers and quietly lowered her hand to the sheet, now cool from the loss of his heat. Unwilling to endure an awkward goodbye—*and because you're a coward*—she'd closed her eyes and feigned sleep.

Jonathan was gone before the first light of morning glowed over the horizon.

They'd both gone into it with the understanding that was all it could ever be—a few hours. That didn't make it any easier to ignore the regret and loss she felt every time she replayed the sound of her front door quietly closing behind him. Not for what they'd shared, never for that, but for what they would never share again.

No. Her mind rebelled at the thought. *You are not giving up.* Damn it, she'd had a lot of time to think during her long flight, and she'd decided she was going to fight for the big, stubborn idiot. Andi had known deep down inside he was it for her when she'd first walked into his office and he'd given her the stink-eye. She hadn't imagined the tender look in his eyes as he'd entered her body. They'd shared a level of intimacy that went beyond a few fleeting hours together. Years, decades wouldn't be enough time for them. When this case was resolved, nothing would stand in the way of her getting what she wanted, and what she wanted was a life with Jonathan and Ashling. And, by default, his big, overwhelming, loving family. Anything less would leave her an empty shell.

Decision made, a sense of calm and contentment had washed over her.

"Andi Swain?"

She looked up and recognized Jarod Raymond from his driver's license photo.

After Jonathan left her apartment, she'd needed something to distract her from the emptiness closing in around her. She'd jumped up, thrown on some sweats and brewed a pot of gut-churningly strong coffee, then started going back through all the files related to the failed FBI op. For weeks, she'd been pestered by the feeling she was missing something.

The first file she'd come across was the one she'd created for Isaac Andrews. He had been cleared of suspicion when she learned his financial windfall was the result of a hefty inheritance from his grandfather. He'd also shown no indications of deception during her face-to-face interview with him.

Halfway through the second box of folders, she'd about fallen out of her chair when she came across Jarod's name on the list of people who'd lived at The Farm. The reason stated for being there was "clearing his soul of man-made demons." She'd immediately arranged to meet with him.

"Hi." She reached out her hand. "You must be Jarod."

"That's me." He gave her a genuine smile and shook her hand. "Sorry I'm a little late. My last passenger changed their mind about where they wanted to go, and it ended up taking a bit longer than I anticipated."

Five-foot-ten and a little on the thin side, he looked older than his twenty-five years, no doubt the result of a hard-lived life. She was glad to see his eyes were clear and bright. His dark blond hair was cut above his ears, and he had an air of I-can-accomplish-anything about him.

"No problem at all." She indicated the other chair at the small, round table. "Please, have a seat.

"Thanks." He shrugged his coat off, draped it over the back of the chair and sat.

The bells on the door jingled, and a nondescript, middle-aged man entered the shop and moved to the counter. After a quick side-eye assessment—*old habits die hard*—she focused on Jarod.

"Would you like something? Coffee? Tea? Their Danish

and scones are incredible here." Scarpetti's Bakery & Coffee Shop was her go-to spot whenever she was in town. Mr. and Mrs. Scarpetti were the cutest little old Italian couple. Mrs. S's handmade pastries melted in your mouth and were a perfect match for the best, old-fashioned, brewed black coffee anywhere. "It's my treat. After all, you were nice enough to meet with me on such short notice."

During her flight, she'd done some research on him and knew money was tight. When he wasn't driving people from one place to another, Jarod attended night school, working toward a degree in psychology.

A young gal with dark eyeliner, long lavender hair and way too many piercings and angry tattoos for someone her age sauntered up to their table. "What can I get you?"

"I'll just have a large black coffee, please," he said.

"That's it?" Pierced brows bunched together, she tilted her head like a dog hearing a high-pitched sound. Poor girl's fancy-coffee-selling world must've been rocked on its axis, since Andi ordered the same thing earlier. "Like, you don't want anything in that? Like, ya know, cream, or like, sweetener or flavored syrup or something?"

"Nah, just black. Thanks." He waited until she walked away. "So, what did you want to talk about? You work with my mom, right?"

"I work for Jeffrey Burke, so our paths have crossed many times. She was super helpful when I first started working there." Andi had to tread lightly with her questioning. She wasn't sure just how much he knew, and she assumed Jarod was very loyal to his mom. "I'm doing some follow-up on a case concerning The Farm, out in Montana."

"Yeah." He shifted in his seat and nodded. "I spent some time out there."

"Do you mind if I ask why you were there?" Most folks

who ended up at The Farm had been running from something.

"Not at all. I was—"

"Here ya go. One large black coffee." The waitress tossed a cardboard coaster on the table and set his oversized, heavy mug on it. "Anything else I can get you guys?"

"I'm good." Andi looked at Jarod. "Sure you don't want anything else?"

"No, this is fine." He lifted the mug, blew across his coffee, then took a sip. Not until their server was on the other side of the room, helping a customer at the counter, did he continue. "I started hanging with some pretty shady folks and got mixed up with drugs."

Jarod didn't mince words, just jumped right to it. Not the least bit hesitant or put out about discussing his indiscretions with her.

"Next thing I knew, I was stealing stuff to buy dope." He took another drink, then set his cup down. "Went from grabbing purses from shopping carts to snatching jewelry from my mom."

He shook his head and stared out the window for a moment.

Andi waited.

He sighed and turned back to her. "When that no longer worked, I became a runner for this guy who controlled the flow of drugs throughout the entire west coast."

Oh, shit. Andi remained silent, even as alarms clanged in her head.

"He paid pretty well, but I was so far gone, it still wasn't enough." He huffed out a disgusted laugh. "Turns out, he didn't much appreciate when I skimmed a little product for myself."

"Let me guess. You weren't just at The Farm to kick your habit." A statement, not a question.

"Not even close." He leaned his forearms on the table and wrapped his hands around the large mug. "One of the other runners, the guy who recruited me into the operation, suggested I head up there until things cooled down a bit. Turned out to be a huge mistake."

"What do you mean?"

"When I first arrived at The Farm, I had to agree to leave my worldly possessions, desires, problems, all that stuff behind. Had to hand over my cell phone. Wasn't allowed a radio or television. Internet access was strictly controlled. Some bull about starting over again as 'God's innocent child.'" He used air quotes and rolled his eyes. "Anyway, Bedaiah, the guy who ran the place, baptized me as a new follower, then gave me a biblical name."

Bedaiah, "the only Lord," was the name John Proctor had given himself. He'd required all his followers to use it. Turned out, he was the furthest thing from being a man of God.

"What name did he give you?" She laced her fingers around her cup. Andi already knew the answer. It had been in the records she'd reviewed, but she wanted to see what he would say about it.

"Elisha, which means, 'God is my salvation,'" he scoffed. "Sick freak said it was fitting, considering my reason for being there."

Didn't sound like Jarod put much stock in his new name or in Proctor's legitimacy as the only Lord.

"I figured I'd stay, play along and quit cold turkey. After all, not like I would be able to get my hands on any drugs way up there."

Lucky for him, Jarod hadn't known The Farm was a front for a lucrative meth operation. In his weakened state, going through withdrawals, he might've been lured down a darker path to a completely different kind of deadly addiction.

"Anyway, one day after I'd been there about six weeks, I

got called to the admin building. I had a phone call from some Russian guy telling me my debt had been cleared and to forget I ever knew his boss." With each word, his body visibly tensed. "If I didn't, they threatened to kill my mom."

"Do you mind if I ask who it was that called?" Each word he spoke added to the picture of what might've happened.

"I never knew his name, just that he was one of Nikolai Radoslav's thugs." His Adam's apple bobbed up and down, and he leaned close. "The only reason I'm even saying his name out loud is because he's dead."

Thanks to Beckett O'Halleran.

"Radoslav is the man you owed money to?" She'd suspected but needed confirmation.

He nodded.

In addition to being in charge of one of the most pervasive drug rings in the country—as well as many other illegal enterprises—Nikolai Radoslav was also an arms dealer. He'd done business with John Proctor's partner, Grady Teague.

Teague ran the meth operation on the compound, and Proctor kept his followers in line and used them as a cover. The disgraced former cop traded his product and funneled some of his profits to stockpile weapons, ammunition and explosives. He'd intended to murder several important people he blamed for his brother's death in Afghanistan. His plans literally went up in smoke when a team from OSI raided the compound to rescue Caleb's now-wife, Dawn, and her sister, Luna. Teague died during the raid, and Proctor was currently sitting in a federal prison, serving a life sentence on a variety of charges.

"How did they know where to find you?" Andi asked.

"The only person who knew I was up there was the guy who told me about the place." He shook his head. "I don't know if he was a snitch for the old man and he set me up, or if he was *compelled* to tell them where I was."

By "compelled" he likely meant Radoslav had tortured the guy to gain the information he needed.

"I never told my mom about any of it. Not about owing Radoslav money, The Farm, or the phone call. None of it. I was too ashamed." His voice became strained, and his chin fell. "I'd disappointed her enough, getting messed up with drugs."

Andi quickly flashed through everything she knew and put it together with what she'd just learned. Jarod had to be more valuable to Radoslav's organization alive than dead. Otherwise, no way would he still be walking around. But why? He had been a low-level runner, far from a major player in the organization. He was a recovering addict who still lived with his mother.

Oh, shit. Her back stiffened, and with a clarity too painful to imagine, she knew.

"Who paid your debt?" Andi asked, though she had a sinking feeling she already knew. Radoslav, the evil SOB, must've blackmailed Nancy with the death of her son. Then turned around and threatened Jarod with the death of his mother. And they'd each kept it from the other.

"I have no idea." His shoulders lifted and fell. "I kept waiting for someone to show up at my door, expecting payback. Nothing's free, right? Then Radoslav was killed after he kidnapped that woman, and The Farm was raided. I'll probably never know."

"I don't suppose you remember when you got that phone call, do you?"

"Actually, I do. It was about a week before I finally blew out of that weird place." He rattled off the date, finished the last of his coffee and set his cup down. "I will never be able to forget the day I left that compound and watched those massive gates close behind me. I always equate it to what a prisoner must feel like when they're set free."

Everything clicked into place and, just as Andi feared, the truth crystallized. Money is not what had cleared his debt.

The timing of the call to Jarod at The Farm—right after Caleb was shot and his K9 partner was killed.

Radoslav clearing Jarod's debt—he'd waited to confirm that the inside information he'd been given about the FBI operation was accurate before letting Jarod off the hook.

And the reason Jarod was alive—he would have been an ace up the Russian's sleeve. Radoslav would've been able to use him as leverage every time he wanted to extort information from Nancy Raymond.

"How are you doing now?" Andi really needed some small glimmer of good news to counter this bleak realization.

"I'm doing really well." His shoulders drew back, and he grinned. "I make decent money driving and can set my schedule around my school stuff."

"That's great, Jarod. Really great." He had gone through so much and come out the other side a better person. Andi hated that she would be responsible for dragging misery back into his life again.

His phone chimed in his pocket, and he slipped it out to glance at the screen. "Looks like I've got another rider."

Andi raised her hand to get their server's attention. When she arrived at their table, Andi gave her enough cash to cover the coffee and tip.

"Thanks. Have a good one." The young woman gathered up their mugs and headed back behind the counter.

They rose from the table. Jarod tugged his coat from the back of the chair and put it on. He held the door for Andi, and they stepped out into the cold.

"Thanks again for meeting with me." She pulled her collar up around her neck and tugged her knit cap over her ears.

"Sure. But I'm not sure I was much help." His eyes locked on someone across the street.

"What is it, Jarod?" Andi turned to see what garnered his attention.

"Eh, it's nothing. Just ... that guy looks kinda familiar." He grabbed his gloves from his pocket and tugged them on.

"Which guy?" There were four guys in dark overcoats gathered midway up the steps of the Eisenhower Building, as well as a few people entering and exiting the main doors.

"The tall one with the bright red scarf." Jarod pointed to the men on the steps. "I know I've seen him somewhere before." He snapped his fingers. "It was at The Farm."

What the hell?

"You saw *that* man"—she dipped her chin in their direction rather than point— "right there at The Farm?"

"Yeah." He zipped his coat. "He must be pretty important 'cause he was coming out of the VIP Quarters. Only real bigwigs got to stay there when they came to visit."

The man was important, all right. He was none other than Senator Preston Etheridge. His snake of an aide, Matthew Roberson, stood right next to him. And those *VIP quarters* were just a fancy name for what was eventually exposed as a front for prostitution. Important men, including one skeevy former deputy director of the FBI now wasting away in prison, visited when they wanted to *enjoy the company* of young girls who lived on the compound. Proctor, the psychopath, had brainwashed them into thinking they were doing God's work.

She and Jarod said their goodbyes, and he strolled to his car parked a few spots down the street.

Andi called Emily and asked her for a favor, then rushed to the airport. She couldn't wait to tell Jonathan she'd figured out who the mole was.

Feet numb in his leather wingtips, Matt stood on the sidewalk, freezing his ass off. Next to him, the senator finished schmoozing with his newest potential donor.

They'd spent the past hour listening to this short, portly, extremely wealthy guy bluster on about how much he hated the current president and the direction he was taking this country. They'd only met with him for one reason. Well, more like a couple hundred thousand reasons, all of which he was looking to donate to a "like-minded" candidate. Of course, there were massive strings attached in the form of a choice cabinet position. No worries. Preston Etheridge wouldn't let a little thing like personal integrity slow his charge to the White House. A man after Matt's own heart.

His boss shook his head as he watched the man waddle away, his lawyer tagging along next him. Etheridge resented every single minute he was forced to spend kissing people's asses to get what he wanted. His home life, such that it was, was no different.

"What's next on the schedule?" Wisps of fog puffed from the senator's mouth with each word. He blew into his gloved hands.

"You have a meeting with Senator McAfee at two-fifteen, and the president and his chief of staff from four to four-forty-five. After that, you have two interviews for the open intern position." Matt ensured they were both male this time. Would be unwise to place temptation directly under his boss's nose again.

"Have Margaret order my usual for lunch and have it sent to my office." Hands shoved in his overcoat pocket, shoulders drawn up to his red ears, the senator started to walk away.

Matt followed. His phone rang, and he dug it out of his inside coat pocket. He spotted the caller ID, and his steps faltered.

"Sir, I've got something I need to take care of. I'll meet you back at the office."

Etheridge didn't miss a step. Just waved over his shoulder and kept walking.

Matt yanked his glove off with his teeth, swiped his finger across the screen and turned his back to the street noise. "Yes."

"I followed your guy to a coffee shop. He met a woman, and they spent about thirty minutes talking."

Matt waited, wondering what this had to do with the senator.

"They just walked out of the coffee shop, and seemed very interested in your boss. And I think you'll be especially interested in her. They're on the sidewalk, directly across from where you're currently standing."

Matt spun around to scan the other side of the street. An icy chill having nothing to do with the shitty weather spiked down his spine. Jarod Raymond was shaking Andi Swain's hand, then they headed off in separate directions.

Shit! Shit! Shit!

"It's the woman you asked me to find." The investigator had continued to hit roadblocks and eventually conceded defeat in trying to identify her.

Matt eventually had taken a risk and asked a few people about her. He'd implied that he was simply interested in asking her out. It had paid off. He'd gotten her name and where she worked, and all it had cost him was the promise of a seat next to his boss at the next state dinner. He'd informed the senator and, as usual, he'd flown into a panic. Matt spent hours talking his boss off the ledge. He didn't dare tell him about his little surprise visit to one of Burke's employees.

Fuck. What was the Swain chick doing in DC? She was supposed to be out of state, consulting for OSI.

"What did they talk about?" Matt kept his voice level, as if unconcerned about her destroying everything they'd worked for.

"Not sure. I didn't stick around. I got a sense the woman would've sniffed me out." A hint of respect wound through his words.

"You didn't give yourself away, did you?" If anyone would've noticed, it would've been her. The woman was said to have an uncanny awareness of people.

"Nah, I grabbed a coffee and left. I waited and watched from the souvenir shop a few doors down. They never saw me." Matt desperately hoped he was right.

"Okay, thanks for letting me know," Matt said.

"Want me to stay on him?" Keys rattled in the background as he started his car.

"No. Follow the woman." Matt cast a quick glance around him.

"Then what?" The PI asked.

"Then nothing. I'll take care of her myself." He hung up, shoved his phone back in his pocket and cursed under his breath.

Things had just gone from bad to catastrophic. From the moment the senator first whispered in Matt's ear that his ultimate goal was to rule from the White House, Matt had begun planning. Now, his carefully constructed plans, built on deception, promises made, and secrets learned and hoarded, were beginning to implode. Something had to be done. He couldn't risk sharing this latest news with the senator. Matt couldn't afford to have him distracted during his meeting with the president.

He jerked his glove back on.

Think, Matt, think.

Anger and desperation fired through his system as he

glanced through the bare trees and caught a glimpse of the American flag fluttering atop the White House. He'd worked too damn long and too damn hard to get them this close to their dream. Matt would destroy anyone who stood in their way. Including an uppity bitch like Andi Swain.

CHAPTER TWENTY-EIGHT

Jonathan paced over and stoked the fire. He'd only done it about ten times in the last half hour. Couldn't say how many times he'd check his phone. He'd even snapped at Christina, who'd just smiled, rolled her eyes and walked away. Frustrated as hell, he'd finally gone over to the gym and spent an hour trying to kill an innocent punching bag.

He'd been acting like a freak since finding out Andi had left town to take care of personal business. What kind of personal business would require her to leave town on such short notice? Did it have something to do with their night together?

He circled behind his desk. His chair groaned as he slouched back against it.

Last time he saw her, she was curled up in bed, the sheets pulled up to cover her gorgeous body, her long, dark lashes casting a shadow on her cheeks. Their absurd *deal* was the only thing that kept him from crawling back into bed with her. And even though they'd both agreed to one night, he'd felt like a pussy for sneaking out of her place. Mostly, he felt cheated. What the hell ever made him think he could get a taste of her and not want more?

"Because you're an idiot, that's why," he mumbled to himself.

As if summoned by his remorse, his door burst open, and Andi charged into his office. Cheeks and nose pink from the cold, she wore her sexy bomber jacket and had a manila folder in her hand. She looked tired yet somehow rejuvenated at the same time.

"Jonathan." She glanced back at Christina, who stood in the doorway. "Oh, sorry. I probably should've knocked first, but I've got some news I think you're going to want to hear."

"It's okay, Christina." Jonathan tipped his chin up at her and waited until she returned to her desk. He leaned his elbows on the desk, working to hide all the craziness he'd just been feeling. "Is it about this *personal business* you had to tend to?"

Andi's brows crinkled in confusion, then she smiled.

"Oh, that." She waved it off. "No, I didn't have any personal business. I was—"

"What do you mean you didn't have any personal business?" He slowly rose from his chair. "You just decided to blow out of town in the middle of an investigation to take a quickie vacation?"

"What?" The frown returned, and she shook her head. "No. I was following up on a hunch I had about Nancy Raymond."

"A hunch? About Nancy Raymond?" Jonathan rounded the desk, braced his hands on his hips. "I thought my instructions were pretty damn clear."

Instead of admitting he'd missed her, that he was happy to see her, he shielded himself. He embraced his anger and disappointment about being lied to by another woman, and for sitting around wondering and worrying about her.

He got right in her face. "When I give an order, I expect it to be followed."

"Excuse me?" Her chin drew back, and her eyebrows shot up until they were hidden under her bangs.

"You heard me." He pointed at her. "I will not have you jeopardizing the reputation of this company so you can go off on some wild goose chase involving the director of the NSA's assistant."

"Wild goose ... " She shook her head and chuckled to herself, but there was no humor in it. "You know what? I'm going to make things really easy for you." She lifted her badge from around her neck and tossed it onto the middle of his desk. "I quit."

A painful silence sucked the air from the room, and she turned to leave. She took a couple of steps, swung back around and marched right back to his desk.

"I get it. Believe me, I do. Something real and meaningful passed between us the other night, and it terrified you. Here's the thing, Jonathan. It scared me, too." She hesitated. Then, as if she'd come to some sort of conclusion, her shoulders rose and fell on a sigh and she shook her head. "If you refuse to let go of the past and let yourself love again, you'll end up very sad and lonely. I speak from experience."

Andi firmed those proud shoulders of hers and, right before his eyes, began rebuilding every one of the walls he'd managed to break through.

She tossed a folder on the desk in front of him. "You might want to take a look at what's in there."

Without another word, she pivoted away and walked out of his office.

"Fuck," he spit out as he dropped into his chair and stabbed his fingers through his hair. Her words clanged around in his head, *something real and meaningful*. She'd felt it, too.

Jonathan's eyes dashed toward the sound of someone clearing their throat. Christina stood in the doorway. He'd hoped it was Andi.

"Um, is everything okay, Boss Man?" Voice uncharacteristically subdued, his assistant stepped into the room.

Shit. He'd neglected to close his door.

"Everything's just great." Which was a complete lie. He'd just done the one thing he'd promised he wouldn't—he'd hurt Andi again. She was right. He was a fucking coward, afraid to take a chance on loving someone again. On loving her.

Christina gave him a long look that was a combination of pity and frustration, then pulled his door shut with a quiet, lonely *click.*

CHAPTER TWENTY-NINE

Andi rushed to gather her things from her office and locker in the training area and managed to make it out of the building without seeing anyone. Fortunately, all the guys were out on the obstacle course. She had zero interest in answering questions right now. Running into Jonathan wouldn't have been fun either.

She tossed her workout bag to the opposite side of the back seat, plunked the box down next to it, then slammed the door. She yanked open the driver's side door and dropped in behind the wheel. Her eyes traveled over the OSI compound for what would likely be the last time. With a twist of the wrist, the engine fired up and she pulled out of the lot. She would go back to her place, pack the rest of her stuff, then get the hell out of town.

Before that happened, she needed to say goodbye to Molly and Michaleen. And to see Ashling one last time. Andi's heart clenched tight and took her breath away.

Never again would she get to see the adorable pixie's chubby cheeks or take in her soft, powdery baby smell. She would never know when she got her first tooth or when she said her first word. And there was a very good chance Ashling would never even know who she was.

She veered onto the shoulder and skidded to a stop in the mud and gravel. She slammed the car into park, and white knuckles gripped the steering wheel tight. Her forehead dropped against the wheel and, this time, when the tears came, Andi let them fall. Shoulders that had always carried so much responsibility and pain shook with great, tormenting sobs torn free from where they had burrowed deep within.

She cried for the mother she never knew. For the father who could never love her. For the big, loving family she longed to be a part of but never would. Mostly, she cried for another motherless little girl who would grow up without knowing how much Andi loved her and, yes, she even cried for Ashling's pigheaded, clueless father.

The Colonel's voice invaded her thoughts, ordering her to *toughen up*. Andi raised her head, sniffed back her tears. "Go to hell, Colonel." With those words, she banished her father from her heart and mind for good. Never again would his inability to accept her for who she was keep her from being the woman she ached to be. A woman unashamed of loving and wanting to be loved. Including all the scary, wonderful, magical things that went with it.

Course set, mind cleared of all doubt, she pulled back onto the road and headed to the O'Hallerans'. She had business to take care of. After a quick goodbye with a promise to return, she would finish this business with Nancy, the senator and his smarmy little aide once and for all.

MATT FELT a surge of panic when the Swain woman pulled to

the side of the road. He cruised by her and turned in to a small gas station just down the street, making sure to park where he could see her car in his side-view mirror.

His PI had followed her to the airport and reported back that she'd jumped on a flight back to Washington. An hour later, Matt was on his own flight into Seattle. As soon as he landed, he'd run to catch the shuttle bus to the off-site rental car station and picked the closest car on the lot. He was lucky he hadn't been stopped, since he had certainly broken a few traffic laws getting to OSI's facility.

Fuckin' O'Hallerans. The place was tucked back in the middle of some dense woods. His damned rental car had come close to getting stuck when he'd pulled into a narrow opening between some trees.

Damp palms clenched and unclenched the wheel. Sweat dripped down his temple, and his heart hammered in his chest. Had she spotted him? This hick town was so small, he wouldn't be surprised if they blasted out an announcement every time a stranger showed up. He glanced around, half-expecting a team from OSI to swoop in and surround him.

His phone vibrated in his pocket, and he checked the screen. The senator. Again. His tenth, no, eleventh call. No doubt wondering where the hell his aide was. Matt didn't respond, just shoved it in his suit coat pocket. What the hell was he supposed to say? *Hey, sir, sorry I missed your calls. I've been busy chasing down the woman who could blow up your entire future and every single chance you have to make it to the White House. Oh, and you could end up in prison. Sooo, there's that.*

Not to mention, Matt had a few of his own secrets to protect. The less his boss was involved, the better chance he had of keeping them buried. No sense him finding out about the questionable donations Matt had accepted—without the senator's knowledge—from a certain Russian.

Movement flashed by his peripheral vision. He hunkered down low in his seat as she drove past him without so much as a sideways glance. Matt blew out a heavy breath, put the car in gear and followed.

Hanging back, he waited until she turned onto a two-lane road that meandered along the water. A large truck loaded with cut timber turned in front of him, wedging its way between them. He cursed and craned his neck to see around it. A few miles later, she made a sharp left turn onto a narrow gravel drive.

Matt continued beyond her turnoff point. The large truck lumbered up the steep hill in front of him, slowing his progress. At the first opportunity, he executed a three-point turn, then slowed to a snail's pace as he crept back to where she'd turned off. Leaning closer to the windshield, he got a flash of her car as it crested the hill, then disappeared around a bend.

The idling engine seemed suddenly loud as he scanned the area. About ten feet off the road, he spotted an old, dilapidated wooden shack. Its moss-covered roof was rotted, and the walls were collapsing under the weight of decades' worth of ivy, thorny blackberry vines, and weeds. It would have to do.

He maneuvered along side-by-side ruts in the tall grass—remnants of an old driveway. The car bumped and shimmied through mud and holes. Dangling branches scraped the roof of the car as he backed into the cramped shack.

Matt stepped out and sank to his ankles in freezing mud.

"Fuck." He gave each foot a quick shake and checked his surroundings. Along one side of the old structure, shafts of dull light pierced through broken and displaced planks of rotted wood. Water dripped from multiple openings in what was left of the roof. Bent and rusty nails stuck out here and there, giving the place the feel of a medieval torture chamber.

He shivered. Slammed the car door. Panicked birds fluttered past him from the darkened depths of the old building.

Matt jumped and cursed again. He took a deep breath, smoothed a hand over his hair and straightened his jacket. Tried to force a calm into his jagged nerves. He stumbled his way to the trunk, popped it open and rummaged through his small suitcase until his hand brushed over steel. Shaking fingers wound around the rubber-sided grip of the revolver, and he slipped it out. And *that* was the only reason he'd checked a bag. He'd shoved towels in with the gun to keep it from tumbling around. *Damned baggage handlers.*

Before getting to Whidbey Cove, he'd stopped at a chain sporting goods store to buy a box of ammo. He tore through the cardboard and dumped the contents. Bullets rained down, scattered and rolled over the carpeted floor of the trunk. Hands shaking, heart pounding, he managed to load six rounds into the cylinder. The rest he scooped up and put in his suit pocket. He lifted the back of his coat and tucked the .38 Special into his waistband, then settled the jacket over it before he ducked out of the old building.

For about thirty minutes, he slogged his way through the dense woods skirting the dirt road Swain had taken. Scratches burned his cheek and forehead. His pants were soaked to the knees, weighing down each step. His best jacket was a total loss—torn and wet from water dripping from the trees above. Not to mention bird shit on both shoulders. Slick-bottomed dress shoes—now ruined—were far from perfect for the hike he'd just made.

Matt spied a clearing ahead, and his steps faltered. The cold air scorched a path from his throat to his lungs. He bent over and put his hands on his knees. Water dripped down his nose, and each heaving breath came out in foggy puffs. He straightened, dragged his cold hand down his face, and noticed her car sitting in the driveway of a massive home on the far side of the large open space.

One corner of his mouth lifted. “Gotcha.”

His eyes traveled over the clearing. Once he felt sure no one was around, arm down along his side, gun tucked tight to his leg, he emerged from the woods. A light rain began to fall as he ran toward the back of the house in a crouch.

CHAPTER THIRTY

Jonathan paced back and forth in front of the fireplace. He held his cell phone to his ear. The other hand was shoved in his front pocket. His steps halted when Andi's voice mail picked up again. He cursed, thought about leaving another message, hung up instead. She deserved a face-to-face apology, not some chickenshit recording.

His head fell back on a sigh, and he stared at the ceiling. The second she left his office and disappeared from sight, he'd felt like a piece of him was ripped away. His heart physically ached without her.

Damn it, he loved Andi and wanted a life with her. She was his. He didn't deserve her, but she belonged with him and Ashling. He would do whatever it took to make her see that.

Jonathan was going after her. Mind made up, he walked over and, just as he reached for his coat on the back of his chair, Emily charged into his office. He was beginning to question why he even *had* a door.

"You need to see something." Her petite form vibrated with pent-up excitement as she hustled across his office.

He started to shove his arm into his coat. "I have something I—"

"Trust me, Jonathan, you need to see this. Now." She tugged his coat off and tossed it onto the guest chair, then rushed around his desk and laid some spreadsheets out on the center of his desk.

Jonathan settled into his chair. "What am I looking at here, Em?" There were four columns—one with names, two with dates, and a third with notes.

"These are all the people who stayed at that creepy farm slash commune at some point in time." She pointed at the date columns. "These are the dates they arrived and left, and this is their reason for being there."

The Farm? Why was she digging through that data?

"Check out whose name I found." She pointed at a specific entry.

"Jarod Raymond?" He cast her a questioning look. "Any relation to Nancy Raymond?"

"Her son." She set that sheet aside and replaced it with another one. "Now look at this. These are all the donations made to Preston Etheridge. The name of the donor, date of the donation and amount are all listed."

"Etheridge?" He sat forward, giving special attention to the rows she'd highlighted. "Why are you looking into him?"

"Andi had a hunch the senator, Radoslav and Nancy Raymond were all connected in some way. Before she got on the plane to come back here, she called and asked me to do some digging. Look." She popped the cap off a highlighter. It squeaked as she ran it across a few entries. "Here, here and here."

A company called Bergenia Corp. had made three very large donations to the senator's last campaign.

"At the time those donations were made, that company

had no assets of record, and the board of directors was a bunch of old guys who were dead long before the corporation was legally formed."

Classic shell corporation, typically set up to launder money, but it wasn't uncommon for them to be used as a source of funds for payoffs to code enforcement officers, cops, corrections officers, judges, politicians.

"What does all of this have to do with Nancy Raymond?"

"I was curious about the name of the corporation, so I looked up the word bergenia." She tugged her phone from her back pocket and swiped her finger over the screen to show a clustered purple flower. "It's a flower native to Siberia."

"Nikolai Radoslav was from Siberia." Jonathan didn't believe in coincidences.

"I figured." She lifted one shoulder. "So, following my own hunch, I looked through his financial records. Which was a bit of a pain in the patoot, since he kept a lot of them in old handwritten ledgers." She mumbled something about living in the dark ages, then continued.

"I narrowed my search to the dates the senator received donations from the Bergenia Corporation. And guess what ... " She flipped to the next page, where she'd prepared a side-by-side comparison. "There are three very sizable donations whose dates and amounts match exactly to what was recorded in Radoslav's ledger. And look whose name is next to each entry."

"Matthew Roberson?" He looked up at her. "The senator's aide?"

"Yep. Seems he personally took delivery of those donations on behalf of the Senator."

"All this tells me is that the senator and his aide took donations from Radoslav." And he would share that information with Burke. He leaned back in his chair. "Again, where does Nancy fit in all of this, Em?"

She straightened, a confused look on her face.

"Didn't Andi come in and talk to you this morning? She said she was going to tell you what she learned from her conversation with Jarod Raymond."

He cleared his throat. "She came in a bit ago, but I ... well ... "

"You what?" She scowled. Her hands slammed to her hips. "What did you do, Jonathan?"

Jesus. It was eerie how much she sounded like their mom sometimes. Jonathan had over a hundred pounds and a whole foot on his little sister, yet he still had to force himself not to squirm.

"Hold that thought." He flipped open the folder Andi dropped on his desk. Her notes were neat and concise.

"Says here Jarod was a runner for Radoslav until the old man found out he was skimming some of the product. Kid got scared and, on the advice of one of the other runners, decided to hide out in Montana while he tried to kick his habit."

He flipped it over, read the back. "While he was there, he got a call from an unnamed Russian telling him his debt had been covered."

What he read next sent ice coursing through his veins.

"The date of that call was right after Caleb was shot." Jonathan had been overseas when it happened. His folks opted not to tell him until he returned home on leave. They felt it would've been a dangerous distraction. He understood and appreciated their worry but would always regret not being there for his brother.

"Soooo ... What?" She crossed her arms and leaned her hip against his desk. "You think Nancy paid off his debt to

Radoslav?" Emily hesitated, then her eyes widened. "Oh, shit."

What the hell had Nancy gotten herself into?

"Yeah, oh shit." His sister was smart enough to figure it out. "Money isn't what she used to repay his date. She used—"

"Information." Her nostrils flared.

"Calm down, Em." An explosion was imminent. His baby sister was extremely headstrong and wasn't exactly known for her ability to control her emotions. He worried it might get her in trouble one day.

"Calm down? That ... that ... *WOMAN* got Caleb shot. Power was killed because of her. She works for Burke, one of the most powerful men out there. She could've gone to him for help. He would've known what to do." Her voice rose, her outrage justified.

"Instead, she said *nothing*. Because of her, Radoslav was out there ... free. And look what happened. Gwen was ... "

Tears filled her eyes, and she turned away.

His little sister had visited Gwen in the hospital a few days after Beck, Caleb and Mason extricated her from Radoslav's compound. She'd seen an up-close example of the kind of damage he could inflict. Their sister-in-law still carried scars from what the sick fucker had done to her.

A quiet sniff and Emily drew back her shoulders, visibly gathered herself. She had such a kind heart, but boy did she hate showing anything that might be perceived as a weakness.

"Even after Radoslav took Gwen, she still said nothing. Jesus, she's been around Mom and Dad, in our home! She has to be punished, Jonathan." Conviction permeated every word. "She *has* to be."

"And she will be, Em." He put his hands on her trembling shoulders and looked her in the eye. "I promise."

She gave a quick nod, took a deep breath and picked up Andi's notes to skim through them.

"Okay, so let me make sure I've got this straight," his sister said. "Radoslav threatened to hurt Jarod to gain Nancy's cooperation. Then the scumbag turned around and told Jarod to keep his mouth shut about his business or he'd kill his mom?"

Jonathan nodded. "Yep. Looks like it."

"I'm glad Beck killed him." Emily grumbled and dropped the notes on his desk. She stomped over and plopped down into one of the big chairs by the fireplace with a huff. "You still have that bottle in your desk? I could really use a swig right about now."

"How did you—"

She cut him off with a look over her shoulder, eyebrows raised like, *really, dude?*

"No, it's not there anymore." He'd dumped it and the one in his bedroom the morning after Ashling's party. Decided it was time to stop wallowing in self-pity and be the father his baby girl deserved.

"Shit. I have to call Burke." He picked up his phone and scrolled to the NSA director's private number. Normally, he would call Nancy Raymond, and she would put him through. Not this time. His head almost exploded when he thought of all the sensitive information she'd been privy to over the years.

Emily opened her mouth to say something.

He held up his finger when Burke answered. The man had no idea Jonathan was about to ruin his day ... week ... hell, his year.

"Burke."

"Jeffrey, Jonathan O'Halleran."

"What can I do for you, Jonathan?"

"Do you have a few minutes?" Jonathan moved over and sat on the front edge of the chair across from his sister. "We've uncovered a few things you need to know about."

Understatement of the year. God, this was going to suck.

"Sure. Hold on." His voice became distant, as if he set the phone down. "Gentlemen, if you'll excuse me, I need to take this call."

A mumbled "no problem" and "absolutely" could be heard in the background.

"Nancy, please hold all my calls. And make sure I'm not interrupted." His door closed.

"What have you got?" He must've sat, because his old chair squeaked.

Jonathan spent the next few minutes outlining what Andi and Emily had learned.

How the senator was seen at The Farm.

How Matthew Roberson funneled mob money to his boss's campaign.

He shared their suspicions regarding Nancy's involvement with Radoslav and how it all started.

The Russian supplied Grady Teague at The Farm with weapons, explosives, and other armament. Teague paid for them with a combination of cash and meth that Radoslav then sold through his distribution channels.

"We think Radoslav knew for some time that Nancy worked for you. Considered her a weak link he might someday be able to exploit. That day presented itself when he learned her son was staying at The Farm." Radoslav finally had his inside source.

"Scared he'd kill Jarod," Burke detailed the rest, "she gave Radoslav a heads-up that the FBI's team was going to meet with a confidential informant from The Farm. The guy was freaked out. Said he had information about a shipment of Russian-made rocket-propelled grenades being delivered to the commune."

Unfortunately, when the team arrived, the CI was already dead from a gunshot wound to the back of the head, and

Caleb, his K9 partner, Power, and the rest of his team were caught in an ambush.

Months later, an alarmingly large arsenal was confiscated during the raid of the compound in the mountains of northwest Montana. Ballistics from the slug that tore through Caleb's shoulder, as well as the two removed from Power's body during the necropsy, matched a gun found on Teague's body.

"Other than hitting a brick wall in her inquiries about Frank Morgan, Andi eliminated all the other likely suspects." Jonathan skimmed her notes.

"Morgan is in the clear." Burke said. "His new job is just a cover. He's actually working for me on a dark op."

Shit. Jonathan kicked himself for not listening to her when she tried to tell him Nancy was involved.

"Other than the donations and VIP visits, did Roberson or Etheridge have any other connection to Radoslav or The Farm?" Burke asked.

"No. We've found nothing linking them to the drugs or weapons." Accepting illegal campaign donations and sleeping with underaged girls who were probably drugged and coerced would be more than enough to destroy them both.

"Send me everything you have via encrypted e-mail." Nothing in Burke's voice gave away what he was feeling. "I'll get a warrant for the senator's place here and in Georgia, as well as Roberson's place. I'm going to try to get one for their offices here, but that might take a bit more time."

"And the other ... situation?" Meaning, his assistant.

"I'll deal with that myself." If possible, his voice held even less emotion.

"Jeffrey, I wish I had better news." Being betrayed by someone you've worked with, trusted and been loyal to for so many years was a bitter pill to swallow. Even for a man who'd been in the trenches as long as Burke.

"Yeah, me, too." He sighed. "I'll look for that information."

"We'll send it right away." They both hung up. Jonathan flipped open his laptop.

"Well?" Emily hopped up from her chair and faced him down from in front of his desk. With each new detail he'd shared with Burke, he'd sensed his sister's agitation returning.

Understandable, really. More than once, Nancy—the quiet, middle-aged woman who had betrayed them all—had been welcomed into their parents' home, spent time around their children and grandchildren. She was with Burke the day they buried Power at Quantico. She'd watched his brother mourn the loss of his K9 partner, then suffer through weeks of painful rehab from a gunshot wound, knowing she was responsible the entire time.

"Burke is going to nail Etheridge and Roberson to the cross." The man's dislike and distrust of those two weasels was no secret. Once again, it seemed the NSA director's instincts had been spot on about them.

"Good. Fine. Great. But what about Nancy?" She crossed her.

"He's taking care of it, Em. You need to trust him." Nancy Raymond was a traitor. Burke would handle her accordingly. "I need you to send me all your data via the encrypted e-mail."

He listed a few other things he wanted to send, including scanned copies of Andi's notes.

"You scan these, Emily. No one else. Got me?" He trusted his people completely but wanted to keep a tight lid on this for now.

She nodded just as his cell phone rang on his desk. He grabbed it and was disappointed when it wasn't Andi.

"Jeffrey, we're—"

"Roberson is in your neck of the woods."

Jonathan slowly rose from his chair. A tingling sensation snuck across the back of his neck.

"I wanted a heads-up on where he and the senator are so I could have them both served simultaneously." The element of surprise would keep them off balance, and one might say something about the other that that could be used against them. They also wouldn't have an opportunity to destroy possible evidence.

"Roberson usually has his nose up Etheridge's ass, but no one has seen him since yesterday. He called the office and told them he was sick and wouldn't be in today. Then he hopped on a flight to Sea-Tac and rented a car. We were able to track his cell and caught a ping off a tower not far from Whidbey Cove." Burke lowered his voice. "Where did you say Andi met with Jarod?"

Jonathan shuffled through her pages. "A place called Scarpetti's Bakery and Coffee Shop."

"Son of a bitch." Uncharacteristic urgency spiked through Burke's voice. "He and Roberson had a meeting across the street from that location around the same time."

Jonathan didn't bother asking how Burke knew that. His ability to gain information was the stuff of legends. It was also a huge asset to OSI.

"So ... What?" The prickling sensation intensified. "You think Roberson might've seen them together?"

"Where is Andi?" Burke asked.

"I don't know. But I'm going to find out." He hung up and dialed Andi's number again.

"Damn it!" Voice mail. "Andi, Roberson is in Whidbey Cove. He knows about your meeting with Jarod Raymond." He blew out a breath, ran his hand through his hair. "Look ... I know you're pissed, but please, *please* call me."

Where are you, baby?

"What is it? Jonathan?"

He swallowed the sharp fear trying to lodge itself in his throat.

"Roberson's here, and he's after Andi."

CHAPTER THIRTY-ONE

Andi sat alone on the O'Hallerans' large back porch. Without knowing it, they had become the mother and father she'd always dreamed of as a little girl. Simply being in their presence made her feel safe and loved. Andi was going to miss them terribly.

No. Don't you dare give up, she scolded herself.

The kid who did odd jobs for the family was heading down the hill and had pulled to a stop next to her and let her know Michaleen was at one of his job sites and Molly and Ashling should be back any time. He'd flicked a wave and torn off down the road.

Her hands rubbed over the arms of her favorite chair. The smooth wood surface spoke of years of enjoyment. Countless tall trees swayed hypnotically in the breeze swept up from the valley below. A momentary break in the drizzle allowed sunshine to peek through clusters of puffy clouds as they floated by overhead. Their shadows danced along the rolling hills to where the land met the dark, gray water stretching all the way to and around the San Juan Islands.

Staring out over such awe-inspiring terrain, she

should've achieved a sense of calm. Nope. Not today. Today, she just couldn't shake her sense of loss. Sure, she'd decided to fight for what she wanted—a life with Jonathan and Ashling—but there was no guarantee he would be on board with the idea. And just because they connected in bed didn't mean they would be able to move beyond their painful pasts.

Her head fell back, and she filled her lungs with cool, crisp air.

One thing at a time, Andi. She'd take care of this nightmare with Nancy, then come back here and fight for what she wanted. Fight for her future.

Her head lifted at the sound of footsteps near the side of the house. Andi rose from the chair. She'd just gotten a few feet from the bottom of the wide porch steps when she spotted a man rounding the corner.

What the hell? Matthew Roberson stood about thirty feet away, looking like he'd taken a tumble down a long, muddy hill. His presence was so incongruous with his surroundings that her brain tripped over the image for a few seconds.

His eyes locked on hers and widened in surprise. He gave his head a quick shake, then raised his right hand. That's when she noticed the gun.

Andi dove away from the porch, tucked and rolled in the wet grass behind the pile of firewood. Two shots rang out. Chips of wood landed in her hair and on her shoulder. She scrambled over on her belly and hunkered down behind Michaleen's large stacked stone fireplace, cursing herself for leaving her weapon and phone locked in the car.

"You might as well come out." Roberson's footsteps squished across the wet grass, bringing him closer to where she hid.

Thanks to Killian's tour, she knew this property. If she could make it to that large maple tree about fifteen feet away, she could lose him in the woods long enough to circle back around to her car. And her gun.

She sucked in a breath, exploded up to her feet and took off at a sprint, zigzagging her way to the woods. Roberson fired. The bullet tore through the thick brush next to her. Andi darted around the maple and bolted past the O'Halleran siblings' trees. Her arms pumped and her boots chewed through sloppy, soggy undergrowth.

Behind her, heavy breaths and crashing footsteps gave away his location. Sounds of him faded as she put distance between them. He took another shot at her, missing horribly. Good thing he was such a shitty shot.

A couple of minutes later, Andi burst from the woods to hear car tires crunching over gravel as it pulled into the driveway.

She heard Molly's voice and picked up her pace.

Oh, no. No, no, no.

"Who are you? What do you want?" Molly's voice was shaky.

Andi's boots skidded on the wet flagstone walkway. Her arms windmilled, and her heart dropped to her stomach.

Roberson had doubled back to the house and now stood next to Molly, pointing that fucking revolver at her, his finger on the trigger.

"Shut up and step back from the car." He was trying to steal her minivan?

"Roberson," Andi called out.

He swung the gun her way. It boomed, and sparks exploded from the end of the barrel.

Molly screamed and threw her arms around her head as Andi dropped to the ground. The bullet whizzed past her and embedded in one of the thick, wooden columns supporting the front porch. She crawled behind a large rhododendron bush.

"Goddamn it, get the hell out," Roberson shouted.

She peeked through the foliage. Molly had managed to duck into the driver's seat. Her arms were locked around the steering wheel. Roberson pointed the gun at her head.

Oh, God. Andi's heart clenched. Ashling was with her. Molly would sacrifice her life for her granddaughter.

Roberson gave up on getting her to move. Instead he ran around the front of the car and climbed in the front seat. "Drive."

When Molly didn't move, he pointed the gun toward the back seat and said it again. "Drive ... now."

Andi stood, ready to charge the vehicle.

Molly looked over at her, a combination of fear and fury in her eyes, then gave a quick nod and reached for the gear shift.

"Noooo!" Andi ran toward the driveway. She got there just in time to hear Ashling's hysterical cries from the back seat as the car headed down the dirt road.

She charged for her car, grabbed her cell phone from the cupholder and called the OSI ops desk. Someone was there twenty-four seven taking calls, monitoring the teams in the field, providing support in any way. Pretty much any activity relevant to OSI could be tracked from there.

As soon as someone answered, she gave them her code number, hoping Jonathan hadn't had time to deactivate it yet, then succinctly conveyed all that happened. Assured backup was on its way, she grabbed her holstered Glock from her glove box and clipped it to her belt.

The memory of that gun pointed at Molly and Ashling's terrified screams filled her head as she tore down the bumpy driveway.

"TURN RIGHT UP THERE to get to the hotel." Matt's palms sweated as he gripped the gun tight in one hand and checked the map on his phone with the other. At least the windows were tinted so no one could see him. He hoped, anyway, since locals would no doubt recognize this mom van.

"I know how to get to the hotel," the woman driving snapped at him, then checked the kid in the rearview mirror again. Thank God it had finally stopped screaming and fallen asleep. Damned kid had a powerful set of lungs. It was all wrapped up in a bunch of pink shit, so he assumed it must be a girl.

"Just shut up and drive." He looked over at her. "Who the hell are you, anyway?"

"Who am I?" She turned to him with contempt. "Who the heck are *you?* You come to my home, shoot at my friend, make my granddaughter cry, then you force me to drive you to a hotel."

Matt popped open the glove box. He dug around and found an envelope with the registration inside. The van was registered to Michaleen and Molly O'Halleran. Which meant the baby was probably an O'Halleran, too. *Shit.* His shoulders dropped. Just when he thought this day couldn't get any shittier. The O'Hallerans were not a family you fucked with.

This was supposed to be quick. Get in, take care of the Swain chick, then get out. Instead, here he was, driving around some hick town with a woman and a kid whose family wouldn't be satisfied with anything less than seeing his head on a pike. How had everything gone to shit so quickly?

The sign for the small hotel came into view.

"Pull in there and drive around back." He pointed to the parking lot entrance farthest from the lobby doors.

He was amazed when she actually did it without arguing. Old bag had been carping his ear off since he jumped in her car.

"Back into that space, right there in front of the door." He hadn't planned to stick around, but he'd swung by earlier and paid cash for a room, just in case. While he was here, he'd scoped out the parking lot looking for the best spot. This particular door could only be opened with a key card, and it was right next to the stairs, which led to his room in the back corner of the second floor. He'd intentionally picked this room because, one, the entire floor was practically vacant and two, it was isolated, separated from the other rooms by the ice and vending machines.

"Shut off the engine, grab the kid and get out." He pointed the gun toward the car seat, careful to keep his finger off the trigger. Killing a kid wasn't part of his plan. "I have no interest in either of you. But if you don't do exactly as I tell you or if you make a sound ... "

He left the threat dangling. Her huge eyes told him she'd gotten the message. She wedged her way between the front seats and climbed in the back. As she undid all the buckles and latches on the car seat, the baby started fussing again.

"Sh-sh-sh, it's okay, honey. Grandma's got you." She cooed at her and stuck a pacifier in her mouth, lifted her from the seat and tucked her close to her chest.

Matt jumped out and opened the sliding door on the side of the van. He scanned the parking lot as she tightened the blanket around the kid and grabbed a big quilted bag.

"Uh-uh-uh. Leave the bag."

She slipped it onto her shoulder. "It's just a diaper bag, you idiot."

Matt smacked her across the face with his free hand.

Her head whipped to the side, then slowly turned back to him. There were no tears, no pleas for mercy. She just glared through the strands of hair that had come loose from a clip and now hung over her face.

"It's not nice calling people names." He dug through the

bag and decided to let her keep the stupid thing. Then he dragged her and the kid from the van and put them in front of him. He pressed the end of the gun barrel to her back and leaned close to her ear. "But the next time you open your mouth, it'll be your last. Now, move."

He slipped the key card into the slot, and there was a click.

"Open it." He continued to check the parking lot and the woods surrounding the place as she tucked the kid close with one arm and pushed through the door with the other.

She stumbled on the steps but managed to keep herself from falling. The whole time the damn kid was giggling and blowing bubbles, completely oblivious.

A few tense moments later, safely ensconced in the room, Matt paced back and forth, casting sideways glances at his captives. What the fuck was he supposed to do now? He made her sit in the chair with her back to the wall. He thought about taking the kid from her—leverage and all—but decided against it. As long as she thought he might kill one or both of them, she would be cooperative.

Matt realized with sudden clarity that he would in fact kill them both if it would further his cause.

CHAPTER THIRTY-TWO

Andi called the ops desk again and let them know she'd followed Roberson to the Whidbey Cove Hotel. By the time she hung up, a team of OSI field operators would be on its way there.

She popped the magazine out of her weapon, checked that it was full, then shoved it back into place. With a rack of the slide, a round was loaded into the chamber, and she tucked the gun into the holster at her hip. She shoved open the door of her car, ran the small distance to the hotel, and headed for the registration desk.

"How can I help you today?" A perky, young blonde in an ill-fitting suit smiled at her from behind the counter. She looked like she had to have skipped school to work here.

"My name is Andréa Swain, and I'm with the NSA." She flashed her badge, then showed her Roberson's picture on her phone. "Have you seen this man?"

Brandi with an "i," according to her name tag, stared wide-eyed. Her mouth opened and closed.

Andi snapped her fingers close to her face. "Did you check him in?"

"Oh, um ... " She blinked a couple of times. "I'm sorry. Yeah, I did. Hang on a second."

Brandi clicked away at a few keys on her computer, then leaned across the counter and whispered, "He's in room two-fifteen, at the very end of the hall."

She grabbed a piece of paper with a pre-printed layout of the second-floor rooms and showed Andi where his room was located.

"It's as far from the front desk as you can get." She kept her voice low. Her eyes darted around the lobby as if he might appear any moment. "Unless someone was looking for him, you wouldn't even know he was there."

"How is the room set up inside? Where are the beds, tables, dresser, that kind of stuff?"

Brandi flipped over the paper and sketched out where everything was in the room, including the TV and lamps.

"I noticed all the second-floor rooms have balconies. Are those real or just for show?"

"What do you mean?" Her perfectly plucked eyebrows drew together.

"Do the windows open or not?" Andi could hear the clock ticking on how long Molly and Ashling had been with Roberson. The longer he held them, the more dangerous this situation became.

"Oh, I'm sorry. Yes, the sliding doors open. They have a regular latch on the handle, but they also have a chain to secure them shut."

Well, shit. That would make gaining entry that much more difficult.

"Brandi, is there an office back there?" She pointed to the area behind the girl.

"Yeah." Her blond head bobbed up and down. "The manager's office."

"Okay, listen to me very carefully. I want you to go back there, turn off the lights and lock yourself in. Don't call anyone. Don't go anywhere. And stay nice and quiet. Do you understand?"

"But I'll get fired if I leave the front desk unattended." Instantly, tears formed in her eyes.

"No one will fire you. Especially after I tell them what a big help you've been." Andi patted her arm to reassure her. "I promise."

Brandi sniffled, pulled back her shoulders and said, "Okay, I'll do it."

"Good. Someone will come get you when it's safe." Andi waited until she heard the deadbolt on the door click into place before turning from the desk. She called the ops desk one last time and gave them the room number, then jogged toward the stairs.

The door to the stairwell opened with a whisper, and she glanced up between the sets of concrete stairs. Weapon in hand, feet silent, she made her way up to the second-floor landing. The door into the hall had a long, narrow window running up from the doorknob. She flattened herself against the wall next to it, took a deep breath and risked a quick peek. Room two-fifteen was directly across the hall and, *shit,* there was a peephole in the damned door.

Andi couldn't risk stepping into the hall for fear he might be looking. Her only option was the balcony. She holstered her weapon and, taking two steps at a time, headed to the top floor. A steel, pull down ladder on the wall led up to a hatch-like opening for the roof.

The first rung was about eight or nine feet up from the floor. She wiped her hands on her butt, jumped up and grabbed hold, then used her weight to drag it down. The gears ground together from disuse, and a loud squeal echoed through the stairwell. She cringed, then scrambled up the ladder, cranked open the giant lever to open the access door and climbed out onto the roof.

Andi checked her watch. *Shit!* Ten minutes had passed since she'd walked into the lobby. She scurried across the roof, trying to find anything she could use to lower herself to the balcony two floors below. Scaling down the wall was possible, but it would take too long. Her eyes landed on a large metal storage box next to the air-conditioning unit. She jogged over to it and, with a grunt, hefted open the heavy lid and smiled. Andi wanted to shout with joy at the sight of squeegees, rags and window detergent wedged in next to a large bucket full of varying sizes of carabiners. Another one held red, green, yellow and blue climbing ropes. There were two seat harnesses and a couple of helmets, a bunch of miscellaneous pulleys, even a couple of battered pairs of leather work gloves.

She grabbed one of the harnesses, the longest rope and some carabiners. The gloves were too bulky and would get in the way of her trigger finger. Her heart raced as she carried everything to the edge of the roof and looked down. This whole plan hinged on her being able to access the balcony to Roberson's room. It was doable, if she lowered herself down next to it. All she'd have to do was swing onto the balcony without him hearing, unlock the door, then get through the door without him shooting anyone. *Just your typical day at the office.*

Andi stepped into the harness and secured it around her hips and legs, fed the rope through a large "D" ring bolted to the roof, then through the loop in the harness. After a couple of quick tugs to ensure it would hold her weight, she stepped out onto the edge of the roof, checked below one last time, then slowly began to walk herself down the side of the building.

The rope slipped through one of her hands, and she began to fall. She wrapped her other hand around the rope and held on tight until she hung from one arm. Her biceps and shoulder burned, and skin was torn from her arm, her palms. She'd managed to conk the back of her head against the wall. Not hard enough to cause concern, but she'd be nursing one hell of a headache later. Her knobby, rubber-soled boots grabbed hold of the rough brick exterior, and she wedged the toes in a crack between the bricks to relieve the strain on her arm.

Andi leaned her forehead against the wall, closed her eyes and took a few deep breaths. Her heart hammered in her chest and pounded in her ears. After a minute, she swallowed and looked around to get her bearings. Miracle of miracles, she was only a few feet above where she needed to be. She rotated her shoulder a few times to loosen it up, wiped the blood from her chewed-up palms onto her pants legs and lowered herself the rest of the way.

The balcony was about two feet away. She tied herself off, reached out and used the hand rail to pull herself closer, then planted her feet on the edge of the concrete slab. Andi waited. Listened. Confident she hadn't been heard, she swung first one leg, then the other over the rail and stood as far from the sliding door as possible. She left the rope dangling, made quick work of the harness and dropped it into the bushes below.

The heavy, lined curtains were closed, but there was a narrow opening about four or five inches wide at the end closest to Andi. It afforded her a sliver of a view into the room. Roberson came into and out of view as he paced back and forth. His right arm hung down, a revolver clutched in his hand; he rubbed the back of his neck with the other. His tie hung loose. His clothes were a muddy, ripped mess, and his hair was all over the place. Anger, frustration and desperation poured off him.

He was on the far side of the bed and, according to Brandi's sketch, the dresser and TV should be on the right. She craned her neck and saw Molly sitting in a small upholstered chair in the corner, across from where a small round table and chair should be. Andi's anger spiked when she noticed the red mark on the side of her face. As if Molly sensed Andi's presence, their eyes connected for a brief moment. Without moving her head, Molly's eyes tracked to Roberson, then to Andi. From the firming of her lips and determined look in her eyes, it was obvious Molly had made some sort of decision.

Jonathan's mother stood and started gently bouncing Ashling. Roberson's pacing halted, and he swung the pistol in her direction. His agitated command to *sit down* was muffled by the thick glass. Andi's heart lodged in her throat. Her entire body tensed, and she found herself involuntarily reaching for the door. If that piece of shit harmed a hair on either one of their heads, she would kill the man herself and feel not one bit of remorse.

Molly's voice was amazingly calm when she replied that the baby was starting to stir and she was simply helping her fall back asleep. He must not have been too worried, because he let her be and went back to pacing. One inch at a time, eyes darting back and forth between the slider and Roberson, Molly managed to position herself directly in front of the latch on the door.

She angled herself *just so* and, using the blanket hanging from Ashling as cover, covertly fiddled with the lock until it released. But there was still the damn chain to deal with, and that would not be so easy. *Easy?* What a joke. Nothing about this situation was easy. Molly gave her a sideways glance. Andi gave a quick shake of her head—it was too dangerous. Apparently, the stubborn women didn't agree. With a slight nod, her eyes following Roberson, Molly turned her back to the slider, bent her arm up behind her and stretched up on her tippy-toes. Ten seconds later, to

Andi's utter astonishment, the chain dangled down the aluminum frame of the glass door. She wasn't sure why it surprised her. After all, the woman did manage to raise six kids and live to tell about it.

Molly gave her a quick wink, *a wink,* then lifted Ashling to tuck her head to her shoulder and gradually moved back toward the corner. Trusting they would be okay, Andi cleared her mind of everything but taking down Roberson.

She squatted against the wall to the side of the door and reached up with one hand. Blood smeared the door handle as, desperate not to rustle the curtains, she slowly slid it open. She'd never been more grateful Whidbey Cove lacked noisy traffic. Her eyes connected with Molly's. They exchanged a slight dip of the chin. Andi drew her weapon and mouthed, *three, two, one ...*

Everything slowed way down. She dived through the door, tucked and rolled, came up on one knee, raised her gun and pointed it at Roberson. He spun toward her, arm up, and they both fired.

THE OSI tactical van skidded to a stop, kicking up gravel and mud in an undeveloped lot down the street from the Whidbey Cove Hotel. They made no effort to hide the damn thing—everyone in town had become familiar with the large, black beast. Hell, it had been the main attraction in last year's Whidbey Cove Fourth of July parade.

Mathias jumped out from behind the wheel. Golden did the same from the front passenger side, their doors banging shut simultaneously. Double doors in the back flew open, and Jonathan and Killian piled out.

Jonathan checked his watch and shook his head. It had taken too damn long to get the guys in from the obstacle course. Unfortunately, the other teams were either deployed or out on remote training exercises.

"Hey, isn't that Andi's car?" Killian walked over, cupped his hand on the window and looked inside. "What the hell is all her stuff doing in the back seat?"

All three men turned to him with varying degrees of confusion and pissed-off looks on their faces.

"Let's load up," was all he said.

Now was not the time to admit to being a stubborn jackass. The only person he wanted to talk to about that particular topic was Andi. And he had no idea where she was or if she was even safe. Jonathan shut down the part of his brain eaten up with worry about her, his mom and Ashling and tapped into the controlled, deadly warrior created during years spent hunting down the worst kinds of human filth. His sole focus now was his team and their mission.

Each man reached into the back of the van and grabbed their weapons. They checked that the magazines were fully loaded and that a round was in the chamber. They'd gotten an update that Roberson was in room two-fifteen. With that critical piece of intel, they were able to analyze every possible scenario and come up with multiple plans.

"Okay. Killian, you cover the front. Mathias, you head around back."

"Roger that," his brothers responded in unison.

He pointed at Golden. "You and I go through the lobby and up the north stairs."

"Yes, sir." The big Viking tipped his chin.

Jonathan tugged on his tactical gloves and squeezed his brothers' shoulders.

"Let's go get our girls."

Their passionate "hell, yeah," "fuckin' A" and Golden's more polite, "let's do this" overlapped as they turned and headed into the woods.

A few minutes later, they exited the tree line about one hundred feet from the side of the hotel. They split up. Jonathan and Golden hustled across the parking lot to take up positions on either side of the glass front doors. Roberson's room was at the opposite end of the hotel. Unless he was hanging out in the lobby—highly unlikely—he wouldn't know they were there until it was too late.

Jonathan gave the signal. They pushed through the doors and wasted no time clearing the lobby. Luckily, it was off season and no guests loitered about. The phone at the front desk rang repeatedly, but no one was there to answer it. If Andi arrived before them, she would've ordered any employees to lay low.

Where are you? he wondered.

"Jonathan?" Mathias's voice crackled in his earpiece.

They stopped at the door to the stairwell, and he looked up through the narrow window.

"Go ahead," he murmured.

"They're inside. Mom's van is back here." Barely restrained anger saturated his brother's words. He and Killian were still butt-hurt because he'd pulled rank and told them to cover the exits. They'd wanted to charge in, guns a-blazing. They weren't fully field-tested yet, and the last thing he wanted was two more family members inside this fucking hotel.

"Stay alert, guys," he ordered. "We're heading into the stairwell."

He nodded once to his partner, pulled open the door and, guns raised, they started up the stairs. An overhead fluorescent buzzed and flickered, casting the whole place in a sickly, yellow glow. Their ascent was textbook until his right boot hit the fourth step from the top.

Boom! Boom! Gunshots echoed through the walls.

"Go! Go! Go!" Jonathan and Golden charged up the

remaining steps, threw open the stairwell door. Nothing would stop Killian and Mathias from coming in after them.

Golden lifted his right foot and plowed his size fifteen boot into the door, right next to the doorknob. One kick was all it took. The wood splintered, and the old door blew inward. They charged in behind it, one going in high, the other going in low.

Jonathan scanned the room. His heart pounded, and sweat trickled down his temple. In that split second, a million images flashed through his mind. His mom and dad's unabashed tears of joy when they were finally allowed to hold Ashling in the NICU. The first time Ashling's eyes connected with his and her first smile. And Andi ... glorious, magnificent Andi. He was bombarded by so many visions of her, he almost couldn't process them all.

CHAPTER THIRTY-THREE

Roberson's shot went wide, but Andi's aim was true. The bullet slammed into his upper right chest and threw him back against the wall like a rag doll. The revolver dropped from his limp hand, and a garish red swath was left behind as he slid to the floor in a heap.

She rushed over, grabbed his weapon, flipped open the cylinder, ejected the remaining cartridges, then tucked the revolver into the back of her waistband. Ashling cried, and Andi spun around. Molly, the genius, brave, wonderful woman, had gotten on the floor and wedged herself and the baby into the corner behind the chair.

"Are you all right?" Andi settled on her knees and wrapped one arm around them both. The other was extended, gun in hand, as she kept a vigilant eye on Roberson.

Before Molly could answer, a loud crack sounded, and the door was ripped from its hinges behind her. She turned, gun raised, ready to kill anyone who dared cause harm to these two people.

"It's me!" Jonathan, both hands up, shouted over the

ringing in her ears. He kicked aside pieces of what used to be the door. "Baby, it's me."

Breath exploded from her lungs, her shoulders sagged, and the hand holding the gun hit the floor with a muffled *thud*. Jonathan stepped over an unconscious Roberson and, before she could react, Jonathan joined them on the floor, encircling all three of them in his warm, strong, perfect arms.

"I've got you." He tightened his hold, and his whispered words of reassurance blew warm across her ear. "You got him, Andi. It's all over."

Golden yanked Roberson's hands behind his back and bound him with zip ties. Mathias and Killian charged in next, frantically taking in the nightmarish scene before them. Doing their *twin thing*, they both turned simultaneously to the group crouched in the corner, then stalked toward them as Golden kept watch over Roberson.

IN ALL HIS years as a Navy SEAL, no high-altitude jumps into enemy territory, no foray into a dark mountainous cave hoping to ferret out terrorists, none of it had ever terrified Jonathan as much as hearing those two shots. His fear had been so visceral, he could taste it, smell it. The adrenaline surging through his system would take hours to abate.

They're all safe, he assured himself as he tightened his hold on three of the most important women in his life. *They're all safe.*

Roberson had begun to regain consciousness and was being triaged by Golden and Mathias. Killian, legs planted apart, arms crossed over his chest, glared down at him. Sirens blared outside—ambulance and local cops, most likely.

"Here, Andi, honey. You take her." His mom wiggled from

his hold and held Ashling out to Andi, as if sensing her desperate need to touch her.

Andi sat back on her heels and tucked her gun in her holster. She put one trembling hand under the baby's head, the other under her tiny bottom, and drew his daughter to her chest. She fussed with the blanket, folding and tucking it around Ashling as she murmured gentle words and rocked her side to side. The sweet, private moment was incongruous with the harsh activity buzzing around them.

Liquid brown eyes gazed at him and, right then, in that moment, with silent tears streaming down her face as she cradled his daughter, he was a goner. Andi owned his heart forever.

"She's okay, baby." Jonathan smoothed his hand over his daughter's dark, downy-soft hair, more to calm himself than her.

Andi's chin quivered. She nodded. Her throat moved up and down. He plopped onto his butt with a relieved sigh, crossed his legs, then scooped them both up and settled them in his lap. She burrowed her face into his neck, curled into him and quietly allowed herself to cry.

"You got to us in time, honey." His mother rested her hand on Andi's shoulder.

Jonathan's beautiful warrior peeked out from under his chin.

"You were so brave." His mom's fingertips gently slid across Andi's cheeks to wipe away her tears. She skimmed dark bangs aside, and looked her in the eye as she said, "I can never thank you enough."

Andi cradled Ashling in one arm and pulled his mom close with the other. His mother returned the hug and smiled at him with a wink.

"Me? You were amazing." Andi sniffled and turned to look up at Jonathan. "I never would've been able to get in if she hadn't unlocked the door. I still haven't figured out how you contorted yourself to do that."

"Guess those yoga classes paid off," his mother said. "I'll never complain about it again."

Ashling gurgled and cooed between them, tugging on Andi's necklace, his beautiful daughter unscathed by all that had transpired. He would never have to worry about his baby girl being ignored. She wouldn't allow it.

His mom made a move for her. "Why don't you let me take her—"

Andi opened her mouth to protest.

"I'm just going to change her diaper, honey. I'll do it on the bed, then I'll bring her right back to you. Okay?" His mom smoothed her hand up and down Andi's arm.

"Oh ... yeah, of course." A dusky glow warmed Andi's cheeks, and she shook her head with a small smile. "Sorry."

She kissed Ashling's head and reluctantly let her go. Her eyes followed as Mathias curved his arm around their mom's shoulder and escorted them across the room, careful to keep himself between Roberson and the two of them.

"Andi." Jonathan waited until she turned back to him. "I love you."

He refused to let another minute go by without telling her.

"Nice timing, dumbass." Killian shook his head and rolled his eyes from where he stood watching Golden triage Roberson.

Shit. His brother was probably right. Maybe now wasn't the best time for such a serious declaration. What could he say? Jonathan didn't have a lot of practice with this sort of thing. Other than his mom and his sister, he'd only ever said those words to one other woman in his life.

"You—" Brows pinched, she drew her chin back. "But I thought—"

"Yeah, I was an idiot." *Again.* He sighed. "I was a coward. My feelings for you terrified me. I've never felt anything close to that before. I was afraid to embrace it, because losing you would kill me."

"You're not going to lose me, Jonathan." She leaned close, her lips a hair's breadth away from his, and whispered, "I'm not going anywhere because I love you, too."

EPILOGUE

Thirteen months later ...

Andi gave Jonathan a warm smile as she slowly weaved her way around the family assembled on the large patio behind their new home. The day they'd gotten engaged, his folks gifted them with fifteen acres of land, which included an area they'd affectionately dubbed Serenity Bluff. The bluff became a place of new beginnings when they'd vowed their never-ending love for each other on the very same spot Jonathan had been standing one stormy night when his father's tough love wrenched him back from despair.

A judge performed the small ceremony. Immediate family had flown in from all over. Jeffrey Burke gave away the bride. Sherm, Golden and a few other guys from the teams were there too.

They'd kept it short and sweet, then slipped simple platinum bands on each other's fingers. The second the judge pronounced them husband and wife, they'd practically jumped each other. Hell, if he'd had his way, he would've skipped the reception and taken her straight to their hotel room. His beautiful bride had other ideas. Andi had tugged her lips away, dug into his inside jacket pocket and snatched the adoption papers and pen he'd placed there before the ceremony. With a twirl of her finger, he'd turned around and, using his back as a desk, she signed them on the spot.

"Here. Now you." She'd thrust the pen and paper into the judge's hand with a *get on with it* look. Only after his signature was scrawled along the bottom did she allow herself to relax and enjoy the moment.

What could he say? His wife knew what she wanted and went after it. Ashling was lucky to have such a strong, brilliant woman as one of her role models.

Jonathan thought about all the things that had happened since that day.

Nancy Raymond was charged with accessory to attempted murder of a federal agent and to harming an animal used in law enforcement, which carried a felony murder charge. To avoid going to trial, and for a slightly reduced sentence, she reached a plea deal with the U.S. Attorney. As part of the deal, the judge made her stand up in court and, with the entire O'Halleran family looking on, she'd tearfully detailed her part in what happened to Caleb and Power. She was currently one year into a twenty-five-year sentence in a federal prison close to where her son lived. Burke once mentioned that Jarod visited her every weekend.

If possible, Burke had become even more secretive. He'd performed a complete review and overhaul of his entire agency. Access to all levels of classified information was tightened. Every single employee, from the janitors to the highest-level analysts, was required to undergo another, more extensive background check. His power continued to grow, and he was tough as nails ... except when it came to his goddaughter, Ashling.

Two days before their wedding, Jeffrey had testified

before a Senate investigative committee charged with ferreting out Senator Preston Etheridge's various *indiscretions.*

The senator's executive secretary also testified regarding some unaccounted-for days in his schedule—days that just happened to match the dates he was at The Farm. Even though it wasn't required, she attended every single day of the hearings, giving him the stink-eye from her seat in the gallery.

As a result of his visits to the VIP quarters at The Farm, the once-esteemed senator was found guilty of child endangerment and multiple counts of statutory rape. He was forced to resign his senate seat, and his wife quickly divorced him, taking her daddy's millions with her. Former colleagues feigned shock and disappointment. Their willingness to discuss it on national television fed the ravenous appetites of the cable news networks desperate to fill a twenty-four-hour news cycle. In a rare show of reaching across the aisle, they all agreed prison was too good for the likes of Preston Etheridge —even those who months earlier had been kissing his ring, so to speak, when they thought he would one day be sitting in the Oval Office. Another example of politicians eating their own.

Not that it mattered anymore, but Etheridge went to prison vehemently denying any knowledge of campaign donations received from a Russian mob boss. Like that was the most egregious offense he'd committed.

Matthew Roberson, the piece of shit, recovered from his gunshot wound, though he was left with limited use of his right arm. He was convicted of attempted murder of a federal agent, two counts of kidnapping, false imprisonment, and breaking multiple campaign finance laws. Having turned down his own plea deal, he was currently serving thirty-five years to life in a maximum-security federal prison. According to Burke, he still wrote one letter a week to his former boss—all returned unopened.

The crackle and pop of the fire drew Jonathan's attention back to his family. Sparks sizzled and hissed and, like a million fireflies, sprinkled skyward. Firelight sparkled in the warm depths of Andi's eyes and captured the varying shades of color interwoven through her short, dark hair. The happiness glowing from his wife's face took his breath away. No matter how often he looked at her, he would never shake the feeling of how lucky he was to have her in his life, in his world—to know she'd given him a second chance at love.

Wanting to spend as much time as possible with their daughter, Andi left the NSA and went to work for OSI as the head of special field training. She could set her own schedule and work from home and still satisfy her need to be physically active, while sharing her vast knowledge and expertise. At work, she was a ball-busting, show-no-mercy instructor determined to hammer as much knowledge into the minds of her pupils as possible to ensure they all came home alive. She only let her guard down around family, allowing the generous heart and unlimited capacity for love she'd suppressed for too many years to shine.

He smiled at their daughter's little hand wrapped tight around her mommy's index finger as she toddled alongside her. Ashling was a healthy, happy, chubby twenty-two-month-old who kept them on their toes with her penchant for climbing and ability to find new and creative places to hide.

"Dare I ask what's going on in that brilliant mind of yours?" Voice husky, Andi leaned down to kiss his forehead, then sat on the arm of his chair. Ashling released her grip, squatted down and played with a bug racing around by his boot.

"I was just thinking how lucky I am." His arm curved around her, and she laughed when he dragged her down to his lap. God, he loved having laughter back in his life again. Especially when it was Andi's. "I'm in love with an intelligent, beautiful, kickass woman. I have a brave, adorable little girl"—he smiled down at Ashling as she was about to put something in her mouth—"who doesn't need to eat that bug."

Andi swooped her up off the ground and set her in her lap. "If you want to munch on bugs, Appleseed, wait until Daddy shows you the right ones to eat."

She brushed dirt from Ashling's fingers and then kissed each one before tickling her tummy. Ashling twisted and giggled, then buried her face against the side of Andi's neck. A minute later, she yawned, stuck her thumb in her mouth and dropped off to asleep.

Both of his girls in his lap at the same time. *It doesn't get much better than this.*

"I'm the lucky one, Jonathan." Andi's tone became serious. She cradled his jaw in her hand. Flames sparked off her eyes and glowed across her smooth skin. "I'm in love with a man who doesn't expect me to change—who loves me just the way I am. A man who has given me everything I always wanted." Andi pressed a gentle kiss on his lips and the top of Ashling's head and gazed out over the patio at the family assembled.

As quiet conversations meandered around them, a sense of peace and contentment washed over him. Andi was his equal, his partner. She was the woman he would love forever.

"I love you, Andréa." Jonathan rubbed his hand up and down her thigh. She might be Andi to everyone else, but to him, she would always be his gorgeous, amazing Andréa.

Andi snuggled her head to his shoulder, their little girl tucked safely between them. "I love you, too, Jonathan."

DON'T MISS OUT!

Sign up at https://www.tjloganauthor.com/subscribe-to-newsletter to receive the "COVERT DETAILS" newsletter. You'll receive advance notice of release dates, get the first look at book covers, have access to exclusive content, and be eligible for fun giveaways.

You can also find TJ on ...
Facebook: https://www.facebook.com/tjloganauthor/
Covert Commanders Private Facebook Group: https://www.facebook.com/groups/2382419041796260/
Twitter: https://twitter.com/TJLoganAuthor
Instagram: https://www.instagram.com/tjloganauthor/
Website: https://www.tjloganauthor.com/

ALSO IN THE SERIES

Watch for DEADLY SECRET and DEADLY DISCIPLE,
Books 1 and 2 in TJ Logan's
O'Halleran Security International series

DEADLY SECRET

He steps into the shadows to pursue a killer ...

F.B.I. Special Agent Beckett O'Halleran values Family, Honor, and Loyalty. A botched undercover assignment results in the brutal murder of his partner. When the killer is set free by a Deputy Director on the take, Beck walks away from the Bureau. He vows to stop at nothing to avenge his partner's death, including using an innocent woman.

She is dragged into the shadows by her mother's past ...

A deadly secret from the past threatens Gwendolyn Tamberley's life. Thrust into the crosshairs of a merciless psychopath who will destroy anyone who threatens his empire, she becomes the center of a firestorm between the Russian mafia, the F.B.I. and a former agent hell-bent on retribution.

Will deadly secrets destroy them?

Gwen's only hope is the man who's been deceiving her.

And Beck must choose between his obsession with vengeance and the woman who's come to mean everything to him.

DEADLY DISCIPLE

An honorable man driven by the need for retribution ...

Caleb O'Halleran is a Tactical K9 Specialist with the FBI's elite Hostage Rescue Team. Finding the traitor responsible for his K9 partner's death is the only thing that matters ... until he meets an enchanting, strong-willed doctor.

A noble doctor determined to help others ...

Dr. Dawn Pannikos is a busy ER doctor with a surly teenage sister to raise and a past that has taught her not to trust love. There's no room in her well-ordered life for an irresistibly charming ladies' man with shadows around his heart.

Two innocent women dragged into a nightmare ...

Dawn and her sister become prisoners of a psychopathic cult leader and are plunged into the middle of a dangerous FBI operation. Will Caleb and his new K9 partner, Jake, find them in time, or will he be too late to save the woman who owns his heart?

ABOUT THE AUTHOR

TJ Logan is an award-winning author of romantic suspense anchored by strong themes of Family, Honor, and Loyalty. Her writing journey began one day, back in 2012, when a bunch of strange voices popped into her head. Hoping to exorcise the craziness, she started typing, which simply ushered in more—as if she'd cracked open some sort of portal for fictional characters to charge through.

Those random voices morphed into the O'Halleran family. The family grew with the addition of lovers, friends, neighbors, and co-workers. Voila, the first six books of the O'Halleran Security International (OSI) series was born.

TJ grew up in a military family, lived all over the country and was surrounded by five brothers ... and, amazingly, lived to tell about it. She was also a key member of a team who managed a Secret program for one of the world's top defense companies. All of these things have given TJ an interesting perspective on life. And every bit of it goes into her writing!

Family, Honor and Loyalty aren't just words in a tagline to TJ, they are everything.

Copyright © 2019 TJ Logan

Learn more at tjloganauthor.com

Made in the USA
Middletown, DE
07 May 2022